GALAXY WARRIOR

TERRY SPEAR

DEDICATION

To Jaclyn Dibona, thanks for being a friend for many years
and for loving my stories.

.

ACKNOWLEDGMENTS

Thanks so much to Donna Fournier who came through for me like always!.

PROLOGUE

3015 Planet Xenon of the Mercurial Solar System

Zaira Cole shifted into her jaguar form, loving the freedom, and loving her limber feline body, and the way she could run full out and race along the Sontron Cliffs. Excited with the prospect, she envisioned what her planet would look like if it were green: treed, birds twittering in among the vegetation, lush, oxygenated, beautiful. It would be, if her brother and she were able to affect the change.

And she was certain it would work, even if her twin brother had reservations. But she worried about what would happen afterward. Right now, no one wanted to inhabit the planet except for those already born and raised there.

Forever, they'd kept their shifter abilities secret

from otherworlders.

A shadow crossing Zaira's path caught her attention. Her brother, Martius, soared above the desert plains in his dragon form—as black as she was. If she and her brother had been like the jaguar shifters, who melted into the shadows of the jungle and were unseen by human types, they would have been the same color as the desert scape and blended in—dusty, mottled, brown. Instead, every time she ran as a jaguar, her black fur would be covered in brown and red dust.

She narrowed her eyes as a dust storm rolled across the rocky terrain. She and her brother knew the consequences of their actions concerning the greening of their planet, that it could cause terrible strife to their people. But they needed to bring life to the planet so her people could really thrive.

They had no recourse but to bring Quad Lassiter and his fighting flying force into the picture. They would need his protection from otherworlders once their planet *wasn't* so inhospitable. Yet she knew, that would be a feat in and of itself.

She was surprised to see her brother flying this morning. Usually he was working hard to create the catalyst that would change their world and their lives forever. He must have had a breakthrough, which was the only way he'd leave his underground lab for a respite.

Good. They were nearly ready to see if their experiment would prove successful this time.

She could barely wait for the transformations to occur. Her father, Carver, was just as adamant about making the alterations to their world to enrich the lives of their people once she had convinced him and her brother of how beautiful Earth world had once been. And how much their world could mirror it. Carver had persuaded the Council that this was the right thing to do. Some were against it—those who didn't like any kind of change. Some feared a world at war as otherworlders tried to take control of their world.

That's why they needed Quaid Lassiter. Except she wanted him for much more than just saving their planet from invasion. Somehow, she had to persuade him to stay and help her people. And *more.*

He would be an acceptable mate. The only one she'd ever considered having. He didn't even know her, and she was certain the bachelor, who swore off any long-term relationships, would be nearly impossible to convince otherwise. So she had her work cut out for her.

She curled her tongue out in a yawn, then roared at her brother, who swooped toward her in acknowledgment. He turned in an arching sweep, heading back to his lab. She returned to her book store and coffee shop situated across from her father's repair hangar.

The time had come to put their plan into action. Quaid Lassiter would be crashing in on them soon, and he would not be a happy fighter pilot. He was the Prince of Orion—and she was as determined as ever to make him her mate.

She knew he wouldn't go along with it. Not willingly. She smiled in a jaguar-caught-the-bird-of-prey way. She had every intention of changing his mind.

CHAPTER 1

Knuckles whitening, Quaid Lassiter punched in coordinates on his Class 1 fighter spacecraft. He was going to crash, die, leaving his men without a leader to fight the constant battles in space. In that instant, he realized, except for his men, no one would notice his death. He would leave no one behind. No wife, children, no parents, family. Which was just the way he wished it.

But he had no intention of dying today.

He was too angry to die—how the hell had he ended up here? And how had his craft lost power so quickly?

Beads of perspiration dotted his forehead. With vision blurring, he clenched his teeth against the ferocious vibration of the failing ionic propulsion drive. Swooping through Xenon's gray atmosphere, he saw the desert landscape hurtling toward him. His heart thundered as he tried to gain control.

His craft made the most gawd-awful screech as it dove toward the sandy plain. His fingers punching in figures, he maneuvered the vehicle into the sole repair station hangar on Xenon, scraping metal against cement, leaving a trail of flames. Foam shot out of the floor, extinguishing the streaks of orange fire. The failing engine screeched to a halt and the sudden stop jerked him in his harness, bruises for sure across his chest as he slammed back against the seat.

The engine dead, Quaid peered out the craft's window and sat in a daze, offering thanks to any god that might listen to him, his heart still banging against his ribs.

Flames shot up above the ship, heating the cabin. Before he could remove his safety harness, foam spewed out of cylinders in the hangar overhead and extinguished the fire. Quaid breathed easier.

Nailed to the north wall of the hangar, a new message posted to the attention of otherworlders finally caught his eye, shaking him loose from his near-death stupor: No Drinking, No Cursing, No Carousing, No Killing—by Order of the Chief Magistrate, Caryndian Bach.

"Of all the damnable places to have propulsion-drive failure. What else can go wrong today?" He really didn't want to know the answer to that question.

As soon as he spoke the words, a silent warning

sounded in his head. His mother's reminder: Ask, and you shall soon receive. As if speaking the words out loud enticed the gods to show any human just what they had in store for him or her. Although he didn't think of himself as a superstitious man, he *knew* not to ask that question aloud.

His stomach grumbling from not having had a decent meal since his food replicator had broken down early yesterday, he was reminded of yet another of the ship's bizarre malfunctions.

He poked the hatch button. With a whoosh, the well-tuned door raised. Steps peeled out of the ship.

Exiting his craft, he spied his long-time acquaintance, Carver Cole, the repair shop's owner, watching him from the office adjoining the hangar. A smattering of gray peppered the middle-aged man's dark brown hair. His brows wrinkled as rivulets of perspiration freckled his temple. He pulled a cloth from his pocket and wiped the moisture away. Carver bowed his head slightly in greeting, giving Quaid pause.

No how-do-you-do? No hearty handshake? No, hell, Quaid, thanks for not wrecking my hangar?

In truth, Quaid had probably taken a few years off the man's life, although he wasn't certain how long Carver's kind lived.

Carver zipped up his silver coveralls and walked into the hangar. Without a word, he crossed the building, then climbed into the craft.

Quaid followed him into the ship's engine room. Carver's slight fingers snapped the engine compartment open. The older man poked his head into the now silent heart of the ship. The silence that confirmed Quaid's little lady was truly dead—*for now*. His spirits in the pits, he hoped Carver could get her back into space pronto.

Carver pulled an ionic pulse meter from his pocket, then ran it over the engine. "Sure thought you were a gonner."

A hint of worry? It was hard to tell even on the best of days with Carver, but something had to be eating at him as quiet as he was.

"Yeah, well, for a second there I wondered if I shouldn't have taken up my mother's field of expertise instead."

A spark of recognition lighting his brown eyes, Carver faced Quaid. "The digs."

Quaid wondered how he knew of such a thing. Then again, it wasn't a closely-guarded secret either. "Yep. My mother had hoped I would have been an archeologist. Had a bit of a knack for it, too."

Carver exhaled deeply.

Was Carver relieved...or something else? Normally, he would give an hour-long lecture on the technical intricacies of the propulsion drive. He would have told Quaid in no uncertain terms how reckless he'd been and that he should have seen to its maintenance much earlier on, just like his father would have said to him. This was not the Carver Cole he knew.

But what Quaid had experienced in the last thirty-six hours had not been normal, nothing that he could have foreseen.

Quaid climbed out of the ship after Carver. "Check out the food replicator and navigational system too, will ya? I was headed for the Feronian home world, when the next thing I knew my destination clicked over to Xenon. Couldn't get the damned—"

Carver glanced at him.

No cursing on the planet. Hell, why did he have to crash land here of all places? Instead of the sweet Feronian planet where everyone went for the most pleasurable R&R and their really were no rules.

"...thing switched over to my intended heading no matter what I tried," Quaid continued. "If I didn't know any better, I'd say somebody tampered with it. Sabotaged it. But of course that's crazy. Who would want to bring me here?"

Carver nodded, but avoided eye contact.

Quaid straightened a bit as he considered Carver's odd behavior, wondering what the hell was wrong. "How have things being going on Xenon since the last time I was here, what six months ago?" Not that he could imagine anything would have changed on the nearly uninhabitable planet where the status quo had remained the same for over a thousand years as far as he knew. Nothing ever changed.

"It'll take at least a week to repair her."

Guess whatever was eating Carver was none of his business. Quaid folded his arms across his chest. "I'll pay you double to get this bucket back into the sky by tomorrow."

"Sorry. I can't rebuild the drive. I told you the last time you were here that she'd need a new one. If you were just taking her for a Sunday spin instead of fighting Rondovins and Caspians...well anyway, the new drive will have to come from Maldovia." Sarcasm laced Carver's words. For the most part, the Xenonians were a peaceful race and detested any kind of violence. Especially Carver.

"Maldovia? But that's not the closest—"

"Orion is at war. You ought to know that."

Quaid knew that, damn it, but he really didn't want to get stuck here for a nanosecond longer than he had to. "What am I supposed to do for a week in *this* place?" Quaid couldn't curb the acid that dripped from his words.

"Stay away from my daughter, for one."

If Quaid didn't know him better, he'd think the old man was setting him up...in an offhanded way. "I didn't know you had a daughter."

"Now you do. She's a nice girl who wouldn't want to get tangled up with the likes of you." Carver gave him a harsh look to punctuate his comment, then ran a cloth over the side of the vehicle. He touched the gash in the sturdy metal. "Looks like you had a bit of a scrape in the last conflict."

"The other guy's ship looks worse for wear, what was left of it. What's there to do around here?" Quaid had never hung around the place, just dropped in occasionally to have Carver check out his craft. But he'd never stayed for any time beyond that.

"Nothing much for your kind. Nothing to kill around here."

Really, I got the point the first time. Quaid rubbed the stubble on his chin. "What's your daughter's name?"

Ignoring Quaid's question, Carver motioned to the craft. "I'll patch up the cosmetic damage while I'm waiting for the new drive to come in. You know the way to the inn. A bookstore and coffee shop have just been added."

Bookstore? Now that was an oddity. He knew Xenonians read many languages as he'd seen the schematics that Carver kept in h,is office. But a bookstore? With real books? Maybe ereaders, 3-D readers, or something.

"Coffee." Quaid rolled his eyes. No bar. "See if you

11

can put a rush on it."

He slapped Carver on the shoulder, then headed outside of the hangar, but Carver said, "Wait."

Quaid stopped, figuring he was going to get a lecture, but Carver said, "Your weapons."

Ah hell. He never left his craft without them. He returned to the vehicle and left his state-of-the-art weaponry, colt laser pistols, throwing stars—not that he'd ever used them—and a couple of daggers in his quarters, but he kept a knife in his boot, just in case.

Carver looked him over as Quaid smiled at him, then headed out of the hangar.

The two-story windowless inn sat directly across from the landing pad for stranded space travelers like himself. The new building squashed against the inn's western wing caught his attention. With no sign indicating the shop's purpose, it was just like everything else on Xenon... gray, blank, and uninviting.

He walked across the platform to the shop's opaque glass door, then hesitated as the roar of an approaching engine shattered the silence. The nearing ship bore the markings of a Terran craft and satisfied it was a fellow Terran from Earth World, Quaid entered the new shop. To his surprise, a bell tinkled his arrival. He'd never heard of sticking bells on a door. Well, for that matter, seeing a door such as this. Most had entrances that zipped into the wall or dissolved to allow entry.

He breathed in the homey aroma of coffee beans roasting in a warmer, then glanced around the room. He had to admit it did smell good and welcoming. Hoping to see that the place offered good home-cooked meals also, he was disappointed to find only leather-bound books lining the shelves of two of the four walls. Tables for ereading or vision viewing sat against a third. Along the fourth, a coffee bar and five round café tables sat. Coffee beans of hundreds of flavors filled colorful jars on shelves behind them.

Yeah, just like Quaid thought. The day wasn't going to get any better.

The scent of jasmine caught his attention next. He turned to the origin of the tantalizing fragrance. His gaze fixed on an ice-blue silk blouse gaping open to reveal a significant portion of firm, rounded tan breasts. Long-tapered polished nails adorned delicate fingers and lingered at a pearl button halfway up the blouse as if the woman was trying to decide whether to slip the pearl in or out of the hole.

In heightened anticipation, Quaid found his heartbeat quickening. He'd been alone in space for two weeks, four days, twelve hours, and thirty-two minutes. Seeing a woman who looked like this...well, he couldn't help but be...interested.

The pearl popped its head in through the

buttonhole, while the slender fingers rose to the next button as if they were climbing to the top of the highest mountain peak with the greatest of difficulty. The blouse slowly covered part of the crevice, then stopped. Heat coursed through his body with great expectancy, but when the fingers didn't move any further, he turned his graze upward to see the face belonging to the breasts that held his interest hostage.

"Disappointed?" Her voice had a sweet softness and yet a hint of power, just aching to be freed. Her dark golden eyes and coils of ebony hair secured high on her head drew him in. For a nanosecond, his brain was controlled by the more primitive part of his body.

"Ahem," he said, trying to clear his suddenly graveled throat and rubbed his stubble-covered chin. He should have shaved. Who would have thought he'd meet such a gorgeous creature as this anywhere on Xenon? "Just wondered if you needed some help."

His stay here was definitely looking up.

***

Zaira considered the captain's appearance from his wavy, nearly raven-colored hair, disheveled by the breeze, to his dusty, leather flight boots before speaking. Her mood swings were out of this world due to her coming of mating age—lusting after the prince, wanting him, knowing she couldn't have him—not until he agreed to everything. "Buttons, I'm not used to."

She had read racy early Earth romances where a handsome hero fumbled with a woman's buttons and how sexy it sounded. So she'd ordered one from a vintage clothing site on a different planet, glad it had arrived in time, especially with the way the prince seemed interested in her buttons. She hadn't been with a man, couldn't be, not until she mated, but her romance books had taught her everything she knew, in an abstract sort of way. At least in the art of seduction, it seemed the books were right.

"I hadn't expected company." She shifted her gaze from his body to study his vivid blue eyes. "Don't get much."

Since the first time she had seen him two years ago while he'd watched her father repair his ship—this Prince of Orion—she had been determined to make him her mate. Subduing the urge to smile, she fiddled with her buttons, wondering how far she could take this charade.

He was quirky, fun-loving, hot, *really* hot, and her vision of the perfect war hero.

His leather jacket, a copy of a WWII fighter pilot's garb of a bygone era, was covered in a thin layer of the dust from her planet, just as if her world had claimed him as well. It seemed he liked old Earth history, too. That wasn't in his file. His sky blue shirt opened partway down his chest. The smoothness of his tanned skin untouched by even a speck of dark hair made her heart skip a beat. To see the rest of what lay under his warrior clothes—to feel his skin warm and naked against hers. She tapped her fingers on the counter. His philosophies conflicted with her own, however.

She knew he'd be the biggest challenge of her life. How could she hope to win his heart, when he was bound and determined never to marry anyone? Her father would put a stop to it if he learned what she had in mind to do. But... she was determined to have her way.

He was a fighter pilot. One of the best. They needed him. She sighed deeply as she twisted a curl of hair with her finger. *She* needed him. If he learned her secrets, would he reject her? She was afraid so. If she could encourage his interest in her first...

His gaze focused on her blouse again, and she cast him the merest hint of a smile. He *was* intrigued with her. Good, that was the first obstacle.

She fought the urge to give herself to him fully. He had to link with her first. As the daughter of the head of the High Council, it was the only way she could mate with him. And now, she was finally of mateable age. Was it wrong to bring him to Xenon the way in which they had done to solicit his help?

She took a deep breath. If he found out they had sabotaged his ship, she was sure he'd want to kill all of them who had been responsible—including her.

She just had to play her part well and ensure he didn't learn the truth.

CHAPTER 2

Quaid chided himself. The woman's dark golden eyes captivated him and for the first time in his life, the clever comeback he had in mind, wouldn't fall off his tongue. The seconds ticked by like minutes, and he took a deep breath. "Sorry, I guess I'm at a loss for words."

"The words are there, you just choose not to use them." She ran her finger over her full, pink lips glistening with a blushing-gloss enhancer, and smiled.

He cleared his throat again. "This planet is normally a downright inhospitable place for otherworlders."

"It's time to change the otherworlders' view of Xenon."

He raised his brows. Now that was a novel idea. Was she as enlightened as she appeared to be? He'd never found anyone on Xenon who was.

He thought she wanted him, like he wanted her,

but she'd have to understand first there could be no commitment to a long-term relationship, ever. Xenonians were an odd sort of race in that respect, descendants of Earth World humans, but unlike his own kind that divorced without regard to the sanctity of marriage, Xenonians were rumored monogamous.

"Would you care for some coffee?" She waved her hand at the jars behind her. "I get them from Celestial Coffee Beans Wholesalers."

His heart sank as his masculinity deflated. Men and women definitely originated on different planets.

"I just came in to—"

"Check out the place? Everyone says that." She sounded disappointed and motioned to one of the chairs. "Coffee?" she asked again. "My father said I'd never do any business here."

"Your father?" All of a sudden, Quaid was getting really bad vibes. "Not Carver Cole, perchance?" Hell, if she was Carver's daughter and Quaid got involved with her, his proverbial goose would be cooked and there would go the repair of his ship.

"Yes, he's the one. He said it's much too isolated. No one ever comes here, except to have their crafts repaired. And most everyone who has to wait for some time wants something... harder to drink. But no drinking spirits allowed in the territory. That's what you're here for, isn't it? The repair of your craft?"

"Ionic propulsion drive failed." This was going to be one long, damn week.

"I heard the most awful noise, then saw you exit Father's shop." She ran her slender hand over the top edge of a chrome chair. "But...I remember you from before."

Quaid tried to recall having seen the stunning woman and her darkened almond-shaped eyes, framed in a ruffle of thick, black lashes, but he hadn't seen her or he would have remembered. "I don't recall having seen *you* before."

"Yes, well, *you,* I remember."

"I'll have a cup of coffee." Although he'd never truly acquired a taste for the stuff, but the woman fascinated him in a way that he hadn't felt in eons. If it made her feel better that he bought coffee when her father said she'd never do well, he was determined to prove the opposite. He'd buy several cups, in fact. He sat at the nearest table. "I'm Quaid Lassiter, captain of the Exiter."

"I'm Zaira Cole, proprietor of the Star Buccaneer Coffee Shop and Candlewick Bookstore."

Surprised, he raised his brows slightly. "Candlewick? Odd name for a bookstore, isn't it?" Almost as odd as having a bookstore. Anyone who read anything did so mostly by IE-Pods. Once Sarysian Gates designed the Interactive-Electronic pods, printed books and dust mites were a thing of the past. On ships, no one could afford to take up valuable space or add weight to their cargo. So IE-Pods were the only way to go.

"In ancient times, folks read by candlelight or natural light. Some of these books are nearly as old as that. Nobody has the time to read anymore. Everyone's too busy trying to annihilate any species not their own, and when they're not doing that, they're going after their own kind as well."

Typical Xenonian—against any kind of fighting. He'd hoped she would be different.

"You mean me?"

Would she rather he was a smuggler or a pirate? He snorted under his breath. Or one of those tourist ships that took people to other planets to show them just how others lived?

"Your kind, yes. Everyone knows you're the hero of the Terrans with more kills than any other... kind of like the Red Baron during the First Great War in Europe on the planet of Terra Firma."

Earth World. "I know the ancient history."

"Been there before?"

"Nope, born and raised on Orion. But the place has too many... troglabites now."

"Troglabites?"

"Too many different human species variants."

She frowned and he realized no matter how much

he wanted to win her over, he wasn't making any points.

"And Xenonians?" she asked.

"Why they're just like us Terrans."

She raised her brows. Yes, they were similar, but they didn't shapeshift. She doubted he knew that her kind did, as much as a heavily guarded secret that it was. "Troglabites. That's a new one on me. What kind of coffee would you like?"

"What do you recommend?" He glanced at the coffee flavors.

"Chocolate, it's my favorite. It has a—calming effect."

His gaze fastened on hers again. "You don't appear to be the sort who needs a fix."

"I have my moments."

"All right, I'll take one of those. Will you join me?"

"Well, I'm awfully busy."

He considered the empty shop.

"I get requests from all over the galaxy from species seeking to improve their knowledge of the world."

"Except for rereading the technical manual for my craft, and even then, I try to avoid it, I haven't read a book in years. They're for children."

Her expression changed again, and he knew he'd lost some more points.

Quaid studied her long, navy skirts reaching past her ankles—nothing of interest there. Her ebony hair twisted into coils of rope and was tucked high on top of her head. Wordlessly, she pulled a copper pin from her hair. Like releasing the floodwaters from a dam, a waterfall of ebony hair slipped down to her narrow hips.

He couldn't take his eyes off her glistening tresses. And craved burying his face in her dark hair and running his hands through the silky strands.

She twisted a strand of hair as her lips rose in a smile. "You say books are for losers?"

"There are those who read about doing things, and there are those who do them." He leaned back in his chair. "I'd rather be doing something, than reading about it."

"You mean like exterminating species?"

Hell, back to the issue of fighting. "Only the fighters. They kill us...we kill them. It's a job."

"I see. Sweetener?"

"Two scoops."

She added blue powder to the coffee, then set the cups on the table. She sat opposite him.

He stirred his coffee, then sipped from the mug, and he found her waiting for some response. "It's very good."

"Thank you, I thought you'd like it." She shifted in her seat. "Been fighting for a while? Kind of gets lonely out there, doesn't it?"

Quaid's interest perked up. "Don't you know it."

"Not much time for female companionship."

A little, but it had been quite a while. "Not that I'd turn any down if I had the chance," he said slowly, testing the waters.

"I don't doubt it. Is your coffee sweet enough?"

"Couldn't be sweeter." His gaze shifted to the cut of her blouse again. He wasn't usually so attracted to a woman that he couldn't quit thinking about how good it would be with her, but he blamed his circumstances, stuck here without anything else to do but ogle a woman who was as hot as the flames that had enveloped his craft.

She stood and reached for the back of her skirt. "I hope it's not too warm in here for you. I'm not used to wearing much of anything at all, but I was trying to make an impression."

"No need," Quaid said quickly as he hoped his enthusiasm didn't show too much. "Did you need help with something?"

"I'm not used to buttons—it's your kind's technology—never took hold much here on Xenon."

He nearly knocked his chair over as he stood. He hastened to help her as she released her hold on the button. Hesitating, he studied the square pearl fastener. For several seconds, he struggled with it as the scent of jasmine tickled his senses. Then he finally shoved the button through the round hole. The skirt dropped to the floor revealing long shapely legs and short blue satin shorts.

"You wear shorts under a skirt?" He focused on the skimpy line of the garment.

"In case I get hot."

She was *hot.* The pace of his breath quickened. *What now? The blouse... the shorts?* His whole body warmed a good ten degrees while he looked for the fastener on her shorts.

"Disapprove?" she asked.

He was not sure he got her meaning. "I didn't know...well, Xenonians were in such great shape." At least this one was.

"Didn't wish to offend." She dipped to the floor to retrieve her skirt.

"No offense taken." His gaze returned to the buttons on her blouse. "Did you need help with any more—buttons?"

"Not at the moment." She sat. "Much better. Are you sure you're not too hot?"

"Come to think of it," Quaid said as he hurried to pull off his leather jacket, "I almost forgot to take it off— just like a second skin." Yeah, he was hot. Really hot, but he wasn't sure she meant that kind of hot.

She nodded. "Fighter's gear."

"Yes, well, no fighting allowed here." He set the jacket on the back of his chair, then sat down.

"Or much else. Ever been married?"

The question of marriage—dead kicker to any new relationship. "No, and you?"

"No, and I don't intend to be."

Life couldn't get any better. He stretched his legs out in triumph.

"Another cup?" She returned to the kitchen.

"Sure." He leaned back in his chair as she reached for the coffee jar. He sighed deeply as he studied her shorts. Satin was unforgiving...a lump here or there would ruin the line, but whoa, she had some of the firmest carynthian melons he'd ever seen and those shapely legs never quit. "Really nice legs," he said under his breath.

"Thank you," she responded without as much as a look in his direction.

His face warming, he hadn't realized Xenonians had such fine-tuned hearing. He'd have to keep his tongue in check in the future. "Don't you hate being in a place like this with nothing to do?"

Zaira poured a cup of coffee for him. "I've met all kinds of interesting folks. I've even met you. I have some orders to ship. You might check out a book yourself. Several adventure stories are on the upper shelves over there. *Kidnapped*, *Rastorian Relief*... all kinds of works."

"Never heard of them."

"Don't doubt it. Nobody ever reads anything

worthwhile anymore. But since you're going to be staying for a week—"

"How did you know that?"

She paused, her cheeks blushing a little, and he swore she looked like she'd made a big mistake. "You mentioned it, didn't you?"

"No." Quaid hated being suspicious of people, but it came with the business. Too many times he'd nearly had his liver sliced in two by a laser gun, just when he'd gotten complacent. He downed the rest of the coffee.

"Well, I guess I assumed it then. You said your ion propulsion drive was out. Only Maldovia will have a replacement with Orion in the middle of the Great Galaxy War."

Okay, he could buy that.

The feeling of being trapped on the desert planet made his skin crawl. Nothing could be worse than being a bird with clipped wings left to rot on an inhospitable planet. Not that the people were, but the desert would fry a body quicker than the double sun of Heliostrate if he had to cross it mid-day. He'd take fighting the worst of his enemies in the blackness of space any time.

"I have some comfortable sofas over there. You can stretch out, read a book, and we could have lunch together later...if I'm not being too forward."

He jumped at the opening. "I thought we might take the time to get to know one another a little better first."

Zaira touched the button of her blouse and smiled. "Later, business first."

No use in rushing things. If he offended her, Carver could very well tell Quaid to fix his own craft. "Can you recommend something to read?"

"Sure... *The Changeling*...fairly contemporary."

Zaira climbed onto a stool, then reached high above her head. Her already short shorts lifted higher. He should have rushed over to help her, but the view from where he stood was too good to be true. He examined the shadow created by the edge of the shorts. The question was did she have anything on underneath those shimmering blue teasers? He could see no line to indicate she did. Straining his eyes revealed nothing further, but the rest of his body reacted impulsively with male interest.

She pulled the book, climbed down from the stool, and held the book out to him. "Enjoy." She disappeared into a back room next to the counter.

She sure knew how to make a man agonize.

Sitting down on one of the sofas, he skimmed through the book. "No pictures." He turned to the first page.

Without hesitation, Zenith dove into the lake, determined to find the lost scrolls of Orion before their enemy did. Darkness enveloped her as she neared the muddy bottom while her heart sank...

Quaid closed the book, then set it aside. "It's a fantasy."

"It's a true story."

Despite doubting the truth of her words, he picked up the book and read further.

The prophecy of the realm will be fulfilled once the scrolls are returned to the High Council, she reminded herself as she gasped for air.

"The scrolls don't exist."

"How do you know that?" Zaira poked her head through the doorway.

"Terran archaeologists have been searching for the scrolls for years. Many say they don't exist."

"Who says?"

"The Terrans, of course."

She gave a short laugh, not amused, more sarcastic than anything. "The Terrans don't know everything."

"We know more than all other human species combined."

Zaira's lips curved up slightly as her brows raised. "I see. Perhaps the book is not to your liking and another—"

"No, I'll read along a bit further. Maybe something will pique my interest eventually." He thumbed the pages for a second. "Is Zenith a changeling?"

"You'll have to read for yourself and see."

He twisted his mouth. "She's a changeling."

"Sometimes things aren't what they seem."

He'd fought in enough battles to know that for a certainty. Nodding, Quaid began reading again.

Zenith readied herself for another dive, but a glint of metal in the woods caught her eye. A dark-haired man strolled toward her, his weapon catching the rays of the sun, and glistening.

"It's a warrior's story." Quaid's interest was snagged. He read another page, then frowned. "Bah, it's a love story."

"What's wrong with that?" Zaira walked into the room, wearing a low cut, snug-fitting, blue sweater-blouse that accentuated her breasts. She pulled her long hair back.

"You were changing in there? I thought you had business."

"I deal with all kinds—some prefer different forms of dress when I communicate with them over the onscreen monitor. Good for business. That's why I was...dressing when you first entered the store."

"Ah." Quaid studied the new look Zaira wore and was instantly impressed, his darned body reacting all over again.

"So you were saying?" she asked.

"Warriors don't have time for families." He closed the book. The image of his dead mother was etched forever in his mind. How could he commit to a woman, then leave her behind like his father did his mother, fighting the big fight in space? And she had no one to fight for her?

"Aren't you going to read any further?" Zaira twisted a fat dark curl around her slender finger.

Seductive damned minx. "I already know what's going to happen. They find the scrolls, fall in love, and save her father from being ousted as head of the High Council...end of story."

"Ah, I see."

Quaid's smile broadened as Zaira looked amused while she strolled over to him. "That's so, isn't it?" he asked.

"It's a true story." Her hair rolled to the side as she tilted her head. "The scrolls haven't been found yet."

"But they fall in love and marry and—"

"If you say so."

He fingered the book. "She's a changeling, and since he's a Terran, they wouldn't want to mix their species...so perhaps things don't work out the way I'd imagined."

"You never know. Truth can be stranger than fiction."

"So true. Once a Rondovin scout ship surrendered to me. I knew it was a trick and was ready to blast them as soon as they showed their true intent. To my surprise, they wanted asylum on a planet untouched by war." Quaid let out his breath. "They were the first to wish peace and asked me to escort them safely."

"Did you?"

Quaid twisted on the sofa. "Yes, it wasn't my usual kind of mission, but it suited my purpose."

"How's that?"

"There would be fewer to get rid of in the usual way."

Zaira took a deep breath. "You mean fewer to kill?"

"Yes, I'm a soldier. That's what I do."

She leaned over the overstuffed sofa. Her lips pouted slightly, while her dark eyes held his captive. "Have you never thought of another occupation?"

He had never met a female who could unsettle him so. Lying to her about his career plans wouldn't have worked with her—he was certain, and yet he wished he could find the right choice of words that would appease her. Others might have said what she'd like to hear, but he couldn't.

"Nope. My father was the captain of his own vessel. He had trained me since I was seven. This is the life for me."

"I see. I'll just let you get back to your book. If you need anything, just holler." She straightened, and his gaze drifted to her sweater. "Did you need anything?"

You, is all that comes to mind. He smiled at her. She

mirrored his expression, then returned to her office. Taking a deep breath, he tried to quell his raging hard-on. He turned his attention back to the book and read a brief passage.

"The Rondovins!" Quaid exclaimed as he hit his fist on the arm of the furniture. "Those short, squat, flat-nosed, big-lipped, thick-necked, war-like, short-tempered humans—"

"What's that?" Zaira's voice was muffled by the humming of a copier-like machine.

"I should've known the treacherous Rondovins would have stolen the scrolls." He studied the entrance to her office.

She had changed her clothes without shutting the door. He hadn't even realized it until now? How could he have missed that?

CHAPTER 3

The bell jingled as the door was thrown open. Drake Jorgenson, Quaid's long-time friend and smuggler by trade, strode into the shop. He hadn't seen him in over a year, figuring he'd gotten himself killed or imprisoned somewhere.

"Quaid Lassiter, what brings you to Xenon?"

"Trouble with my drive."

"I *thought* that was your craft at the repair shop. Looks a bit scraped up."

"Be as good as new…soon. What brings *you* here?"

Drake shrugged.

Quaid closed the book. "You wouldn't be here unless the trip was worth your while."

"I've been commissioned to come here," Drake said.

"So what are you looking for that could be worth

anyone's interest here?"

"The scrolls."

Quaid stared at Drake for a moment. "I thought the Rondovins had them on Orion."

"Nope, they're here now. So, you reading anything interesting?"

Quaid lowered his voice. "Just some story about a changeling who was searching for the High Council scrolls."

"You mean Zenith? She's no changeling...just Darrant. I'm surprised you haven't read the story before this." Drake sat across from Quaid on the arm of a wide-winged chair.

"I don't make it a habit to read. Nothing of interest like living the real thing."

"Don't let Zaira hear you say that."

"Zaira Cole?" Quaid sat taller in his seat. "What difference does it make to her?" His brows arched slightly with the level of his voice.

"Books are her first love." Drake motioned to her shelves. "Haven't you noticed?"

Quaid considered Drake's spotless appearance. His boots shined to a mirror-like image, his beige shirt sported a necktie, and his wavy red locks were smoothed down behind his ears. Fine lines imprinted across Drake's suede jacket indicated a brush had swept away the dust. "Kind of a new look for you, isn't it?"

Drake smiled. "Looked forward to seeing Zaira again."

At once, Quaid's blood heated. Drake was after the woman? "She's rather difficult to get to know."

Laughing, Drake slapped Quaid on the shoulder. "I wouldn't try, if I were you."

"Is there something going on between you and the lady?"

Drake leaned down to speak in private. "Mating season just began on Xenon, and she just turned of age."

***

The ball was already rolling and Zaira had been instrumental in giving it the first big shove, but now the time to set her brother's plan in action had arrived. Green the planet, then prepare for war. Her relatively peaceful people would have to understand, if they wanted the benefits of a green planet, they'd have to fight to keep it. And Quaid Lassiter had the know-how and the men to help them.

Now that Drake had arrived as Quaid's right-hand man, though the two men wouldn't realize her father—as head of the High Council—planned it that way, she had to set the controls that would begin the greening of the desert planet.

As soon as she entered the caves, she smelled the strong odor of speckled spider droppings permeating the normally wet soil smell of the caves. They hadn't been here the last time she was here.

She hadn't planned for any trouble, not this early in the game, and yet now, she had a new menace to deal with.

The spider must have smelled her in the dark and began its warning sound, a raucous clicking noise to alert any others nearby.

For a second, she hesitated. Should she leave the caves? Or fight the spiders, hoping she'd make it safely to the lever room without injury? Injury, she scoffed at herself. If one of their poisonous fangs dug into her skin, injury would be the least of her—

The creature appeared from the black abyss, and she swallowed the scream that issued from her throat.

***

Quaid stared at Drake as the heavenly aroma of coffee lingered in the air of Zaira's shop. "Mating season?" he said under his breath.

Even now he could envision Zaira's breasts squeezed together in silk with half of the buttons on her blouse still undone—he preferred that to the sweater blouse she now wore. His gaze returned to the small office beyond the coffee counter. He was interested—real interested, but he hadn't a clue what mating season on Xenon entailed.

"Yep. Just better watch out."

Rubbing his stubbled chin, Quaid frowned. He must have looked like a wild barbarian to her, not like a fighter pilot and Prince of Orion. He couldn't have Drake spoiling his time with her...all spiffed up for the occasion. Never had he seen his friend's jacket dusted or boots shined, ever...not in all of the years he'd known him.

Quaid cleared his throat. "So after you get a cup of coffee, can I go with you for a spin?" He just had to get Drake out of here. It wouldn't do for him to hurt his chances with Zaira. "I'd need to be back by lunchtime, but that would give us a good two hours still."

"Why would you want to go with me?"

"I'm stuck here, don't you know. It'll take a week for my propulsion drive to be replaced."

"Why so long?"

"Carver has to order the drive all the way from Maldovia."

"I don't know if I should tell you this then, but Carver has the replacement drive in his shop already. I just dropped by there to see about a new solar panel. While I was there, I had to use the latrine. You know how nobody in this place posts signs, so I walked into the wrong room and a brand new ionic propulsion drive—with your name written on it—was sitting in an open crate."

Quaid stood, dropping the book on the floor. "I'll

have to have a word with Carver—"

"He stepped out. Said he wouldn't be back until later this evening."

Quaid glanced at the office. "I have to have a word with Zaira."

He crossed the store, then walked into her office. The place was empty. What the hell?

His mind raced. She was just there. He had just spoken with her.

A particulate-manipulator machine hummed as it scanned a document in a corner of the room. He grasped the handle of the only other door in the room. With a quick flick of his wrist, he twisted the doorknob, but found resistance. The door was locked, with no visible means to unlock it. He walked back into the shop and grabbed his jacket.

"You must've whispered the words to Zaira. I didn't overhear a thing the two of you said."

"Seems she had other business to take care of as well. She's gone."

Quaid had a gut feeling something was terribly wrong on Xenon. First, Zaira's father had acted so oddly when Quaid nearly crashed his craft into the hangar. Sure, he had attributed it to Carver's concern he might have wrecked his repair station. Now Carver had lied about the drive taking a week to arrive from Maldovia? More than that, he had already ordered the replacement drive some weeks prior and had it in stock with Quaid's name on it? Quaid hadn't had any plan to drop in there. Not until he had engine trouble.

Was it a mere coincidence that Zaira just vanished, too?

His neck muscles tightened into knotted rope. He didn't believe in coincidences.

Ever since his navigational system switched over to destination Xenon for no known reason, nothing had gone well for him. Not until he met Zaira. Her doe-like eyes and her attire had made him lose his train-of-thought more than once. He'd never seen a woman with so many curves, in all the right places.

He strode to the entrance of the shop, then jerked the door open. "I'm going to take a look at that ion drive."

"I'll show you where I saw it."

They crossed the dusty platform, and Quaid studied the vehicle parked nearby. "New spacecraft?" He couldn't believe Drake would've already replaced the last new one he owned.

"You know me...new model every year."

"Have you been doing much smuggling these days?"

"Sure, business is good."

They walked into the storage room crammed with repair parts for virtually any model of spaceship in the universe.

Quaid stared at the crates. "So how did the scrolls get here?"

Drake shrugged. "Apparently, the Rondovins didn't believe anyone would ever discover them on this desolate planet." He pointed to an empty plastic crate. "I swear the drive was right here." More crates stacked along the walls towered to the top of the twenty-foot ceiling behind it. "That's where your drive was sitting, right there."

"Maybe you were mistaken, Drake. You haven't been drinking the liquor you've been smuggling into this place for the poor souls who live on this dry planet, have you?" He had no reason to believe Carver had lied to him, and Drake was known to imbibe a bit too much on occasion.

"Nary a drop." Drake scratched his head, mussing up his red hair. "Perhaps Carver already replaced your drive."

Quaid hurried out of the room with Drake on his heels as they strode to the hangar. They walked into the building built large enough for four fighter craft. He couldn't believe his eyes. His ship was gone. Quaid's knees weakened as the blood roared in his ears. "I'll kill Carver when I find him. Of all the—"

"Come on, Quaid. My business is south of here, but we'll take a look for your craft while we're at it. I can't imagine why Carver would have taken your ship like that. He doesn't even know how to pilot one, I don't believe."

"Well it sure as hell didn't walk out of here on its own! What in the hell is going on?" Quaid climbed into Drake's spacecraft, angry, determined to get to the bottom of this as soon as he could.

***

Drake's Silverado Class spacecraft soared high above the sandy planet as Quaid peered through one of the dust-covered windows. Brown leafless shrubs dotted the landscape in a madcap way, reminding him of the home he'd left behind. Orion was no more than a bombed-out shell of a planet now...nearly as inhospitable as Xenon. "I can see why I never bothered to take a sight-seeing trip here."

"The reason the Xenonians settled the planet in the first place was nobody ever had any interest in it. They're about the only truly peaceful people I know." Drake smiled at Quaid. "Ever been here during one of their dust storms?"

"Don't like dust. Deep space with its black velvet atmosphere is just the kind of backdrop I'm suited for." Quaid leaned back in the leather-covered, high-backed chair and fingered the soft material, just as smooth as he imagined Zaira's skin would feel. To have run his hands through her hair, to have slipped his fingers into that ice blue blouse of hers and felt her warm breasts waiting for his caress...he wished.

His whole body stirred into action. Even when he was apart from her, he couldn't stop thinking of her and her hypnotic voice—spoken like a woman in the throes of passionate lovemaking.

Wondering what the hell was going on with her and her father, he turned his attention to the craft. "Nice touch."

"Top of the line."

Quaid glanced down at the switch for the shields and frowned. "Only Class 3 shields system?"

"I outrun 'em."

Surveying the instrument panel further, Quaid ran his hand over it. "This craft has barely any firepower. A laser cannon, tube cannon, and pulse emitter...that's it?"

Drake's green eyes heated in anger. "It's not a bird of war, Quaid."

"Not enough fire power or shields for my liking." Quaid studied the panel. "Nice 20th century touch with the wood paneling." His own craft was strictly functional. It was a craft of war and well-built for the job. Still, he admired the special amenities of Drake's bird.

Drake laughed. "All right, enough with the critique. She's not a warship." He pointed to an irregularly-shaped lake. "That's where we'll land."

"You don't mean to tell me the scrolls are hidden in that lake?" Quaid's brows furrowed while the ship descended.

"No. Caves are nearby, but the entrances are impossible to detect from way up here."

Before they could set down, Drake ran his hand over a touch-screen panel to raise his shields. "Hold tight!"

A swirling mass of dust and debris headed their way, and Quaid grabbed onto the arms of his chair. "Set her down before—"

"Too late!" Drake shouted as the funnel slammed into the craft.

Debris swept across the ship at speeds over 200 miles an hour. Quaid's voice shook with the vibration of the craft. "Use the jump-drive!"

"Can't at this altitude and can't land as we've been shoved from our previous location. I can't tell if we're right over the lake now or not...and believe me, these crafts aren't amphibious."

The craft's hull lifted as the funnel tilted the ship upward, and Drake kicked in the rear thrusters. "Got to break free or this storm's liable to flip us on our top...then Caldoria, here we come."

Inwardly, Quaid was shaken. He'd never encountered anything so bizarre. "Caldoria?"

Drake pushed another switch. The sound of the thrusters roared as the ship struggled through the funnel. "Don't read much, do you?"

"No interest." Quaid stared into the debris, trying to glimpse light on the other side of the storm. Finally seeing a speck of white in the gloom, he gestured to the northeast. "There's clearing in that direction."

Drake turned the ship toward the scant light and soon sped out of the funnel. "Whoa, that was close. Never experienced anything quite that violent." He glanced down at the scenery and frowned to see the lake had vanished. "Guess we got thrown off from our course a bit." He touched the navigational panel and turned the ship southwest.

In disbelief, Quaid stared as the mile-wide funnel headed in the same direction only half-a-mile ahead of them. He couldn't let Drake see how much the storm had affected him. His old buddy would never let him live it down. He wiped his brow with his sleeve while Drake concentrated on flying the ship back to the lake. "Never seen anything like it. Now I know space is the only place for me."

Drake smiled. "Thought you were more of an adventurer than that."

"Fighting dust storms is not my idea of an adventure. I like being able to fight back." Quaid pointed at the lake. "There it is."

Drake switched the controls to automatic landing. "Sorry, that we haven't seen any sign of your craft. Do you want to keep me company for a bit?"

"Nothing else better to do, except to wring Carver's scrawny neck when I get hold of him." Despite being angry with Zaira's father, he still wanted to play it right with Zaira. "Just remember, I need to return to the coffee shop by lunchtime." Maybe she would know what her father was up to.

The craft landed on the rough, rocky surface with a jolt. Drake turned off the engine. "Have we a date with a particular individual?"

"Lunch."

"Ah, with Zaira." Drake reached down for his Millennium Colt blaster. "There's another in the compartment above your head. Grab a couple of those portable lanterns, if you would."

"Dangerous mission?"

"Never know."

They clipped the lanterns on their jacket pockets and exited through the forward hatch. After sealing off the entrance, Drake pulled out his map and pointed to a raised mound in the earth. "This looks to be the place. Search for an opening in the ground somewhere near that hill."

They walked off, their boots crunching on top of the rocky soil as they headed in different directions for several yards, then Quaid stopped. "Over here!" He peered into the hole that dropped into the darkness. "Looks a bit like deep space."

Drake ran to join him, then took a ragged breath as he stared into the hole. "Well, I'm not fond of enclosed spaces. If you wouldn't mind leading the way."

Quaid's mouth quirked up slightly. "Didn't think you were afraid of much of anything."

"Not me." Drake frowned at him. "Just thought you could clear the cobwebs as you walked ahead of me."

Surprised to hear that Drake was afraid of anything, Quaid grinned. Not in all the years they'd traipsed through the galaxies, he had known Drake to show any fear. "Afraid of subterranean speckled spiders? They don't bite...too hard."

"Yeah, well, maybe you haven't seen one close up...like I have."

They climbed down into the abyss on a man-carved stone staircase. Drake's lantern flickered. "Should've charged these up a bit longer, I'm afraid."

"Now you say so. We'll never make it out of here alive, if we don't have a lantern to light our way."

"They'll be all right. Come on, I want to get this over with and hurry on out of here."

"Is there something that you know," Quaid asked, as he walked into a pool of ankle-deep, ice-cold water, "that I don't?" He was quickly coming to the conclusion not all was as it seemed.

"Caves give me the creeps. That's all."

Quaid took a deep breath of the cold, musty air. He shifted his gaze upward to the forty-foot-high ceiling where bats dangled in an ebony blanket. Dripping water caught his attention, then his light reflected off a metal object leaning against one of the natural rock shelves. He reached out to touch the silver metal.

Drake shouted, "No! Don't touch that!" His words of warning were shouted too late.

Quaid lifted the halberd from its resting place. A blast of fire shot out from a cannon poised above the shelf. Quaid and Drake dove for the floor, the fiery inferno barely missing them, heating and drying the air above them.

"Well, you could've warned me." Quaid stood up and wiped the wet mud from his trousers.

"You're the warrior. I thought you would know about booby traps."

"Whoever heard of such a thing? I'm used to fighting ship to ship." The halberd poked out of the mud near Quaid's boot.

"If you'd read some of the great literature about early wars on Earth, Terra Firma, you would've learned how often the enemy booby-trapped objects for their unsuspecting foe."

"*You* should know with the kind of shady business

you conduct."

"Killing is more honorable?"

Quaid shrugged off his friend's comment. The same banter had played between them for years. "At least we all know what we're there for."

They walked into a tunnel, wide enough for the two to stay abreast. Quaid turned his lantern light brighter. "Who's the party paying your commission, by the way?"

"Members of the High Council."

"It no longer exists. It was disbanded, what...forty years ago or thereabouts?"

More bats clustered together high above on the jagged rock formations. They twittered slightly as the men's voices echoed off the cave walls.

"They exist. They're still trying to bring peace to the world," Drake said.

"Why wouldn't they have come for the scrolls themselves? If they already knew where they were—"

"I asked, but they wouldn't say. The money was right, so I took the job." A drop of liquid hit Drake's cheek, and he stopped abruptly.

Quaid smiled. "Just underground water, Drake. You sure are jumpy."

"Don't like caves."

Quaid glanced at the somber tone to Drake's voice. "Had some troubles in them before?"

"Some." Drake clamped his mouth shut in a grim

line.

Quaid wondered what that was all about.

They continued through the narrow passage in silence, then the sudden smell of acrid sewage caught them by surprise. Quaid whispered, "Speckled spiders."

Drake nodded as he readied his weapon. "Let them come to us." His voice was darkened with concern. "They can't get through this narrow passage—"

"Unless we're dead," Quaid reminded him, leveling his weapon at where the passage opened into another cave.

"Don't aim to get that way." Drake's shaky voice indicated killing spiders wasn't his favorite pastime.

Quaid's eyes narrowed as he watched for any sign of the spindly-legged creatures that reminded him of daddy-long-legs, only of giant proportion. Their mouthparts could put the fear into any warrior's heart as the jagged teeth vibrated up and down when the creature taunted its foe.

Drake's neck muscles tightened.

Quaid turned his attention back to the entrance. "So about Zaira, have you made any headway with her?"

Drake smiled. "The last time I visited the shop, her father popped in—said he wanted a cup of coffee. Rather, I think he wanted to keep an eye on me."

"Don't blame him there." Quaid studied Drake's

polished appearance. "And today?"

"Thought I had a sporting chance with Zaira this time, with Carver taking his leave like he did."

"Guess it's not meant to be."

"Well, not at the moment," Drake said. A high-pitched squeal from somewhere ahead of them in the dark peeled through the cave. "They've caught our scent."

They stared into the inky gloom for several minutes as they strained to see any sign of the spiders. Hearing a clicking sound, they readied their weapons for the first sign of the beasts. The creature's fluorescent eyes glowed in the dark. Quaid and Drake fired simultaneously. Their blasts woke the sleeping bats overhead, sending them flying in a screeching mass into the blackness. The spider shrieked in its death throes, adding to the ruckus.

"Good thing the spiders aren't any match for these weapons." Drake wiped his brow with a cloth.

"Let's just hope there aren't too many of them."

Several minutes passed in silence. Drake ran his hand over his blaster. "They're trying to figure us out."

"They're not that clever." Fighting spiders wasn't something Quaid normally did. A fighter pilot...that was his kind of job. Still, a fight was a fight and the adrenaline coursed through his blood as he faced the challenge. The thrill of war filled his soul, just as it had his father's and grandfather's. Yet, if the Rondovins hadn't killed his mother, would he have chosen his current occupation?

He could still remember her gentle voice as she shared archaeology finds with him. He had her gift, too—interpreting the ancient ruins—something few could do. All of that was but a memory of his youth, long ago. A warrior was what he was, and he knew he'd die someday, battling the great fight...maybe even today.

The clicking sound returned. Quaid waited for the sight of the eyes and fired. Burning, putrid flesh filled the air. He wrinkled his nose, then cleared his throat. "Whew, thought their droppings smelled bad."

"Two down."

"Click, click, click," the sound echoed in rapid succession, and they fired at them again.

"Three," Drake said. Another spider attacked, and another after that. He soon lost count.

The clicking and the squealing continued for half-an-hour as the spiders hurried to protect their lair while the intruders attempted to protect themselves.

Drake reloaded his weapon. "How are you doing?"

"Getting low. We won't last much longer if there are many more of them." The fragrance of jasmine wafted on the air, and Quaid said under his breath, "Zaira."

"Now isn't the time to think of the woman of our

dreams, lover boy." Drake fired his weapon again.

Shrieks farther into the cave followed, and Quaid turned to Drake as the onslaught of spiders ceased. "Sounds like the spiders are focusing their wrath on some other intruder."

Drake checked his weapon, his forehead dotted with perspiration.

"Shall we assist?" Quaid asked, intending to and figuring Drake would automatically agree.

"No telling what the other creature could be."

They paused as they heard more shrieks.

"He's having all of the fun without us." Quaid motioned to the cave.

"After you." Drake mirrored Quaid's hand signal.

Quaid climbed through the long-legged carcasses and headed for the center of the cave. Four more tunnels cut into the rock facing.

Drake examined his map. "To the right."

"The sounds are coming from the tunnel to the left." Quaid studied the tunnel's narrow entrance.

"Let the other intruder handle the spiders, and we can continue on our way," Drake said.

Quaid headed for the tunnel to the left, then turned to Drake. "Coming?"

Drake refolded the map in a hurry, then shoved it into his pocket. "Or not." He hastened to join Quaid.

Quaid dove into the tunnel without regard for his

own safety now. The scent of jasmine grew stronger. It couldn't belong to Zaira. She'd never have lived two minutes in a cave filled with the poisonous spiders. Yet, he just couldn't shake the feeling that he was breathing in her fragrance. He skirted around a dead spider in the center of the tunnel that the other intruder had killed, then heard another shriek.

Gripping his weapon tighter, he and Drake climbed over six more bodies in their rush before entering another cave. They waited, listening. The clicking sound began again. They turned with their weapons raised, fired their guns at the creature, and silenced its shrieks forever.

Quaid strained his eyes as he stared into the abyss. Moving into the center of the cave, he saw Zaira dressed in a skin-tight suit of a leather-like material as black as the cave itself. Her dark hair rested over her shoulders in waves as she reached up to touch her head.

"Zaira," he whispered as if saying her name any louder would make her vanish before his eyes. "Zaira!" he hollered as he ran toward her. "What in the devil's name are you doing here?" He touched her cheek. "You're trembling." *Not good.*

He took hold of her arm and eased her onto the cave floor. Looking up at Drake, he said, "Let me have your water pouch."

"She wouldn't want what I have in here." Drake

patted his pouch.

"Mine's in my ship."

"I'm really all right," Zaira responded, her voice shaky. Unable to sit any longer, she lay down on the floor.

"You're shaking even worse now." Quaid took her hands in his. "And your hands are ice cold." He studied her dark eyes as they lost their luster. A pang of guilt filled him with remorse. He'd lusted for her, wanting nothing more than to fill her with his desire. And now, she could die, just as a flower torn from its stem would perish. He touched her cheek with a tender caress. "She's been bitten."

Just saying the truth made him shudder. She wouldn't have long to live.

"She'll need an antidote."

"No." Zaira whispered. She waved her finger slightly in the air. "You have the map, Drake Jorgensen. You must...retrieve the scrolls."

"Later." Quaid lifted her off the cold, wet floor. "Come on, Drake, we've got to find her father and a healer fast. Keep a look out for any more signs of spiders."

"No need." Her voice was barely a whisper. "Coffee?"

"A little later."

Zaira's gaze studied his. Despite the poison's effect,

she still drew him in with her warmth. Never had he been so taken with a woman.

"Disappointed?"

"Shh, keep your strength." Quaid held her tightly in his arms as he dashed across the uneven floor with Drake leading as they backtracked to the entrance. His heart thumped as his head pounded with a mixture of emotions. He was angry...damned angry. What was she doing in the caves anyway? A woman who looked like she did should be featured on *Pinups of the New Millennium*...only he wouldn't want anyone else to get an eyeful of her.

"Whatever made you..." he asked.

Her eyelids were closed now. His anger faded as concern for her health took its place. He tried to recall his emergency medical training. Last he'd remembered—only the antidote for the poison could save her now.

"We've got to hurry, Drake."

"Depending on Xenonian's resistance to the poison, if they're anything like the Terrans, she hasn't more than two hours at the most to live."

"What if Carver isn't back at the hangar? Do you know where we can get medical treatment?"

"Except for coming here to get my craft repaired, I haven't bothered to explore anything further. This place is a desolate way-stop, nothing more."

Quaid held Zaira tighter, her body shivering nonstop. She had to be all right. She just had to be. He took a deep breath as he studied her silent features. The adrenaline flowed through his veins as though he was in a fight for his life...only this time the fight was for hers. How could he feel this way for a woman? Just a good time if she had been of like mind. That's all he had wanted.

He couldn't get tied up with a woman—any woman—not for good. But, God, she was more beautiful than any woman he'd ever met on any of the worlds he'd ever been. He'd never seen a more perfect body...well, better than perfect. Those full pink lips of hers, silent for words now, still shimmered with gloss, waiting to be kissed.

Quaid cleared his throat. "Can't you walk any faster?"

"I can't race through this uneven—"

"Just hurry."

"I'm hurrying. I'm hurrying."

When they reached the hole stretching to the desert plain, Drake carried the weapons. Quaid climbed after him with Zaira slumped over his shoulder like a rag doll as her body remained motionless.

As soon as they reached the rocky surface, Drake bolted to his craft while Quaid ran after him, huffing and puffing, cradling Zaira in his arms. Puffs of dirt rose in the air, kicked up by the tromping of their boots.

Drake entered the code on the side of his craft. The hatch started to lift. Quaid hurried up the steps while they were still unfolding from the craft. The door closed with a whoosh, and he strapped her into a chair. He pushed a button, causing the seat to recline.

"Grab a chair!" Drake jumped into his seat, then reached for the controls while Quaid headed for another. "Uh, Quaid." He stared out of the window as Quaid joined him. "We have company...the really bad kind."

CHAPTER 4

Quaid's blood heated when he saw the black-haired, squat-built men surrounding the ship as they aimed heavy-duty canons at the craft. "Rondovins! What are you waiting for? Take her up! Blast them!"

"Not this time, buddy. This craft isn't half as maneuverable as yours and certainly not as well-armed."

"But we've got to get Zaira—"

Quaid's speech was interrupted as one of the Rondovins indicated they wanted Drake to open the hatch to his craft. As soon as the hatch drew up, five Rondovin soldiers dressed in black uniforms barged onto the ship. With gnarly hands, they yanked Drake and Quaid toward the steps.

Quaid twisted to break loose from the soldier's firm grip on his arm. "Speckled spiders have bitten the lady."

Two of the Rondovins unfastened the belts he had secured Zaira with. One lifted her and carried her out of the craft. Quaid frowned. "Damn, Rondovins. Can't get a word out of them."

"Their ship probably has a medical tech aboard. At least they'll attempt to make her well before they execute us."

"Comforting, Drake. Remind me not to bring you along when things get rather grim." The Rondovins set charges to Drake's craft, making him scowl. "Somehow, I don't believe the commission I was going to make on this venture will even cover expenses."

They climbed aboard the Rondovin command ship of prey, marked with its distinctive gold trim. One of the Rondovins carried Zaira into a room, while two more shoved Quaid and Drake into a room opposite hers. As soon as they were inside, their doors slid closed.

Two cots, two chairs, and one small table furnished the typical sleeping quarters of a craft of war. They sat down quickly on the beds as the spaceship lifted with a roar.

Quaid rubbed his brow as he stared at the handle-less door. "Why would a Rondovin command ship of prey be in this vicinity?"

"Beats me."

Quaid spied the ventilation shaft directly above his head.

Drake followed his gaze. "You're not thinking of—"

"I don't know about you, but I always figured I'd go out with a more glorious end than this." Quaid moved a chair beneath the air vent.

Drake gave a small shrug. "I hadn't really given any thought to the subject, but I'm game if you are."

"All right. If we can find the weapons' cache, then head back through the ventilation shaft to the control room—"

"Let's do it."

Drake steadied the chair as Quaid opened the grate.

After he climbed into the shaft, Quaid pulled his jacket tighter around his neck. His husky breath smoked in the frosty air, and his fingers quickly numbed. Light poked through the grill from their room, illuminating the section for several yards. As he crawled along, wiggling his torso flat against the narrow passage, the shaft grew dark.

He had to concentrate on getting them safely out of the bind they were in, but he couldn't stop thinking about Zaira. Did the Rondovins know how to cure her? Would they bother? And why did they take them prisoner in the first place? Xenon wasn't at war. Never had been. It was one of the few neutral planets. Not that any of that mattered to them right now.

Focus, Quaid. Use those instincts of yours and

Drake's to get out of this pickle of a mess. Still, I wonder. The longer he was on Xenon, the more muddled the situation became. What was really going on? Something Carver knew, but had been afraid to speak to him about it?

Quaid maneuvered around a bend in the vent, and Drake bumped his foot with his head. Quaid stifled the urge to cry out. Filtered light ahead caught his attention, and he worked his way to the next grill.

Voices were spoken below and Quaid paused.

"Yeah, he says he's getting promoted, but that was *before* the general found him with his daughter."

Laughter followed.

Another Rondovin said, "He should've known the girl was underage—won't be twenty-five for another three revolutions of the moon."

Quaid crawled past the vent and arrived at the room where they were holding Zaira. "Zaira," Quaid said under his breath. He pointed to the grill.

"Weapons?" Drake whispered.

Disheartened to see her lifeless body strapped onto a table, Quaid studied her. Her dark hair draped over the edge and her breasts rose slightly with every breath she took. The medical tech stepped out of the room.

Hating to leave her, Quaid knew he couldn't help her right now. He crawled farther until they reached a grate above a room filled with treasures from conquests of other cultures: sabers from Cranyor, golden statues from the Caspian home world, even crystalline sculptures from Orion. Noticeably absent was any relic of Xenon. He didn't imagine they had any.

Quaid moved toward the next room.

Ivory satins trimmed in gold and black draped the next set of apartments. A larger-than-normal bed filled the room near to capacity while a small ornate 25th-century, mahogany bedside stand sat next to it. "Captain's quarters," Quaid whispered. "Weapon's room should be nearby."

He crawled to the next vent, then peered into the room. A metal desk covered in papers made him pause longer than he intended.

Drake tugged at Quaid's boot. "What's up?" he whispered.

"Possibly war plans."

"Another mission."

Quaid frowned to have to bypass important documents, if that was what they were, but he knew Drake was right. With reluctance, he headed past the vent.

An ear-shattering rendition of some Rondovin war song in a typical gruff Rondovin drawl yelled out above the sound of the shower. Quaid peered down into the steam-filled room. If the captain only knew his prisoners were listening to his singing in the shower. He passed the room by and Drake chortled behind him when he crawled over the shower room.

"Weapon's room." Quaid hurried to pull the grate free. He slipped into the unguarded but secure room. Drake waited in the ventilation shaft and watched through the opening. Quaid selected his weapon of choice and Drake nodded in agreement.

"For the first time in my life, I'm glad the Rondovins stole our technological advancements in weaponry. It'll certainly come in handy." Quaid passed the weapons to Drake. Then he pulled a crate underneath the grate and climbed atop it, then reached up to Drake, who helped to lift him into the shaft. Drake replaced the grate while Quaid continued through the passage.

Twenty minutes later, they found the control room empty and the automatic controls in place due to the lateness of the hour.

Quaid dropped into the room and studied the controls. "What do you think?"

Drake dropped out of the ceiling. He rubbed his hands together to get the feeling back into his cold-numbed fingers, then leaned over to observe the dials. "Piece of cake. If we switch this here, and turn that there, the craft should make an unscheduled landing."

"And then?"

Drake stared at the on-view screen and smiled. "Looks as though we're crossing the Craterton Lake.

Rondovins can't swim."

"What about Zaira?" Quaid asked.

Drake rubbed his chin in thought. "If they've given her the antidote—"

"No, can she swim?"

"I'll help her."

"How will we get to her?"

Drake pointed to an internal ship's screen. "The crew members have retired for the night. If you take the corridor here, then turn left at the next hall, her door is four rooms down. I'll deactivate the lock to the door. Meet me where they brought us in initially."

"All right." Quaid waited for the door to the control room to slide open. The day hadn't gone well at all. He hoped there would be no more complications tonight.

As soon as the door opened, he ran down the hall to Zaira's room with his weapon at the ready. Encountering no further trouble, he rushed into her room.

"Zaira," he whispered, but she didn't move a muscle. He slung his weapon over his shoulder, then unbuckled her. After lifting her off the table, he headed for the doorway. Suddenly, the room and hallway turned pitch black.

"Damnation!" he exclaimed as he tripped over a stool and nearly dropped her. The lights flickered on, and he hurried into the hall. He hastened to the hatch where they first had entered the craft. A warning bell's shrill ring suddenly spilled into the halls. He held his breath, his heart thundering.

Drake ran toward him, an intense look of concern on his face. Quaid anticipated seeing a slew of Rondovins following on his heels, but to his relief there were none. Quaid turned his attention to the buttons covering a rectangular panel.

Bang! The craft set down on the lake's surface, causing Quaid to stumble back against the wall as Drake staggered. Regaining his footing, Drake dashed to the instrument panel.

For an instant, he studied the colored buttons marked with cryptic symbols, then punched one, causing a squealing, thundering beat of music to pelt their senses.

"Guess my Rondovin is a little rusty." Drake pushed another button. A grinding noise sounded. Stars sparkled in the night sky as the hatch drew open. "Come on. Got the Rondovins locked up in their quarters. As soon as they figure out that they need to use the ventilation shafts, it'll be too late."

The sound of metal-edged boots clanked as Rondovins ran down the corridor in their direction.

"Maybe not." Drake grabbed Quaid's arm and yanked him up the steps and through the hatchway with Zaira. Drake pulled the two into the water with him before Quaid had a chance to object.

All three went under with a splash into the lukewarm water, then finally resurfaced. Quaid floundered in the lake while trying to keep Zaira's head above water. Drake took hold of her arm and wrapped his other around her neck to keep her afloat.

"I'll take her, Quaid." Drake swam toward the shore as Quaid followed.

Flashes of light struck the lake surface near Quaid, heating the water as it circled around him. His skin prickled with the sensation and the unease ramped up about twenty notches.

Two Rondovins fired at him from the top of the ship.

"Out of range," Quaid said under his breath, then dove under the water and swam underneath the surface just in case.

His heart still beat out of control, the worry plaguing him as to whether Zaira had been given a poison antidote or not. She hadn't stirred, not once in his arms, though her body seemed warmer than it had been. The slight hope kept him splashing toward the beach, annoyed with himself that he wasn't a better swimmer and had to give her up to Drake.

When Drake, Zaira, and he reached the shore, they collapsed. The silver metal ship sparkled with lights like a Christmas spectacle while it wallowed in the placid lake. Like fire ants from Terra Firma exposed to flood waters, Rondovins boiled out of the top of the sinking ship, seeking higher ground.

"You're sure they can't swim, Drake?"

The Rondovins screamed obscenities at them. Flashes of light pierced the darkness as they fired blasts from laser weapons aimed at the beach. Suddenly the ship tilted on end, dropping its Rondovin crew into the lake. The great war machine slipped silently into the black waters. The cries of the men soon died away.

"Positive."

"But you didn't think they could get out of their rooms—"

"Sure they could get out of their rooms. I just didn't think they could do so that quickly. There must have been a manual override switch somewhere."

Quaid leaned over Zaira. "She's still sleeping." He couldn't believe she would have been in the caves without protection. What had she been thinking?

"Both the bite and the antidote cause sedation," Drake assured him.

Xenon's three moons lighted the featureless plain stretching as far as the eye could see.

Drake stood. "Sorry about the lights on the warship, by the way."

"You switched them off?" Irritated that his friend had done so, Quaid lifted Zaira off the beach.

"My arm bumped the wrong switch. Shook me up for a second as I sat in the dark trying to figure out who'd shut them off in the first place."

Unable to hold a grudge, Quaid chuckled. That sounded like his old friend, and if Quaid had attempted to get them out of there, things could have gotten a whole lot more heated. "Nearly broke my neck stumbling over a piece of furniture in the dark." He studied the plain to get his bearing. "Due east, to Carver's place then."

"I'll spell you whenever you need me to, Quaid."

They started their slow-paced trek across the rock-littered dirt. "How did you know so much about the craft?"

"Privateers get all kinds of booty. Happened to pick up one of their command ships of prey once. Those men back there didn't realize it, but I've got quite a bounty on my head for it."

"Don't you think that's why they picked us up? Probably recognized your craft." Quaid frowned at Drake. "I don't know how we could have gone to all the same schools together and turned out so differently."

"It's this blamed war."

Zaira stirred. His hopes lifting he could speak to her, Quaid said, "Zaira?"

"Scrolls," she whispered while her lids fluttered but remained shut.

"That's a good sign. She's dreaming," Drake said.

"Or hallucinating." Quaid couldn't help worrying.

"Either is a good sign, Quaid. The bite causes total paralysis, then death. If she's beginning to speak, she's going to be all right."

The notion would have cheered Quaid further if she'd been walking and talking and sharing her winning smile. The color had returned to her cheeks—that was encouraging. But the lethargy concerned him. He had his doubts too, that Carver would even be at the repair station. Then what would they do?

He turned to Drake. "Whatever would she have been doing in the caves like that?"

"Beats me—unless she was meeting a Xenonian there in private. I've heard tell the mating season has quite a pull on those who come of age. Even so, Carver Cole might not approve yet."

"How old is she?" Quaid asked.

"Twenty-five."

Quaid's brows rose.

"They feel an older age makes for more compatible mates."

"But if she's of age—"

"She'll go through the same process for the next ten years until her father agrees to her choice of mate. In the meantime, if she can slip away and see a male without her father knowing about it..." Drake smiled.

***

After walking for over an hour, the beating of drums, jangling of tambourines, and lilting of flutes drifted on the slight breeze, raising Quaid's spirits that they'd come across a Xenonian village.

Drake asked, "What do you think?" Quaid shifted Zaira's weight in his arms again. "Are you sure you don't want me to carry the lady for a bit? I know she's light, but even so, she's got to weigh a ton by now."

"I'm all right." Zaira stirred again and Quaid quickened his footsteps. "Let's head toward the music. Doesn't sound like anything the Rondovins would play." Not that they were known to camp out on the planet either. Fighting in the sky was their business.

The two stumbled over the grassy uneven terrain as orange-red flames flickered into the night sky. Quaid and Drake stopped as they grew closer to where twenty women danced around the fire in a circle chanting like the sirens of the sea.

"What do you think?" Drake whispered.

"Looks to be Xenonian women partying a bit."

"Looks like a safe spot to alight for the rest of the night." Drake eyed the women in their low cut gowns.

"Maybe a healer's among them."

The women's hair hung in dark curls in a tempestuous way while the strands twisted to the shaking of their narrow hips. The length of their skirts split into sections allowing their shapely legs to dance about freely. The music suddenly ceased. The dancing women stopped and stared in Quaid and Drake's direction.

"Guess we've been discovered." Quaid considered Zaira's sleep-cloaked features. She just had to be all right.

"Looks like a standoff."

The women began to speak to one another in hushed tones.

Quaid frowned, concerned they were in for more trouble than they'd bargained for. "Maybe the sight of an unconscious Xenonian woman in my arms isn't helping matters any."

"Hadn't considered that. Want to continue east toward Carver's station?" Drake asked.

"Yeah, I think we ought to," Quaid said.

Quaid and Drake turned back east. Rapid footsteps crunched on the soil behind them. They turned to face the women, running to catch up to them.

"Where are you going?" one of the tallest of the women asked, her eyes wide with intrigue.

"Do you not want to stay a while?" another asked, motioning back to the campsite.

"What has happened to Zaira?" a third inquired, studying Zaira's sleep-filled features.

Quaid said, "She was poisoned by a speckled spider.

We believed she received an antidote, but she—"

"Bring her with us. I'm Lynonia." She directed them to a tent some distance away.

Surprised to see such a large canvas building that hadn't caught his eye before this, Quaid realized from a distance it blended in with the desert soil.

When he reached it, he hurried in through the entrance as Lynonia signaled to a bright blue mat on the canvas floor. Different colored mats covered the canvas floor.

"We'll look after her, and we'll look after you."

The latter she said with deep interest that forced a new slice of concern sliding through Quaid. He felt things were not as they seemed.

"Come, did you wish to watch us dance?" she prompted.

"I'll stay with Zaira." Quaid lay her on the bedding, then brushed a strand of hair off her face. "Go ahead, Drake, if you want."

"If you don't mind..."

Quaid sat on the pillow offered him.

"Something to drink?" Lynonia asked him.

A woman hurried Drake out of the tent while another woman examined Zaira.

"No, thank you." Quaid's gaze focused on Zaira.

After a few minutes, she opened her eyes with a dazed expression. His heart skipped a beat, and he reached for her hand. "How are you—"

Her eyes narrowed as she listened to the music. "We must leave this place at once." Her voice was whispered, but firm and worried.

"No rush." Lynonia ran her hand over Quaid's leather jacket. "You should get your rest, Zaira."

"She's right." Quaid raised Zaira's hand to his lips and kissed it. He wasn't sure why he'd done such a thing afterward. Her eyes widened, and he feared he'd breached some kind of etiquette. "Sorry, guess I shouldn't have done that." He patted her hand.

No way could he get involved with a woman—any woman—permanently. He'd sworn he'd never do such a thing. And yet, someone as sweet as Zaira could surely make a difference in someone's life. Yet he didn't wish her to be anybody else's. Still she couldn't be his, either, not with the life he'd chosen.

Frowning, he envisioned his mother's lifeless body in the rubble of his home. Her blue eyes stared vacantly without vision—murdered, when she had harmed no one. What good would it do to have a family in such a war-torn world?

"We must leave at once, Quaid," Zaira repeated with urgency, tugging weakly at his arm.

"You were bitten—"

"Where's Drake?" she interrupted, her tone of voice harsher now.

"Watching the dancers."

She glowered at Lynonia. "He must get the scrolls."

"Later." Lynonia strolled out of the tent.

"Drink this, Zaira," the other woman said. "It'll make you feel better."

Zaira tried to sit up, but she didn't have the strength.

"She must drink this," the lady said to Quaid.

"No." Zaira waved the cup away.

"I'll stay right by your bed, Zaira." Quaid helped her to sit.

"No," she said, as the lady tried to get her to drink the concoction. Quaid managed to hold her hands hostage, while the lady was able to coax Zaira to drink. When Quaid helped her to recline, she reached for his hand and whispered, "You must do something for me."

"What, Zaira?"

She glared at the lady who curtsied to her, then hastened out of the tent. "Quaid, you must wear this ring. It's not safe for you or Drake to be here, but this ring will protect you."

"And you?"

"I'm perfectly safe as long as you do not leave my side." She closed her eyes.

"Zaira, safe from what?" *Damn, the drink put her back to sleep*. He touched her cheek. "Zaira?" No amount of coaxing stirred the dark-haired siren from her sleep.

Lynonia soon entered the tent and smiled to see Zaira asleep. "Come, dance with us. Your friend is having the time of his life."

"I promised to stay by Zaira's side."

A queer look crossed the woman's face, and she glanced down at Zaira's hand, then turned her attention to Quaid's. "You wear her ring."

"Yes, she asked me to."

"Blasted, Zaira." Lynonia whipped around in a huff and hurried back outside.

Quaid took his seat beside Zaira, and he touched her soft hair. He took her hand and ran his fingers over her satiny skin, thinking if he hadn't chosen the life he lived, hadn't had the life experiences he'd had, she wouldn't be a bad choice.

The tent flap waved in the wind as the odor of canvas filled the room. Colorful bedding covered every square inch from one side to the other. Then boots tromped toward the tent in a run. Before Quaid could react, he feared more trouble was headed their way.

Drake rushed inside, his cheeks as flaming red as his hair and his green eyes wide with alarm. "We've got to leave now! Trouble of the worst sort is coming!"

CHAPTER 5

Adrenaline flooding his veins, Quaid jumped to his feet with his weapon readied, worried that the ones who had captured them had sent word Quaid and his friends had escaped before the Rondovin's ship sank in the lake and now more had come for them. "Rondovins?"

"Hurry, Quaid. Come with me. Xenonians, of the male persuasion, are on their way here now. One of the ladies said there's bound to be fighting over the women. Since we're otherworlders, we don't stand a chance at living through this sordid mess."

"Killing isn't allowed—"

"When it comes to the mating ritual, everything's game."

"Zaira has been given some kind of drug—"

"She'll be safe here."

"I promised I wouldn't leave her side. She said we'd be safe if I wore her ring." There was no way Quaid was leaving her.

Drake stared at the ring for a moment, then laughed out loud. "Should have read up on other cultures a tad, Quaid. You've gone and married the lady. Sure, nobody will mess with you *or* the lady now."

Quaid's heart did a somersault. Then he breathed a sigh of relief when he realized she'd done it as a hoax. "She only did it to save our skin. She knew the medicine would make her sleep."

Drake smiled darkly. "They mate for life. No divorce here. She offered her ring to you and you accepted it...right?"

Quaid rubbed his whiskery chin as he frowned. What else could go wrong while he was stuck on this blasted planet? "But if I'm protected and you're not—"

"Best man at the wedding." Drake slapped Quaid on the back. Then he scratched his forehead. "Of course if you haven't kissed the lady yet—"

"I haven't."

"Anywhere will do."

"I did." Quaid recalled the kiss to Zaira's hand and the shock it seemed to have on her.

"In front of witnesses?"

"Two of the ladies."

"It's official then."

"I kissed her before she gave the ring to me."

"Ah, but did she ask you to kiss her?"

"No."

"Then you kissed her freely. In so doing, you tied the first part of the knot—the ring was her offering." He chuckled. "Wonder what old Carver Cole will do to you when he finds out you married his daughter without his permission."

Stay away from my daughter. That's what Carver had said and the words rang loud and clear.

"It's just a ruse."

The roar of several spacecraft announced their approach. Quaid glanced down at a still sleeping Zaira.

"Marriages are one of the most sacred happenings on this planet. Just think, the next time I visit here, a couple of little Quaid Lassiters could be dashing through the prairie, fighting each other with toy plasma guns."

"Not another word of this, Drake." It was bad enough Quaid had gotten himself into this mess, but Drake's rubbing it in wasn't helping one bit.

The soft lilting of flutes floated on the breeze again. A shadow stretched into the tent. Lynonia entered the canvas building with a big male, black-haired and beady-eyed Xenonian holding her arm. She waved her hand at Quaid and Drake. "These two are with Zaira. The one, Quaid Lassiter, is her mate. The other, Drake Jorgenson, helped to rescue her from the Rondovins. He's Quaid's lifetime companion and now serves as Zaira's private guard."

The man stared at them for a moment, then said in a darkened, deep voice, "He received permission from Carver Cole?"

Everyone looked at Quaid, whose ears must have turned red as hot as they felt while he considered what to say. Lying was never something he could do easily, even if it meant saving his skin.

Drake spoke up. "Zaira made all of the arrangements."

"Some will be sore over the matter that she chose an outsider." The Xenonian turned and headed back outside.

Drake said to Quaid, "It's your chance to be with the lady now."

Quaid's emotions were tied in knots. The notion of making love with such an exquisite creature appealed, but marriage was another story. A wave of heat, the anxious kind, washed over him this time.

***

After eating roasted fish flown in from the southern coastal region of Xenon, Drake sat down next to Quaid on his guest mattress. "You know here, the female chooses her mate. Of course, her father is supposed to approve of her selection just in case she makes an unwise choice."

"But Carver Cole hasn't approved—"

"Sorry, it's still a done deal. The two of you sort of eloped."

Quaid couldn't believe the mess he'd gotten himself into.

"I really don't see the difficulty. She's chosen you from all the males of Xenon, and you should feel quite honored." Drake sipped from a flask of Orion ale.

"I can't believe we're here in the middle of an illegal mating party, and you're drinking liquor to top it off. I suppose you were the one who brought it here in the first place."

Drake smiled. "Sure thing. Consider this, Zaira's selection would've been based on three things: your position—"

"I'm a fighter pilot. She's against my fighting even."

"It's your family's position she's interested in. She's one of the highest-ranking females on Xenon. Similar to a princess, the daughter of a ruling family in medieval times on Terra Firma, only on a grander scale. We're talking of all the colonies scattered this side of the planet, you know. She could've chosen any mate among the Xenonians, and any one of them would've jumped at the chance to mate her."

"Carver Cole is *what*?"

"Head of the High Council."

"He repairs crafts and does a darn good job of it.

What you speak of is pure fantasy. Besides, what has my family's position got to do with anything?"

"I imagine she sees you as a prince leading our people. You're quite a hero to the Terrans as was your father and his father before him. Your grandfather was the ruler so by all rights you truly are a prince, although we don't have such a designation on Orion any further."

Quaid couldn't believe any of this, but he'd play along. "What else?"

"Then she'll select you based on your personality traits—"

"She knows nothing about me."

"You can bet the lady knows everything she could find out about you. Her passion is research. I imagine the lady has read your personnel files down to your psychological report even." Drake took another swig of ale. Two Xenonian males shouted obscenities at one another outside the tent. Drake smiled. "Glad they're leaving us out of this one."

"If she's read my psychological report, she'd know I wasn't suited to marriage."

"The final major thing she'd consider, in choosing you as her mate, is your physical stature." Drake took another drink of his ale. "That is to say they have this notion about continuing their species in the best form possible. If she felt your physical characteristics were unsuitable for her offspring, she'd have rejected you,

GALAXY WARRIOR

despite your position or charming ways."

"She chose wrong and Carver will have my head."

"Probably. I certainly wouldn't want to be in your flight boots. I've never known the old fellow to have a sense of humor." Drake ran his hands over his chest. "You know, she's untested. As high a position as she holds, nobody would have dared to have touched her."

"You said she might have been in the caves to rendezvous—"

"With an outsider...I realized afterward, she would have had to have been seeing an outsider because of her position." Drake leaned back on his mattress. "She's yours to have. She's willing and she's waiting. I don't see what the difficulty is. If it were me—"

"It isn't." Quaid stood, then walked over to Zaira's bedding across the tent from the one he'd chosen for his own. He studied her face framed by her dark hair while her lashes hid her beguiling eyes. "She's the most desirable woman I've ever met, Drake. I can't get my mind off her. But if I fulfill my desires for her like I'd love to, I'll have cemented the commitment I'm not willing to make to her or to any woman. Worst of all, I'll have hurt her in the process."

"I'd take your place in a heartbeat, Quaid."

That notion didn't appeal in the slightest bit as Quaid returned to his mattress. Despite the fact he felt he couldn't be committed to Zaira, he didn't want Drake to take his place with her either.

A Xenonian male shouted, "An outsider did what?"

Drake raised a brow. "I suspect he's talking about you. Can't be me. And it sounds like we're in for trouble."

The man towering six-foot-five-inches tall stormed into the room tent. One of the women tugged at his arm to keep him from reaching Quaid and Drake. "Tagaron, Quaid Lassiter has married Zaira properly. You cannot interfere or else you'll have to face prison on Vaschon."

"Nobody has to know." The man dragged the woman with him as she refused to let go of his muscular arm.

Quaid jumped to his feet as the big man reached for him. Ducking under the man's fist, Quaid quickly turned as the man stumbled forward, causing Drake to jump back to avoid being hit next. Seemed Zaira's plan was going to get Quaid killed, not saved.

"You cannot do this," the woman pleaded with the Xenonian. "Come, watch me dance further."

"Which one is Quaid Lassiter?" the man growled as his blurry eyes shifted from Quaid to Drake.

"I am," Quaid said as the man balled his fist and readied it to strike Drake. He swung instead at Quaid, and Quaid ducked the Xenonian's gnarly, clenched fist, then stepped back.

"What can I do?" Quaid dodged another blow. He

was game for a fight, though he figured he was well outmatched with this one, but he didn't want to have the whole male population beating him up if he chanced to make the wrong move.

"What do you mean?" Drake took a couple of steps back to keep out of the fracas.

"I know I can't kill him, but can I hit back?"

"No," the lady said, "otherworlders are not allowed to strike Xenonian citizens on their home world."

"But he can hit *me*?" Quaid jumped away from another powerful swing as the air whooshed past him.

The man tripped over bedding and landed on his face, making Quaid smile. The incident made the Xenonian madder, cursing that Quaid had tripped him. He rose soggily to his feet, then lunged at Quaid with murderous intent. Quaid dove to the side and the big man fell on his face again. Drake laughed.

"Don't make him madder than he already is."

"You're next," the man said to Drake as he got to his knees.

He knelt there for several seconds while Quaid caught his breath. The Xenonian wavered in place.

Seeing he wasn't going anywhere, Drake said to him, "Want some more Orion ale?"

The man nodded slightly, and Drake handed the flask to the woman. She took the container and walked gingerly over to the big man, then reached it out to him.

"Tagaron, the otherworlders offer this ale to you in greeting. Drink it in peace."

The man reached for the flask, but the woman withheld it from him. "Drink it in peace," she repeated. He nodded and she gave it to him.

He drained the flask.

Drake grimaced. "I didn't expect him to drink the whole blasted thing."

"You bring ale?"

"Yes." Drake folded his arms across his chest. "I brought the ale."

"Friend."

"Yes." Drake pointed at Quaid. "He is too."

"He married Zaira."

"Yes."

"He's not friend."

Without another word, the big man slumped over on his face on the dirt floor. The woman kicked his shoulder with her bare foot. "Idiot. Now I shall have to find another mate."

She turned to Drake who threw his hands in the air. "I've already been asked."

Quaid considered his friend's sincerity. No way was Drake planning on settling down anytime soon either.

"Who?" The woman placed her hands on her hips.

"Catarina."

"Ahh!" The woman stormed out of the tent.

"Catarina?" Quaid skirted the Xenonian, then sat down on his mattress, relieved he was still in one piece.

"The woman who warned us to get away before these fellows arrived."

"I'm not sure that woman believed you." Quaid glanced at all the bedding. "Looks like we're going to have quite a crowd."

"Should be interesting when everyone beds down for the night."

As the music drew to a close and sand extinguished the fires, lanterns hovered near the tent. "Looks like we've got company," Drake whispered.

Soon men and women stumbled into the canvas building and headed for the bedding. The soft glow of the lantern light illuminated the circus-sized tent while the sweet waters the women wore scented the air. A mix of voices spoken in hushed tones filled the tent as women and men wrapped their arms through each other's while they maneuvered to their mattresses.

"Hey," one of the men said as he tripped over Tagaron, "somebody help me to move this gregoron bull out of the pathway."

As four of the men dragged Tagaron to a corner of the tent, Lynonia sauntered over to Quaid. "Are you not going to sleep beside Zaira?"

"She needs her rest."

"Did you wish to warm me a while?"

Quaid said, "No."

Lynonia turned to Drake. "Wanna mate?"

Drake smiled as Catarina brushed past her. She curled up next to him on his borrowed bedding. "He's spoken for. Run along, Lynonia."

The woman stormed off, but soon found a willing male to bed her on the far end of the tent. She slipped out of her scanty gown. Catarina cast her an annoyed look. "She'll never truly have a mate. She's been pleasured by half of the bachelor males on Xenon."

Drake's lips broke out into a full-fledged grin. He touched Catarina's cheek. "What are the rules here?"

Lying back on his mattress, Quaid ran his hands through his hair.

Catarina unbuttoned a button on Drake's shirt. "We can do what Zaira and Quaid did, and what most of the folks here are doing...eloping without the permission of the female's father. Or we can wait and get my father's approval."

"What do you wish?" Drake ran his fingers through her light brown curls.

"My father has a temper like Carver Cole has."

Quaid groaned. He wasn't going to live long in this desolate place.

Drake chuckled.

"I believe we should wait," she said, "but we can get *real* close."

Drake hurriedly tugged at the rest of his buttons. "Sounds like a plan."

A rustle of blankets followed as Drake and Catarina buried themselves under the covers. Quaid turned his attention to Zaira. For over an hour he watched her, then his eyes grew heavy with sleep.

Nestled with his cheek against the silken bedding, he saw Zenith from the book, *The Changeling*.

Zenith was dripping wet in her golden gowns. Reaching out to touch her face, he felt her smooth skin at his fingertips. "We must find the scrolls," she whispered and when she disappeared into the lake, he frowned.

"The scrolls," the woods murmured. "Find the scrolls."

He studied the dark waters, then raised his brows a hint when the dark-haired nymph rose from the lake. Her ice-blue blouse clung to her breasts and his gaze centered on the rose-colored nipples that poked against the wet fabric.

"Zaira," he tried to say, then twisted on the bedding.

"Wear this ring." She reached her hand out to him. "Wear it and we'll be safe."

Zaira.

"Hurry, Quaid, we must leave here at once," Drake said.

The warm, gold metal encircled Quaid's finger.

Drake chuckled. "Gone and married the lady; should've read up on other cultures a tad, Quaid."

"Leave my daughter alone. She's a nice girl." Carver's gray-streaked brows knitted together. "Leave her alone."

Sweat beaded on Quaid's forehead as the desert hurtled toward him. His fists clenched, he gritted his teeth. His heart pounded in his ears as he heard the screech of the Exiter as it pulled to a halt in the empty hangar, flames shooting everywhere. He climbed out of the vehicle and it vanished.

Drake slapped his shoulder. "Don't know why Carver would have wanted your craft."

The scent of coffee beans permeated the air as Zaira's darkened eyes considered him. His gaze shifted to her long polished nails fingering her pearl buttons. "In or out, Quaid. The choice is yours."

I can't marry anyone, ever. Not ever.

Groans of ecstasy enveloped him, and he frowned at the intrusion. *Zaira licked her lips. The full-pink forms glistened in the light as he studied their curves. He looked up to see her eyes considering his. She touched her sugarcoated finger to her tongue. "Don't get much." Her voice was shaded in tenderness.*

He reached his hand out to her, but tangled it in the blankets. *Zaira.*

"Don't get much." *She leaned over the cushions of* *the sofa he sat on. He studied the sweater cut low,* *snuggling over her rounded breasts.*

He reached out to touch one. The blanket hampered his movement, and he tugged to pull it away.

He woke and bolted upright. A figure in the semi-dark, leaned over Zaira. Jumping from his mattress, Quaid dashed across the tent, and pulled the Xenonian male aside. "She's mine!" Quaid growled. "Leave her be!"

The Xenonian stared at Quaid with a dazed look, then collapsed on the bedding behind him. There was a grumble from a couple he squashed, then the man crawled toward his own mattress. Harsh words shattered the quiet as the man pressed his weight against a sleeping couple. Another man bolted upright, readying his fist to strike the offending party, then realizing the Xenonian was not attempting to steal his female, he lay back down while the man continued his crawl over the mounds of blanketed bodies. When he settled in with his own female, Quaid turned his attention back to Zaira.

She licked her lips and stirred. He reached down and touched his finger to her cheek and felt the softness. *Zaira, I can't have wed you.* Lifting her slender fingers in his hand, he pressed his lips to them and sighed deeply. The soft scent of jasmine touched his senses. He studied her dark lashes as they fluttered gently. His gaze drifted to the skin-tight, leather-like material that covered her curvaceous form. *I can't ever marry.*

***

Before first light, Quaid woke while Zaira sat on her mat across the tent watching him. Her amber eyes wore a fluorescent cast in the semi-dark, and he jumped up to see how she fared. As soon as he reached her side, she stood. "We must go now."

"Of course." Quaid grabbed her arm to steady her. "Are you feeling all right now?"

"I'm all right." Her voice masked a new hurt, and he sensed trouble was brewing ahead for him.

Drake sat up and smiled broadly at Quaid. Quaid waved to him to come with them. Drake leaned over and kissed Catarina on the cheek, then hastened to join his friends. The three exited the tent without speaking a word while everyone else still slept.

They headed across the prairie and Drake said, "Quite a night, eh, Quaid?"

Quaid took a deep breath. "Listen, Zaira, about last night..."

Zaira turned her doe-like eyes to study his. He looked down at the blond grass beneath his boots as they covered the ground at a quickened pace. "I appreciate all you did for Drake and me back there..."

She turned her eyes toward the south and Drake said, "Hey, folks, aren't we kind of going in the wrong direction? East is back that way." He motioned with his hand in an easterly direction while Zaira kept on her southerly heading. "What do I know?" Drake shrugged a shoulder and shoved his hands in his pockets.

"He's right, Zaira." Quaid squeezed her arm slightly.

"He has a job to do...get the scrolls. The scrolls are this way." Zaira forged ahead.

"Oh no, you're not going anywhere near those caves again," Quaid said.

Drake smiled. "Husbandly advice?"

She stopped in her footsteps and waited to hear Quaid's response.

Quaid glowered at Drake, then turned to her. "What we did back there...it was just a ruse, right?"

She stormed south again as the two men watched her.

"Think you've riled her some, Quaid. First husband-wife spat, I do believe."

"Shut up, Drake." Quaid ran to catch up to her. "Listen, Zaira," he pleaded. He took hold of her arm in as gentle a manner as he could while he walked at her fast pace. "I'm not familiar with your culture—"

"My mistake, Quaid Lassiter. You're free to return to my father's shop and—"

"My craft disappeared." The notion infuriated him,

but he tried to keep his cool.

"I'm sure Father test-drove your craft to ensure the drive was working properly."

"But he said it would take a week—"

She stopped walking abruptly, which made him take a step back to give her a little space. "There's no need for you to be here any further. Go fight your wars." A tear rolled down her cheek, and she headed south again.

"Well, Quaid, you've really gone and done it now. You've married the lady, then rejected her and now she's rejected you."

"Then that's the end of the marriage."

Drake said, "The Xenonians mate for life. I already told you so. Sure, you can leave here and do as you please just like you've always done, but the lady will never have the chance to have another mate."

Quaid walked a hundred yards behind her as Drake walked beside him.

"What are you going to do, Quaid?"

"She can't go with us. It's too dangerous."

"Then you're going to help me get the scrolls?"

"I guess it's the least I can do now."

"And Zaira?"

Quaid observed her as her narrow hips swung with her stride while her rich ebony tresses followed the movement.

"You could do an awfully lot worse. An *awfully* lot worse."

Quaid quickened his pace to catch up with her. "About the ring—"

"You can bury it in the desert, Quaid Lassiter, if you no longer wish to wear it, but you can never return it to me."

He grabbed her arm and pulled her to a stop. No way was he going to let her get hurt in the caves again. "We can sort this out later, but for now, you can't go back into the caves."

"You tell me this because?"

"I don't want you to get hurt again."

"Because?"

He knew what she longed to hear, but he was already in a deep enough mess and was bound and determined not to dig the hole any deeper. How could he tell her he could have murdered the guy who leaned over her in the tent that morning...just for getting too close to her? How could he admit his heart raced uncontrollably every time he caught sight of her? How touching her body made parts of his rise to the occasion when his mind ordered him to resist such feelings?

He was drawn to her like he'd never been before to anyone he'd let remotely get close. But he'd promised himself, he'd never commit to a woman. Children followed, parents died. Children were orphaned. Better to be a loner, a fighter, and a damned good one at that. Husbandly duties and fatherhood were not for him.

"He cares for you." Drake threw his hands up in the air in an exasperated manner. "Heck, we both care about your safety."

Zaira folded her arms.

"It's just as Drake says," Quaid blurted out. Zaira turned on her heels and headed toward the caves. "I've never seen such a stubborn woman in my life," Quaid said under his breath as he slowed his pace.

Drake walked beside him. "We can't let her go in there again."

"She won't listen to reason."

"You just have to tell her as her husband, you forbid it. It's as simple as that."

Quaid studied her. "I can't do it."

"Why not? That's what she's waiting for."

"I'm not truly married to her—not in my own mind. And if I were, I wouldn't command her to do anything. But I'd sure as heck try to convince her not to go."

She slowed her pace. Drake smiled. "She has awfully good hearing, did you know?"

Quaid took a deep breath. "I forgot."

***

Though Zaira had tried to get Quaid to leave her before the male Xenonians had arrived, he hadn't listened to reason. The only thing she could think of on the spur of the moment as out of it as she'd been that could save his handsome hide was to make him her mate. She hadn't planned on that. But any one of the males would have killed him if she hadn't. Except now her father would be furious with her. But worse, Quaid wasn't buying it.

Deep inside, she'd hoped he might change his mind about her. After all, she had saved his life. And, too, he seemed physically attracted to her.

She couldn't believe her mission was suffering such setbacks though. Drake at least appeared to be on her side. Maybe with more of his encouragement, Quaid would change his mind. Of course then there was the problem with Chief Magistrate Caryndian Bach, and her most fervent admirer. He wouldn't take the news lightly that an outsider wed her.

She took a ragged breath of the warm desert air. Maybe after she and her brother greened the planet, maybe then Quaid would be interested in staying. After all, according to his psychological report, the devastation of his own home world had been life-altering for him. Would he wish to see the same thing occur here if he didn't agree to help her people?

Soliciting his help should have remained the focus of her attention. But the urge to mate with him forced her body to heat at the thought of him touching her naked skin. She knew some of it was turning of age, but she was drawn to him, no other man, so she knew some of her biological need was based on having offspring with the right man. And he was the only man for her.

She glanced back at him. He looked hopeful she'd give him some words of encouragement, and the frown faded across his brow.

"We're mates, Quaid Lassiter," she said, matter-of-factly, whether he could deal with it or not. They were, and as soon as she could get word to her father, she'd let him in on the secret.

Quaid shook his head, whether in disagreement or disbelief, she wasn't sure. But it didn't matter. They were mates, *forever*.

She knew her people would wonder why in the world she'd chosen him, when he didn't want the commitment. But she figured the more they could tie him in to helping them with their cause, the better chance they had at repelling the invasion that was sure to occur next.

With her enhanced jaguar hearing, she heard a sound from the heaven's above. Her stomach clenched, sure it was a hostile spacecraft. She looked toward the sky for a moment. She didn't see even a speck in the clear gray sky. But she heard it, clear as she heard her heart beating as the blood rushed to her ears.

"Rondovin scoutship!" she yelled, then sprinted for a patch of peculiarly out-of-place green grass dotted with purple daisy-like flowers, the secret trapdoor to the caves that she and her brother used to reach the laboratory.

CHAPTER 6

"I don't see anything!" Quaid yelled as he headed in Zaira's direction.

She reached down and pulled a flap of grass up. "Hurry! Down here!"

Quaid and Drake darted down the black wrought-iron steps into the manmade tunnel after her, then pulled the secret hatch closed behind them. Their eyes soon adjusted to the low light that cast twisting shadows among green leafy, tendril climbers gripping the glistening-wet walls.

The party walked down the narrow, snaking, rock hallway covered in more green leafy vines. Red flowers, their throats spotted in dots of violet, scented the air with the fragrance of oranges.

"What is this place?" Quaid whispered to Zaira.

"This is where my brother works."

Drake poked Quaid in the arm and pointed at the golden ring on his finger. Quaid frowned at him. Yep, matters could *only* get worse.

As the tunnel exited into a cave, Quaid and Drake stared at shrubs wearing sharply-toothed, green leaves, filling the corner of the room. At least a hundred other different varieties bloomed in profusion, all with subtle to extreme color variations while flowers or berries clustered amongst their leaves.

"Does he harvest the plants for food—" Quaid asked, but was cut off.

"No, not exactly." Zaira indicated another long tunnel, this one covered in whorls of oval, light-green leaves. Half-hidden in the fine greenery, red berries and purple-tinged flowers peeked out. Zaira ran her hand over the soft mass of plants, releasing the scent of peppermint into the otherwise damp-earthy air. She took a deep breath. "Like it?" Quaid nodded while rolling a berry between his fingertips. "Edible too."

"But he's not harvesting—"

"Not at the moment."

When they entered another cave, Zaira waved at her brother who strode across the floor to welcome her. "Greetings, Martius!"

He kissed her lips, and Drake whispered, "The familial greeting."

"Looks to be a little too familiar to me," Quaid

whispered back. He hadn't realized how friendly family members were with one another. Seeing her brother kissing Zaira like he did, raised Quaid's ire. To his annoyance, a feeling of jealousy gnawed at his gut. He wasn't allowed such feelings if he couldn't accept the notion he was married to the woman.

"This is Martius." Zaira wrapped her arm through his, then walked him over to meet Quaid and Drake. The family resemblance was astonishing. His black hair hung to his shoulders and his dark amber eyes replicated Zaira's. His same satiny complexion and oval shaped-face was uncanny.

Quaid took a deep breath as Martius glanced down at the ring resting on his finger. Now he was really in trouble.

"Congratulations." Martius kissed her again. "Seems you beat me again, my sister. But I don't remember Father having mentioned that he'd made any marital arrangements for you."

"You know how concerned Father has been about the scrolls."

"Certainly. So what brings you down here?"

"A Rondovin scout ship passing overhead."

Martius turned his eyes upward, then nodded. "Well, gentlemen, would you like to take a tour of my work?" He didn't wait for a response as he took Zaira's arm and led them through the cavernous room to another tunnel. "Has Zaira told you I'm a mad scientist?"

Zaira smiled at him. "He's a genius, he means."

"Yes, well, to some—mad, but I intend to turn the gray planet green. I've nearly completed the technology for the transformation."

They walked into a cave where ferns stretched their fronds ten feet high and rubber plants towered to forty feet. Quaid leaned over and studied the brown spots on the underside of the fern's giant four-foot long frond.

Martius crouched down next to him and ran his finger over the rough-feeling spores. "They'll produce an abundance of fern."

Quaid stood. "You have jungle plants here and yet it's not a hot, humid environment." He was overwhelmed by the notion. Greening a desert planet? He'd never heard of anyone attempt such a thing. The idea fascinated him though. He wondered if the technology couldn't be utilized on his own scarred home world.

"These plants come from a cooler, dryer planet. In this way, we'll have a variety of plants from every climatic region that'll grow here. With a special seeding of the atmosphere, rainstorms will feed the plants. Then once they're established, the plants themselves will transpire and this will cause a natural water cycle. We already have lakes and rivers and abundant underground water, but it hasn't been enough to create an adequate global rainfall to support a lot of plant life until now."

"Grand undertaking." Quaid followed Martius with the others through a brief passageway that emptied into a deciduous forest. Trees filling every square inch of the next cave watched over smaller shrubs crouching at their feet. "Amazing how these can grow in here like this with very little light." He squinted to see the vegetation where natural light streamed through an opening in the plain above filtering down to cast a scanty light on the tips of some of the trees.

"Sorry." Martius hurried over to a wall and pushed a button. A naturally-simulated light washed over the room. "I turn the light off for thirteen hours to simulate nighttime."

"Ah." Quaid considered the colorful collection of red, purple, gold, green, orange and yellow-leafed trees of various ages from foot-tall saplings to seventy-foot tall trees dwarfed only by the height of the cave. A brown-and-dusty-pink-speckled mushroom, its cap nearly stretching a foot in diameter, clung to a rotting oak log.

"Edible too." Martius pointed to forty more growing nearby.

"My favorite sautéed in salysin." Zaira squeezed her brother's arm. "Grown by Martius especially for me."

"It's hard not to do what she insists you do." Martius led them into another cave. "And over here is where we've created meadowlands—good for grazing domesticated animals for food and for harvesting our own crops."

"This is truly remarkable." Quaid considered the fine dark green wisps, bearing spikes of bell-shaped lavender flowers. Yellow and green variegated stalks reaching four-foot in height bumped up next to these. Black clumps of spreading grass covered in lilac flowers tipped with black fruits grew nearby. Taller, bolder, stiff-pointed, wine-red grasses bearing tiny red, daisy-like flowers added additional color.

Drake fingered a burgundy rose petal's velvet surface in a corner of the cave as Quaid turned to watch him.

"The roses, jasmine, and honeysuckle are Zaira's idea," Martius explained.

"Jasmine." Quaid considered Zaira's smile.

"I make my own fragrance from the flowers."

He took a deep breath. Every time she drew near, that scent of hers drove him mad with desire.

"And in here, a conifer forest. My favorite really. I cannot wait to grow these on the surface of the planet, smell the fragrance of the pine needles, hear the whoosh of the breeze as it dances through the firs' fine leaves."

"You're a genius, my brother." Zaira squeezed his hand.

Martius sighed deeply. "The only problem really is that once the planet is cloaked in vegetation, the Rondovins will try to take us over. Right now, there's no interest. However, they've gotten wind of the project and have been scouting the area to find out if there's any truth to the rumor."

"The Xenonians are a peaceful race." Quaid rubbed his chin. He frowned to feel the stubble turning into a fuzzy black beard. "How do you intend to stop the Rondovins from getting their way?"

Zaira ran her hand under one of the plant lights. "That's why we must have the scrolls. The scrolls give the council legitimacy."

"The Rondovins won't care about that," Quaid said, not believing Zaira and her brother could be so naïve.

"No, but several other worlds do. We'll have their support should we need it. The Rondovins won't want to fight that many."

"All right, so Drake and I will return the scrolls to the High Council, but you'll remain here, where you'll be safe from speckled spiders and the like."

Martius grinned. "Seems your husband desires your obedience."

"He must earn it, as a good husband should." She tilted her chin up. He liked a spunky woman, but not one who would endanger her life against his wishes.

All eyes turned to see Quaid's response to the challenge. He was determined to keep her safe at all costs, but it irritated him that her brother did nothing to discourage her foolish notions when he seemed to care for her a great deal.

Quaid cleared his throat. "Zaira, can I have a word alone with you?"

"Certainly, you're my husband. You may have as many words alone with me as you like."

Martius pointed to his bedchamber off the cave and Drake laughed. Quaid headed toward the room, his neck hairs bristling at Drake's apparent amusement concerning his predicament, but when he didn't hear her footsteps following him, he turned to see why Zaira hadn't joined him.

Zaira smiled, amused at the way Quaid's ears turned red. All he had to do was admit he was her husband, and she'd agree to anything...almost. But she and her brother had worked on the greening project for too long to have anyone stop either of them now. "Did you wish something of me?"

"Come speak with me."

"Of course." She walked into the room, and he shut the door behind her.

"Do I displease you?" She hoped with all of her

heart he would say no.

"No, Zaira."

She sighed inwardly.

"You're attractive and fascinating. Well, just totally intriguing. It's just that—"

Now the part that she knew was the biggest hurdle she had to maneuver over. "You're a warrior?"

"Exactly and as such it wouldn't be fair to a woman...well, to you, Zaira, to be married to a person like me."

She sat down on the bed, determined to prove to him that the notion he had about not having a family could be changed.

"Then you agree."

"No."

"All right then, I want you to stay here."

"Because?" She knew he felt something more for her than he was willing to admit.

"I don't want you to get hurt."

"Because?" Somewhere deep inside his heart, he could love her. She was sure of it.

"You're a woman, confound it."

She smiled. That wasn't the reason. He'd gone on many a mission with women, and never had he wanted them to stay behind to remain safe. "Kiss me goodbye, Quaid."

"You'll stay then?"

She closed her eyes as she puckered her lips slightly. He leaned over and brushed his lips lightly against hers. She opened her eyes and frowned at him. "Even my brother shows more feeling toward me than you do."

"He shouldn't." Quaid hurried toward the door. He couldn't touch her any more than that. His trousers were already tighter than he could bear. "As soon as we retrieve the scrolls, we'll speak with your father and straighten this other matter out."

"Whatever you say, Quaid." She stood and pulled the zipper to her jumpsuit down slowly.

He glanced at her, but hurriedly slammed the door shut behind him.

"How did it go?" Drake grabbed two lanterns resting on the floor next to one of the plant beds.

"Where's Martius?"

"Made himself scarce. His hearing is as good as Zaira's, and he didn't want to be eavesdropping on your intimate moment. So...how was it?"

"I convinced her to stay." Quaid hurried toward the exit from the lab.

"What concession did you make?"

Quaid frowned at Drake, making him laugh in response. "I should probably let you learn this on your own, but female Xenonians shouldn't be trifled with."

"I don't understand it. I thought you were interested in Zaira."

"It seems you had more of a draw then I ever did. But I believe Catarina is truly the one for me. She's waiting for my return once I get the scrolls."

"Don't get yourself locked into anything you can't get yourself out of."

They climbed out of the hidden hole, shut the hatch, and hurried south across the prairie.

"I'm tired of the single life. I'm ready to settle down and bounce junior on my knee. It wouldn't hurt for you to do the same. You're not getting any younger, you know."

"Can't ever happen, Drake. I swore when I was a kid, I'd never marry. You, of all people, should know why."

***

Four hours later, they arrived at the caves where the scrolls were supposed to be located, and Drake switched on his lantern. "Phew, it's working. Martius said he hadn't charged them up in a while."

Quaid checked his and nodded. "Got the map still?"

"Right here." Drake patted his pocket.

"Let's get this done then."

They walked past the halberd still poking out of the mud. Quaid glanced at it while Drake slapped him on the shoulder. "Don't *even* try that trick again!"

"I'm a quick learner." Quaid headed through the narrow tunnel, and then exited into the cavern. He studied the black stains on the rock floor. The idea that something ate all of the bodies in record time slightly unnerved him. "Where are the bodies?"

"The bats here are scavengers. They'll eat anything that's dead."

"Learn something new every day."

Drake pulled out his map to verify they were to take the tunnel to the right while Quaid walked toward the left passageway. "We need to go right, Quaid." Drake folded the map and tucked it securely in his jacket pocket.

"What was Zaira doing here?" Quaid continued toward the left-most tunnel. He still couldn't shake the eerie feeling he'd find her in here again, half dead from the effects of the poison.

"Didn't you ask her?"

"Kind of slipped my mind because she was unconscious or angry most of the time."

Drake pointed to the correct tunnel. "Well, we're to go right. So, maybe you could ask her when you see her again, but for now, let's find the scrolls."

Quaid entered the left tunnel.

"Or not." Drake hurried after him.

Quaid tilted his nose up and sniffed the air. "Do you smell the scent of jasmine?"

"Don't smell a thing, Quaid. The mold count must be pretty high in here due to the dampness. My sinuses are really backed up. Unless, of course, we run across more spider droppings, which will clear out my sinuses in a hurry, I can't smell a thing."

"Would Zaira's fragrance linger here that long?" Quaid searched the cave the tunnel exited into.

"Wouldn't think it would." Drake studied the four tunnels that led out of the cave. "I'm afraid if we get off the path we were supposed to take, we might lose our way."

"Do you hear anything?"

"Other than the dripping of water, no."

"Then maybe the spiders are all gone. If Zaira was meeting an outsider in here, why didn't she link with him?" Quaid shouldn't have cared what Zaira had been doing in the caves. He had no right to her and yet the thought she might have been rendezvousing with another outsider, one who might have had all the attributes necessary to make him her perfect mate, made his blood boil.

"Maybe he was killed before she could?"

Quaid's thoughts reverted to the dark cave when they first saw her. "We didn't see any bodies."

"We didn't exactly look. Once we saw Zaira, that's all that we were concerned about."

"He must have been the one who killed the spiders

then. Zaira had no weapons on her."

"I don't imagine she would've known how to use one."

"Right." Quaid headed for the tunnel to the left with an impatient step.

"*Now* where are we going?" Drake hurried to catch up to him.

"I want to know how she got in here and what she was doing." Even if he didn't find a whole body left, maybe some remains would give him some answers. He just had to know.

"The scrolls, Quaid. Let's get the scrolls."

Quaid stopped in his footsteps. He'd never considered the scrolls. "You don't think she was trying to find the scrolls on her own, do you?"

Before Drake could answer, Quaid forged ahead again.

"Where are we going?"

"The scent of jasmine grows stronger this way."

"She can't be in here again."

A glint of shimmering green poking out from gray-green moss as it sparkled with moisture, caught Quaid's eye. He reached over and touched the wall.

"What's wrong, Quaid?"

"Emeralds?" Quaid mused. "The walls are covered in emeralds."

Drake raised his lantern to the wall, then smiled. He

rubbed some of the moss away. "Appears to be."

"The Xenonians don't even know what they have here."

"If you noticed, no one wears jewelry."

Quaid glanced down at the ring gripping his finger.

Drake laughed. "Well except for wedding bands."

"Probably didn't know they had any valuable gems they could use in the making of other kinds of jewelry."

"Or no interest."

They entered the next cave and found a light glowing in the wall as if a door was cut into the rock and the light from within seeped through the opening. Quaid hastened to the rock facing, and then ran his hands over the wall.

Drake clenched his teeth. "Don't pull any levers or push any..."

Click! The stone door rumbled open.

CHAPTER 7

Quaid and Drake peered into the room where vines wrapped along the wall intertwining in a graceful dance. Quaid's adrenaline pumped through his veins as he hurried through a small tunnel with weapon poised while Drake followed close behind. They entered into another cave filled with shrubs. "The scrolls couldn't be here."

"No." Drake pulled out his map. "They were supposed to be some distance from the right-most tunnel. We took the left one."

Quaid moved closer to the wall, illuminating it with his miniature lamp. A green button caught his eye and he depressed it. A generous light illuminated the cave while the shrubs cast eerie shadows on the walls behind them.

"Some more of Martius's work?" Drake asked.

"I imagine so." A table and two chairs sat next to the wall and Quaid walked over to examine the papers lying on the tabletop. "Looks like some of his greening plans. He's divided the planet into sections." Quaid pointed at a small room unencumbered by a door and another where a faint light escaped the outer edges of a door. "What do you think?"

"May be a bedchamber like at his other workshop."

Quaid strode across the floor to the closed door.

"Somebody may be in there—" Drake warned.

Pushing a button, the door slid open and Quaid nearly dropped his weapon as Zaira concealed her bare breasts with her hands while her long skirts covered her legs and torso.

"Sorry." He shut the door in disbelief.

Drake's mouth gaped wide while he stared at the door. Quaid grabbed his arm and led him away from the room. Quaid couldn't believe she had entered the caves alone, again despite his telling her not to. And yet, he couldn't get his mind off her breasts barely covered with her hands. The woman was harder on him than any firefight he'd ever had in the galaxy as he tried to get his mind on the reason they were really here in the first place. Hell, the reason he was here was because of her and that damned fragrance she wore. Luring him like a bee to pollen, she had drawn him to her again.

"Wow." Drake slumped down on one of the chairs.

"I can't believe you deny having married such an exquisite creature."

The door slid open, and Drake jumped up from the chair as Quaid turned.

Carrying a pack in her hands, Zaira walked into the room, frowning at him.

Quaid scowled right back at her. "What are you doing here, Zaira? I thought I'd made it perfectly clear that I didn't want you coming to this place."

"I have work to do. Did you get the scrolls?"

Her tone of indifference further annoyed him.

"We got sidetracked. Seems that fragrance you wear has some power of attraction for Quaid."

Not commenting, Zaira hurried across the floor. She entered the small room while Quaid and Drake followed her. They stared at a large, gray slate covered in designs, then turned to see Zaira struggling with a once-brass lever, now colored verdigris, sitting in a slab of smooth marble. She tugged at a lever, frozen in place. She pulled off her sandal, and then hit the handle with the heel.

Quaid chuckled. She glared at him.

She needed him and the notion assuaged his pride. He grabbed hold of the lever and twisted. Damn was it stuck. His brow creased and his knuckles whitened with his struggle. The lever wouldn't budge. His whole body warmed. He couldn't let her see he hadn't the strength to turn a stuck knob.

Drake said, "Let me try."

No way. He wasn't about to be shown up by his best buddy. After several more attempts, the handle creaked, and he felt at once exonerated as his spirits lifted.

Zaira turned it to the proper setting, then walked over to another device and had the same difficulty with the lever. Quaid struggled with it next. He wished they'd step into the next room. No sense in everyone watching his battling with the knob.

Zaira pulled her hair back behind her shoulders. "The high water vapor in the air has caused the levers to stick. Once they're in the proper place, they won't have to be moved again."

His work was temporarily distracted as the cut of her blouse caught his eye. He shifted his attention back to the lever. "You mean you're beginning the greening of the planet?"

"Yes."

"But you don't have the scrolls, yet," Quaid said. She folded her arms as she furrowed her brow at the men. "Is this where you were headed when the speckled spiders attacked?"

"I haven't been down here in a while. I didn't realize they'd made some nests here."

"Who killed the other spiders?"

"I did."

Now he was pissed. She'd come down here to meet some other guy, and she was covering up the fact. Not that it was really any of his business, but he'd have preferred she'd said so...not lied to him. "Who are you protecting?"

"I have two more levers to move. Then I'll be done and you can get on with your task."

He sure wasn't handling the situation well at all. Sure he was mad, but his first priority should have been keeping her safe. He attempted to smooth things over. "Will you stay and wait for our return?"

"Martius needs my help. He cannot do this job alone, but everyone thinks he's mad and won't aid him."

Man, she was exasperating. "Will you stay here and wait for us, Zaira? We'll escort you to where you need to go next. Will you promise you'll do this for me?"

"Will you promise to be my husband?" Zaira didn't wait for a reply. "Then I cannot promise you such a thing, Quaid Lassiter."

Okay, tit for tat. "Listen, if you don't stay, I won't help Drake get the scrolls."

Drake cleared his throat. "Now wait a minute. I was kind of getting used to your being around as long as you don't set off any more booby-traps."

"Sorry, if Zaira leaves here, I'll have to stay with her for her own protection. You're on your own."

Zaira walked across the room, then twisted another

lever. This one moved with only slight resistance. She set it to its predetermined setting, then turned her attention to the last. After moving it to the correct position, she faced Quaid. "I'll go with Drake." She snatched up the pack she'd laid on a chair, then threw the straps over her shoulders. "Then you can protect us both." She grabbed Drake's arm and led him out of the lab.

Quaid hurried after them. He studied Zaira's skirts as they swished with her step. "Can you manage the way you're dressed, Zaira?"

She reached for the button on her skirt and struggled with it.

"Stay here, Zaira."

"Do you need help, Zaira?" Drake offered.

"No," Quaid said. He didn't want Drake seeing her in those tiny blue shorts, and he didn't want her joining them.

Zaira turned her button toward Drake. "Thank you, Drake."

He pushed the button through the hole. Her skirt dropped to the floor. They caught sight of her short blue shorts and both Drake and Quaid took a deep breath.

"Wow." Drake grabbed up his weapon. "I don't know what the difficulty is."

Zaira picked up her skirt, then hurried back into the bedchamber. When she returned to Drake's side, Quaid closed the door behind them. "There's no talking any sense into *you*. I can see that."

Zaira ignored him as she walked with Drake. He glanced down at her shapely legs, then turned and smiled at Quaid.

"Keep your mind on the task at hand, Drake."

"All work and no play makes Jack a dull boy," Drake replied.

Quaid was ready to sock him.

The three headed down the correct tunnel this time while Drake confirmed their trek on the map. "Finally, we're getting somewhere."

They traversed through three more tunnels, then finally entered a cavernous room filled with a lake. An eerie wind howled through a tunnel high above as a pitch-black blanket of bats suddenly rose from the floor. Shrill squeals erupted as the bats sought solitude in another cave nearby.

Quaid studied a half-eaten beast lying on the floor. "Can't make it out, can you?"

Drake told him he couldn't while Zaira stared at the lake in silence.

"It appears this is a dead end, Drake. Are you certain we're in the right cave?" Quaid asked.

"Yes, a tunnel leading into another cave directly across from where we now stand is just below the water's surface."

"Whoa," Quaid said, "nobody said anything about swimming through a tunnel."

Drake frowned. "You swim."

"Not that well and what about Zaira?"

"I swim." She moved toward the edge of the lake.

"This has been some experience," Quaid said under his breath and not the kind he ever wanted to repeat either.

Zaira smiled coyly.

"I won the Orion galaxy swimming championship for four years in a row in my youth." Drake set his weapon on the ground, then pulled off his flight jacket. "Not coming, Quaid?"

"I'm not much of a swimmer."

Drake stared at him for a moment, then he smiled. "I thought you knew how to do everything well."

"It's not that I don't know how to, I'm just not a champion swimmer like yourself."

"Do you want to stay back here and wait for me then?"

"Us." Zaira dove into the lake.

Drake shouldered his weapon. "She's a natural."

She crossed the lake, swimming across the entire length underwater, then paused to wait for Drake at the tunnel's entrance.

"Can you do it on your own?" Quaid asked, concerned.

"No problem. See you in a bit."

Drake dove into the lake. He surfaced, turned back to Quaid and waved. After diving under again, he swam half of the length of the lake before resurfacing. Then he dove under and this time arrived where Zaira sat on a small ledge, half submerged. She spoke to him. He nodded, then they both disappeared under the water.

Quaid stared at the location where they had vanished. Minutes passed by, then he read the time on his watch. He should have checked it before now. He sure hoped they knew what they're doing. No way did he want to swim through an underwater tunnel to rescue them.

The minutes continued to tick by slowly. He closed his eyes and saw the image of Zaira's eyes as they studied his face. How could he get out of this marriage contract without causing her too much grief? And how could her father have lied to him about his drive, then have stolen his craft? This place was becoming a real nightmare.

A sudden cry echoing off the walls of the cavern made him strain to hear further sounds while he searched for any motion within the cavern. He paced across the rough rock and stared at the lake.

Another cry screeching in the darkness made him drop his weapon, then rip off his jacket. If Zaira was in peril, he couldn't leave her to just Drake's care. He removed the lantern from his jacket pocket and attached it to his shirt. After grabbing up his Millennium rifle, he pulled the strap over his head. Without further hesitation, he dove into the lake.

After swimming only a quarter of the distance across the lake, he rose to get a breath of air while checking his bearing. Again he dove under, only this time his leg touched something in the water, making him shoot to the surface as he struggled to keep his wits about him.

With his heart pounding, he floundered in the lake, staring at the black water. Should he return to the safety of the shore? Another scream made him plunge into the depths of the lake again and headed for the place Drake and Zaira had disappeared to.

Again, something touched his leg, sending chills up his spine. Reaching down to his pants leg, he struggled to pull his dagger free from his zippered pocket. His fingers numbed by the cold water, he fumbled with the zipper. He finally rose to the surface to get a breath of air. *Halfway across.* His fingers struggled to unzip the pocket without success. With arms outstretched, he used the breaststroke to swim across the lake's surface this time.

When he reached the other side, a narrow ledge half submerged in the ice cold water welcomed him. He sat on the ledge as he considered diving to search for the tunnel. He wasn't sure he could make it.

He sat there for several minutes. Then not hearing any further sounds, he dove under the water and stretched out his hands as he felt for the tunnel entrance. Finally discovering its location, he resurfaced for air before attempting to swim through it.

After taking a deep breath, Quaid dove again into the lake and headed directly for the tunnel's entrance. The tunnel was wide enough for a land-rover spacecraft to manage and the spaciousness gave him some peace of mind, but as he swam for some distance through the natural tunnel, his lungs screamed for oxygen. With no sign of relief ahead, he glanced back to see if he could make it back to the surface if he returned that way. *He'd gone too far. He'd have to go forward now. It was his only chance.*

With his mind blackening from lack of oxygen, he desperately fought the urge to breathe. He kicked his legs and pulled the water past him with his arms in a dire attempt to find the end of the tunnel. The water swirled around him in frantic bubbles as his mind drifted to thoughts of Zenith.

Her dark eyes lured him to follow her as she swam before him in the water. Her golden gowns clung to her body as she waved for him to swim with her, but he couldn't follow her any longer. He shook his head at her. She swam to him instead. She pressed her lips to his and the sweet air from her lungs filled his.

He studied the golden flecks that carved patterns in the amber pupils of her eyes. Then she pulled him toward the surface of the water. When they broke free of the water, she pushed him against the shore of the small cave.

"What...," Quaid said, but she covered his mouth with her hand.

She whispered, "Shh, Quaid Lassiter."

After catching his breath, Quaid stared at the golden gown embracing her rounded breasts as ribbons criss-crossed between them accentuating their form while the neckline dipped down to her waist. He whispered in confusion, "Zaira?"

"Yes, Quaid, it's me, but we must be quiet."

"You're a changeling."

"The genes are dominant. My grandfather was a changeling. I'm only a quarter, but I have many of the same abilities."

Quaid sat in silence for a moment, considering the news. Drake had said Darrant was a changeling. He couldn't believe Zaira was one, too. "Darrant was your grandfather?"

"You should have read the book, Quaid."

He ran his finger over her neck in surprise. "But you have no gills." The peaks of her breasts willed him to touch them, but he had to satisfy his desire with only feasting on the sight. Still, his wet clothes clung to his arousal, and she seemed to enjoy viewing him, too.

Smiling, she said, "No, I have to come up for air, too, only like the porpoises in the seas of Orion, not as often as regular humans."

Taking a deep breath, Quaid turned his head to survey the cave. Not seeing any sign of Drake he grew concerned. "Where's Drake?"

"He has gone ahead." Zaira squeezed the water from her hair, then reached down and grabbed the pack.

"What was that shrieking I heard?" Quaid pulled his weapon from his shoulder.

"I'm not certain. We must catch up to Drake now."

Quaid hurried with her into another tunnel. "Do you know the way...I mean, without the aid of a map?"

She nodded. "I drew the map."

He studied her figure. "What can you change into?"

"Not now. Listen, I hear a sound."

He listened, but he couldn't hear anything except for the beating of his own heart and the sound of their footsteps crunching on the rock floor. Zaira was a changeling. And he'd married her?

He was just getting himself deeper and deeper into a quagmire of trouble. What next? He'd wished now he'd read up on other species a bit. A changeling? He had no idea what that entailed.

She stopped in her footsteps, then listened. "Come on!" She ran toward the entrance of another cave as he ran with her, his weapon poised for action.

Drake's double-barreled gun blasts echoed off the cavern's walls. The ensuing screeches made Quaid and Zaira sprint faster. As they ran into the cave, Drake waved at the two of them.

Quaid stared at the oversized rat-like rodents scattered about the room, then turned to Drake. "Why did you leave Zaira behind like you did?"

Drake raised his eyebrows. "I left Zaira, then forged ahead first to ensure the place was safe for her. Then she yelled you were attempting to join us and you were struggling in the tunnel. She said she was going to help you. These critters attacked. I led them away from the lake so you'd have a chance to get to your feet after you exited the tunnel. That's about all of the story." He considered Zaira's golden gowns and smiled. "When did you change?"

"Don't like the feel of wet clothes—only after I changed into the gown while you were scouting ahead, I realized Quaid was having trouble in the lake and I had to assist him. Now I don't have another change of clothes."

Drake ogled Zaira's gown further. "That's a shame."

Quaid punched Drake in the shoulder to get him to divert his gaze from Zaira. "So where to now?"

"This way." Zaira entered another tunnel.

They hurried down a long corridor, then soon arrived at a rectangular room.

"This is it?" Quaid words were hushed. "No guards, no door, nothing to protect its precious contents? That's saying the scrolls are really here, of course."

"We have looked but couldn't find them," Zaira whispered. "A weight-release mechanism is in one of the walls that'll probably reveal the scrolls when used properly, but we haven't figured out how."

"I don't like the looks of this." Quaid surveyed the open doorway.

The two men readied their weapons as they headed for the room. Finding not a soul in the place, Quaid frowned. They observed the large room furnished with only one long table and several chairs. "It appears to be a conference room. Are you sure this was the place where the scrolls were hidden?"

Zaira was glad that Quaid didn't seem too bothered that she was a changeling and was focused on the business of obtaining the precious scrolls. "Yes. Some of the Caspians caught Rondovins trying to raid their food supplies and found a note about this place on one of the Rondovin officers. Since the scrolls were shown to be hidden on Xenon, they turned the note over to us."

"Caspians," Quaid said with hatred, then seeing a lever in one of the walls, he pointed to it. "Wanna try it?"

"I don't know, Quaid. It could be a trapdoor or some such thing," Drake warned.

"A trapdoor? You read too many fantasies." Quaid strode across the natural rock floor and pulled at the wooden lever, but nothing seemed to happen.

Drake let out his breath. "You've probably pulled a silent alarm."

"Search the walls. See if there's anything out of the ordinary on any of them." Quaid considered a smooth, glass-like wall, then ran his hand over one of the others covered in rusticated stones. A stone moved slightly. He pulled at the stone and it slid out of the slot with ease. He peered inside to see a safe with the door already ajar. "Maybe the lever pulled it open." He reached inside the safe.

"Wait!" Zaira pulled another stone out of the wall. She studied the heavy metal square resting on a small shelf sunk partway into the wall. "This is the weight-release type of mechanism I mentioned."

Quaid glanced back at the scrolls. "We have the scrolls, Zaira."

"No, it's too easy."

Quaid grabbed the soft parchment and smiled. "Here they are." He pulled the papers out and studied them, then he grimaced. "They're military plans. Search further. They're not the scrolls."

Drake pushed the stone back into place while Quaid shoved the papers into his shirt. Zaira still considered the metal shelf while Drake found another loose stone. "Bonanza! Well, maybe."

Quaid stared at the locked door hidden behind the stone. "Must be another lever somewhere that will release it."

The two men searched the stones for further hidden niches, but not finding any, Quaid leveled his blaster at the safe.

"No!" Zaira shouted. "What if the blaster damages the contents of the safe?"

"I'll go lightly." He set his weapon on low.

"I don't think that's such...," Drake said as Zaira folded her arms, but his words were never finished as Quaid hit the safe's door with a blast.

The door blew open. Quaid smiled. "See?"

A grating noise followed and the three turned to see an iron grill closing off their entrance.

CHAPTER 8

Zaira couldn't believe that Quaid had triggered a gate to close!

The iron grate began descending across the entrance to the room.

"Get out!" Quaid yelled, reaching into the safe and pulling the scrolls out.

Drake managed to squeeze under the grate before its pointed spears dropped to the floor, but Zaira made no effort to leave. Quaid frowned at her. "Why didn't you get out when you had the chance?"

Drake disappeared and Zaira assumed he searched the outside walls for a release for the gate. Quaid opened the scrolls and read the contents. "Looks like the genuine articles to me." He handed the scrolls to Zaira.

Relieved to have made progress, despite the fix

they were in, she had to admit Quaid did get the scrolls. "These are three of them, all right. Now we must retrieve the remaining six."

She shoved the scrolls through the bars to Drake, her priority above all else to safeguard them. "Take these to my brother. He'll be at the lever room where you met me. We were to rendezvous there about now. Martius will get these to the High Council."

"If you were to meet Martius at the lever room, why in the devil did you come with us?" Quaid asked.

"I didn't believe you'd ever get the job accomplished if I didn't aid you."

Drake looked for a release mechanism on the gate. "What about the two of you?"

Zaira wrapped her fingers around two of the cold bars, hard, immovable. The room was like a vault, except for the bar-covered entryway. It felt like a dungeon below the earth, confining, smelling of cave water, though the walls were clean of moss or lichen.

"The Rondovins have undoubtedly rigged this place so they'll be warned someone has been here. They're sure to come to learn who they've caught in their trap. But the scrolls must be given to my father. My brother can advise you on how to reach the next set of scrolls."

Looking more than concerned, his heart pounding wildly, Drake said, "I can't leave the two of you behind."

"Go, Drake. If the Rondovins come back and grab

the scrolls, there's no telling where they'll hide them next," Zaira said.

Quaid nodded. "Don't worry. I didn't relish the idea of swimming through that tunnel again."

Drake frowned. "I'll deliver these and hurry back here as—"

Zaira grabbed his hand through the grate and squeezed tightly. "Do *not* return here. Find the next set of scrolls. It's imperative."

"Do as the lady says, Drake. I've been in worse scrapes than this before," Quaid said.

"All right, but if the two of you get yourself killed over this, I'll never forgive you."

Quaid smiled.

Zaira shoved her pack through the gate. "It's waterproof. Place the scrolls inside." She turned to Quaid and reached her hand out to him. He pulled the war plans out and handed them to her. Turning the plans over to Drake, she said, "Make haste and may the gods be with you."

Drake shook his head, and she thought him admirable that he worried so for their safety, but the scrolls were so much more important. He tucked the rest of the documents into the pouch. He readied his weapon and ran off toward the lake, his boots pounding the rocky floor, echoing off the walls.

Zaira leaned against the smooth wall, then slid to

the floor while Quaid studied her still-wet bodice as it revealed the rosebuds of womanhood. "I'm sorry, Zaira. I got us into a mess this time."

"It's not your fault. You're a fighter pilot. This kind of thing isn't what you're trained for, after all."

He sat beside her. "Yes, but I should have listened to you." He stared at the wall opposite them, then let his breath out in a heavy sigh and wrapped his arm around her shoulders, pulling her close.

She loved how sensitive he could be even if he was fighting wanting to mate with her.

"I've always wanted you," she said softly. "Do I...not appeal?"

He kissed the top of her head and squeezed her tighter. "I'm not the one for you. I'm not the one for any woman who needs a man who will stay with her always. We have to straighten this out with your father." He sighed deeply. "Why didn't you leave when I told you to?"

"You are my husband. I couldn't abandon you in your time of need. Xenonians don't do such things to their mates."

He leaned his head against the wall and stared up at the ceiling. "You just don't understand. I can't be married."

"You are the key to ending this war. Don't you see that?" It was time to reveal the truth to him whether he could handle it or not. If she was ever to win his heart, his help, she didn't have a choice.

"Don't be ridiculous." He closed his eyes.

"Your grandfather started the Great Galaxy War when your grandmother left him to become the Caspian's leader's wife." There, she had said it, told him that which she was certain he wouldn't wish to hear, or believe. But she'd had to tell him.

He stiffened against her, stared down at her with such a growly look she thought he would have made a perfect jaguar, if he'd had the ability to shift. She knew he would not take the news well.

***

Quaid couldn't believe what he was hearing.

"She was taken by force against her will!" His blood was hot with annoyance at the mention of the Caspian leader who had stolen his grandmother and caused the whole great rift to begin. Nobody could convince him his grandmother had left his grandfather willingly.

"No. Your grandfather was so busy flying missions that when the Caspian ruler visited Orion, your grandmother fell in love with him."

Quaid stared at Zaira in disbelief. "You're wrong." How could Zaira know such a thing?

"She wrote a journal outlining the love she shared with the Caspian and detailing the loneliness she'd experienced with your grandfather. It wasn't that she didn't love him—"

"I don't want to hear this." Quaid leaned hard against the stone wall.

"She tried in vain to convince your grandfather to stop the war, but he hated the Caspians for what he felt they'd stolen from him. Embittered, he passed these feelings of hatred to his own son, and from him, to you."

"I don't believe you."

"I have a copy of her journal at my bookstore. You're welcome to read it, if we manage to free ourselves in time."

Quaid stared at the floor for a moment. His head was spinning. All of these long years his father and he had fought for nothing? Just for his grandfather's revenge? His thoughts shifted to the role Zaira seemed to play in all of this. "I suppose your father is a member of the High Council, then." He said it mockingly, not believing that any of this could be true.

"The *head* of the High Council, actually."

"Carver Cole?" Quaid said, with such an incredulous tone to his voice that Zaira frowned back at him. "He repairs ships and—"

"He loves tinkering with engines. It works as a great cover while he continues to serve as president of the High Council—underground, so to speak."

"He's not the ruler of the colonies."

"So say the people."

"And your coffee shop and bookstore?"

"Certainly, I love operating the shop. But I use it to further our cause as well. When we end the conflict and our planet is no longer an inhospitable wasteland, I hope my shop will draw the kinds of crowds it deserves."

He still couldn't believe all of this. "None of this has anything to do with my not wishing to marry."

"If there was no more Great Galaxy War to fight—"

"No, even if miraculously the Great Galaxy War ended."

Zaira rested her head against the wall. "A woman you would never get to know sufficiently, nor would you learn enough about her—died. You never let the past go, never learned to live with it."

"How do you know so much about me?"

She smiled. "You're in our history books."

"You don't know anything about it." He stared at the floor.

"The Rondovins raided your homeworld. Your mother was killed during that raid on Orion. Your father was fighting a mission at the time. You hid from the Rondovins, terrified they would find you in the rubble, angry you couldn't end their miserable lives when they killed your mother, and horrified they'd taken the one person away from you who showed you the only love and compassion you ever knew. An aunt raised you, who wasn't thrilled with the task until you reached the age of seven. At that time, your father took you aboard his warship and trained you to be the fighter you are today."

He studied her expressionless face. "Your history books wouldn't have said that."

"I've read all there is about you. You do not think I would have selected the wrong mate, do you?" She closed her eyes. "You are the only one for me, Quaid Lassiter. Hopefully you will realize this, sooner...rather than later."

"None of that will matter when the Rondovins take us prisoner."

Her eyes still closed, she said, "And you have a very high and active sperm count."

"What?"

"Being as you descend from such important lineage, but still have failed to create your own offspring, the sperm bank on Orion requires a monthly deposit from you."

"That information was supposed to have been kept strictly confidential."

"Not if you can afford to buy it."

Quaid couldn't believe it. What else had the vixen learned about him? "I hope you don't think I enjoy fulfilling my obligation like that."

Zaira's smiled. "If you would pleasure me, you

would no longer have to make a donation at the bank."

"Your father won't be happy you didn't receive permission to marry an outsider like me."

"Ahh, but there's no killing allowed on the planet, so you are safe."

He couldn't help himself but smiled a little at her sense of humor, despite the timing and the predicament they were in. "I thought that when we were with the women on the plain, you said the men might—"

"That's different. During mating rituals, otherworlders who try to mix with Xenonian women, often vanish without a trace."

Zaira suddenly opened her eyes and stared at the rock ceiling. Quaid squeezed her hand. "What's wrong, Zaira?"

"I'm not certain. I hear a strange sound like nothing I've ever heard before."

"Like?"

She patted her legs in a rhythmic beat as she tried to copy the noise she heard.

Quaid frowned. "Rondovins?"

"It doesn't sound like any kind of footstep I've ever heard. It's a continuous pitter-pattering on the surface above the caves."

"A desert storm?"

"A dust cinderfall? No, they make more of a roaring sound. I cannot fathom what it could be." She took a deep breath and closed her eyes again.

Quaid ran his fingers over Zaira's. "If the Caspians captured the Rondovin documents showing where the scrolls were hidden, why did the Rondovins not move them to a new location?"

She cuddled closer to him. "First of all, they do not consider us to be a very bright people. In their culture, if you do not fight, you are considered not very intelligent. I'm sure they figured we could never solve the puzzles so that we could retrieve the scrolls. I'm certain, too, they assumed we'd never realize the scrolls were hidden on our very own planet. They were right about that. Also, they knew the Caspians, who took control of the documents in the first place, would have no need of the information. What the Rondovins didn't know, was that we've always been on good terms with the Caspians."

"I see. Are you tired?" He had to admit he enjoyed holding her close, smelling her sweet fragrance, feeling her soft, warm body pressed against his.

She nodded.

"Rest your head in my lap." He pulled at her arm to get her to lie down.

She lay her head on his crotch, and he groaned inwardly. He moved her head slightly to reduce the agony of the pressure building in his groin. When her breathing grew shallow, he sighed. She was sleeping and she didn't know just how hard she was making his life.

"You are a sight to behold." He brushed her ebony curls away from her cheek and wished he could be the kind of man who could settle down to family life. There wouldn't have been a better woman than Zaira to have shared marital bliss with, if he'd been that sort of man.

He shut his eyes, then as he rested his hand on her shoulder, Zaira bolted upright. "What's wrong?" he asked, his pulse quickening.

She sprang to her feet and he jumped to his.

Quaid readied his weapon as Zaira listened to the sound in the distance. "Someone's coming. Two...two pair of boots."

"Hey!" Drake yelled out as he ran toward them.

Zaira rolled her eyes as Drake grabbed at the grate. She scolded, "You were supposed to have—"

Martius hastened to the gate. "A messenger has been sent with the scrolls to Father. Why haven't you just—"

Zaira frowned at her brother.

He raised his brow as he considered Quaid's concerned face, then smiled. "All right then. It'll take me a minute to get you out of there, but we have to move fast. I heard a Rondovin war bird landing only moments ago."

He strode to the wall where Quaid and Zaira

couldn't see his work. Drake watched Martius. "I hadn't seen the loose stone over there." He crinkled his brow. "Don't think I could have figured out how to manipulate those wires the way you did."

After a few seconds, the grate rose and creaked as it moved. Zaira grabbed Quaid's wrist and jerked him underneath the grate when it was only halfway up. "To the lake!"

They all dashed toward the lake and when they reached it, Quaid said, "I don't like this one bit."

"Should I take him?" Martius asked Zaira.

"I think my husband would prefer for me to assist him."

Before they had time to dive into the lake, they heard the sound of metal-edged boots. Zaira yanked Quaid into the water to his surprise. As he came up for air, she pulled at him to follow her to the underwater tunnel. When they reached the entrance, Drake and Martius hurried beneath the surface of the lake. The heat from a plasma blast struck the water, singeing Quaid's eyebrows.

"Dive!" Zaira disappeared under the water.

Quaid took a deep breath, then dove beneath the surface of the black lake. Halfway through the tunnel, he saw her darkened eyes as she waited for him. He swam as fast as he was able but three-quarters of the way through the tunnel, his lungs screamed for oxygen again. Wasn't it shameful enough Zaira knew how inadequate a swimmer he was, but to have her brother and his best friend know, too? Absolutely humiliating.

She took his hand and pulled him close while she locked her lips on his and breathed sweet air into his lungs again. Her eyes never parted from his as she continued to pull him along through the tunnel. As they exited to the other side, she rose to the surface with him. When they broke water, she continued to embrace him and Drake laughed. Quaid kissed Zaira with such longing her cheeks reddened, making her brother smile. He couldn't help it. He wanted her like a man craved a woman, despite not wanting to make anything permanent of the relationship.

"We have to go," Zaira said softly as she touched Quaid's fuzzy cheek, "as much as I'd love to continue this with you."

"I'm sorry, Zaira." Her gown clung to her full breasts and he couldn't help but stare at them. "I shouldn't have—"

She smiled as she touched his lips with the tip of her finger. "Shh, Quaid. I love you, too."

Love. He had loved his mother, and his father. Could he ever learn to love a woman who would be his forever?

The four swam across to the other side of the lake, then Quaid looked back at the underwater tunnel.

"You're sure the Rondovins can't swim?"

"They can't as far as I know." Drake climbed out of the water. He and Quaid grabbed their jackets. "We'd better get out of here, just in case, however."

After climbing through the hole to the caves and reaching the surface of the planet, Quaid couldn't believe his eyes. Everyone's mouths gaped wide as they took in the changed sight.

The desert planet had turned into a jungle.

CHAPTER 9

"What in the world..." Quaid reached out to feel the rubbery leaf of a tree more than seventy feet tall.

"Guess my theory worked," Martius said and Zaira hugged him.

"You mean the whole planet is a jungle now?" Drake poked at a violet-colored flower, center dripping with yellow pollen on pink stems.

"No, of course not. My brother thought of everything. There are meadows and jungles, deciduous forests, everything that exists on other worlds. We smuggled seeds from all over the galaxy, seeded the planet, then began the transformation. It's taken years."

The canopy of the jungle blocked out the sky, and she frowned. "What was that strange noise I heard while we were in the cave, Martius?"

"Rain."

"Rain." She nodded. "I wondered what such a thing would sound like."

"But the size of the vegetation...the plants appear to be full-grown," Quaid said.

"They're more of the vigorous varieties from other worlds, Quaid. I didn't want to wait until we were old and gray to see the transformation," Martius said.

Zaira turned her ear toward the south and frowned. Her brother nodded. She took a deep breath. "The Rondovins have exited the caves at some other point and are now searching for us above ground. We must get the other scrolls at once."

"Anyone have a machete?" Drake pushed away some of the fern-like leaves.

Quaid held up his blaster, but Zaira rested her hand on the barrel. "We just made them grow. We wouldn't want to kill them off so soon."

Point taken.

As the four began their trek through the jungle, Martius touched Zaira's shoulder. She nodded. "The Rondovins are concerned that some very lively vines are covering their craft. A search party is still looking for us, but the rest are returning to the ship and will probably leave the area."

Quaid stared at Martius, then turned his attention to Zaira. "You can understand each other without speaking your minds?"

"Certainly. We're twins. All Xenonian twins can do such a thing."

"Tell me, Zaira, if you already knew where the scrolls were, why didn't your people try to retrieve them?" Quaid asked.

"Twenty tried and failed. They thought a privateer like Drake would succeed where our people could not."

Drake rubbed his red-whiskered chin. "I wonder if Catarina is still waiting for me."

Zaira smiled. "She'd wait an eternity for you. She's always wanted to mate with an outsider but she says your red hair really caught her eye."

"Hope she doesn't mind the beard too much." He ran his hand over the fuzz again.

Zaira said, "I'm sure she'll desire you just as much as before."

"About the scrolls—" Quaid said, trying to press on.

"We'll split up. Martius and Drake will go south and you and I will head north."

When the party reached the green meadowlands, Martius reached for Zaira and pulled her close. He kissed her goodbye as Quaid looked on with annoyance. "Here we part." Martius took Quaid's hand and gripped it firmly. With one shake he said, "Be safe and keep my sister out of harm's way."

"I'll certainly do my best," Quaid said, then nodded

at Drake. "Drake, see you when I see you."

"Sounds like a plan." Drake began the trek with Martius in a southerly direction.

As Quaid walked with Zaira, she said, "If we encounter any Rondovins, you cannot kill them, you do realize?"

"But, Zaira—"

"Not a one. No killing is allowed on Xenon."

"Except for during the mating—"

"That's different." She quickened her pace.

He glanced at her as she breathed the air as if she were taking a leisurely Sunday stroll. "I've never seen a woman capable of walking as fast as you. And certainly if one could, she'd shortly be out of breath."

"Good lung capacity." Zaira patted her breastbone.

"I'll say."

"You know, Quaid, my brother is concerned that we haven't coupled yet."

Quaid stared at her. "He said this to you?"

She reached for his hand. "I cannot hide what goes on between you and me from my brother. Nor when he chooses a mate will he be able to keep secrets from me."

Quaid took a deep breath. "So what conclusions does he draw from this?"

Zaira squeezed his hand. "He assumes you're shy."

Quaid raised his brows as he considered Zaira's

serious expression. "You're not serious."

"Certainly. It's the only explanation he can think of for a mate of mine not already pleasuring me."

"Zaira, it's not that I wouldn't love to—"

"I know, Quaid. Truly, you're just shy."

He'd been called a lot of things over the years, but shy wasn't one of them and the notion irritated him. "I'm not shy. It's just that—"

"It's quite all right, Quaid. I have a confession to make to you, too. I'm really quite shy myself."

Quaid frowned.

"Seriously, I don't mind tantalizing you a bit, but if you insisted that we unite as husband and wife right this instant, I'd wilt like a carpel beetle that has been too long in the noonday sun."

Quaid considered Zaira's bodice as her breasts bounced with every step she took. "You're tantalizing all right." He looked due north. "But it's hard to believe you're shy."

"Disappointed?" Zaira's voice softened with a tinge of hurt. Her eyes puddled.

Quaid pulled her to a stop. "What's wrong, Zaira?" He'd upset her again, and he had no idea how this time.

A tear rolled down her cheek, and she dropped to her knees.

"Zaira." He knelt down before her. "What's the matter?"

"Nothing." She looked up at him with teary eyes. "And everything. I'm sorry for tying you to me. But we need you. My people need you. It doesn't matter about us. I understand how you feel. I only...I only was trying to protect you because you wouldn't leave me when I was so drugged. You were in danger. Don't you see? I did what I had to do. I thought...I thought we'd have more time to get to know each other. I can't ever be with another man. But it doesn't matter as much as your safety did, or the help you can give us. It doesn't matter that I'll never know the touch of a man inside me, nor be able to nurture my own set of twins."

"Twins?" Quaid's voice rose slightly. The idea of having one child bothered him, but two...at the same time?

She groaned and slapped the ground with her hands. "Nothing I say or do pleases you."

"Anyone would be pleased to have a mate as beautiful and as sweet-natured as you, Zaira." Sweet-natured when she wasn't having a meltdown. He reached for her hand.

"But you."

He caressed her fingers. "I can't ever marry. I wouldn't make a good husband for any woman."

She pulled away from him. Wiping the tears from her cheeks, she studied the grasses wavering in the breeze, then jumped to her feet. "Return to the way station, Quaid—at once! Your craft awaits you! Never come back!" She stomped north.

He jogged after her. "Your father will straighten this mess out, and you'll marry some decent fellow and—"

"Go, Quaid! Get out of my life!" she screamed, then turned northeast.

"I won't leave your side. The Rondovins are searching for us now—"

"Good! Then you can lead them away from me while I retrieve the scrolls!"

"No, I won't leave you."

Her brows knit tightly together in a perpetual scowl while her small chin jutted toward her destination as she strode through the grasses.

"These mood swings you seem to be having...," he said with an air of caution so as not to upset her further.

"I need to be pleasured by my mate." Her voice softened. "I cannot help the way I feel. But I will not accept your attentions toward me now. You are unworthy."

He scratched his head. What a fool he was. To think he could couple with such an exquisite creature—satisfy her needs and his own at the same time and yet... He just couldn't do it. On the other hand, the unconscionable notion he was shy, curdled his stomach. "I'm not shy," he said under his breath.

Zaira stopped walking, totally exasperated with herself. She was a powerful jaguar, bowed down to no one, never got teary-eyed over anything. This...this need to mate had thrown her for a loop. She couldn't believe how stupidly she was behaving, and it wasn't helping matters one iota. She needed to find the scrolls, get them to her father, and find a way to get Quaid's agreement to provide fighter support in the meantime.

She didn't want him to make love to her unless he truly wanted to, but not here or now, for goddess sakes. But she pushed his buttons anyway, annoyed he was so adamant that he couldn't be the one for her. "I can prove you are shy."

"Oh?" He folded his arms across his chest.

"Take off your clothes."

"Now is not the time—"

"I will not touch you. Just remove your clothes." She folded her arms and lifted a brow.

He frowned at her. "We're trying to find the remaining scrolls, and there's a good chance we have Rondovins on our tail."

"You are shy." She hastened north again.

"My not removing my clothes has nothing to do with—"

"Why can you just not admit this to yourself?"

"I am not shy."

"How many women have you pleasured?"

"I won't discuss—"

"None. You are shy."

"Dozens and I am not shy."

"Dozens? You've been with dozens of women that you have not married?" A tear cascaded down her cheek, and she quickly brushed it away. Damn these emotional outbursts when she was normally a completely rational woman.

"They meant nothing to me—"

"You pleasured all those women for no reason?" She let out her breath in annoyance.

"My doctor said being with a woman would help to reduce the number of headaches I was having."

"Did you ever think of changing occupations? Dozens of women!"

"Well, one of the women didn't really count."

She glared at him. She assumed he would have been with women before, but a dozen? Including the one who didn't count?

They walked in silence, then as they caught sight of red cliffs streaked with green vines like the striations of color in marble plunging into the deep canyon, he cleared his throat. "I'm curious, Zaira, how many children *had* you intended to have?"

"That's an idiotic question."

He stared at her, then looked back to the canyon. "Tons, I suppose."

She folded her arms. "You really are quite uninformed about my people. Female Xenonians can only have one child. It's all they're capable of. Unless of course, they're a twin. Then they have one set of twins." She considered the vines dripping over the edges of the canyon. "Coupling afterward is purely for pleasure and done quite frequently, I might add." She poked his chest. "But in your case, you'll never know anything more about it."

His neck muscles relaxed. "I just wondered."

She took a deep breath, getting her mind back on the mission. "I hadn't realized the canyons would have been overgrown with vegetation. It'll make the climb easier, but finding the waterfall, more difficult."

"Waterfall?"

"It was just over there." She pointed to an outcropping of rocks. "But if it's still there, I don't..." She glanced up at the wisps of clouds drifting across the sky. "Rondovin war bird!" She scrambled down one of the vines. "Hurry!" she shouted, "before their scanners catch sight of us in the open!"

CHAPTER 10

Quaid reached for a vine, then shimmied down behind Zaira. She was already halfway to the bottom when he glanced down. She sure was athletic. He considered her dark hair as it draped over her shoulders and back while the muscles in her arms strained with the climb. When he joined her on the rock bed below, she grabbed his arm, and yanked him across the shallow river. Then as a shadow covered them, they looked up to see the sky darken.

"What's happening?" She dashed across to the shelter of the trees growing on the opposite bank.

"Appears to be a sudden storm. Your brother probably wasn't aware of all the consequences of unleashing—"

"He's a genius." She ducked through the screen of a seven-foot tall fern.

Streaks of white light slashed across an angry dark sky and thunder crashed overhead, making Zaira cry out. Rain pitter-pattering at first with a gentle touch quickly turned into a torrent with the roar like ocean waves crashing all around them while quarter-sized drops pelted the leaves sheltering them. "Keep moving," she urged, and ran through the thick vegetation close to the wall of the canyon. "It has got to be here somewhere."

"If your father is the ruler of the planet, your brother will take his place once your father—"

"Yes." She shoved a tree branch aside.

The branch snapped back and slapped Quaid's face. "It's proper etiquette to hold the branch for the person following you and not let it strike him upon its release."

"Sorry, not used to plants." She continued to run. She stopped suddenly, causing him to collide with her. "It's muffled, undoubtedly from the blanket of plants covering it, but I hear its roar some distance hence." She darted off again.

"If your brother will be the next ruler, then what place do you hold?"

"What do you mean?" She stopped still.

He ran into her again and frowned. "You should warn me when you're going to stop so suddenly like that."

"What are you asking?"

"Well, if your brother is the ruler, but you are a princess—"

"For now, my father rules. My brother will continue with his experiments. He has many notions on how to improve our living conditions here. I will help him when I'm able. In the meantime, I have a coffee shop and bookstore to manage. Remember?"

She waited for his reaction as he rubbed his chin. "Yes, but what of your husband?"

She smiled. "Ahh, that's what you are getting at. My husband will have the most arduous of tasks." She dashed off again and Quaid bolted after her.

"What, Zaira? What will he be required to do?"

She stopped. "We are a peaceful people, Quaid. We have no defenses. But you, now, you are a warrior. You've trained in the most advanced procedures and have trained others. You will be our Minister of Defense."

"I thought there was to be no killing—"

"Policies will change I'm certain, as the word spreads that the planet is no longer a desolate desert. The plan was that you would develop a network of defensive measures, train Xenonians to become fighter pilots, and lead the missions."

"As a fighter?"

"That's what you do best, isn't it, Quaid?"

"Your father had this in mind for me?"

"All of the High Council, actually."

"They talked you into marrying me?"

Zaira let out her breath. "That wasn't planned. All right? Me being poisoned, running into the Rondovins, you carrying me to a mating party. None of that was planned. It. Just. Happened. And I did the only thing I could think of doing. Do you know how important I am to my people? With you hovering over me, unwilling to leave before the men arrived, you were in danger. And I was in danger of being mated to someone I wouldn't have wished for a mate because I was so out of it. Though I am pleased to be your mate, which is the reason also that I offered you my ring. You kissed me. I had not asked you to do so. My father has no knowledge of this. He will be quite angry with me. No telling what he'll do."

"Did you think if I married you, I'd do what the High Council wishes?"

"I can tell you all of the times that you'd visited the way station. I could only hope you wouldn't marry before I had a chance to..." She paused. "You wouldn't know the kind of fantasies I've dreamed I've had with you." She sighed deeply. "Guess they'll remain my fantasies." She turned and ran off again.

He stood, watching the ebony-haired nymph as she darted through the vegetation. She had fantasized about him? Nobody had ever been that interested in him before. The other women in his life had just wanted some companionship, nothing more...no strings, no commitments, just a little human comfort.

"Here!" she shouted, as she observed the leaves of the plants soaked with water, then as she continued farther, she waved at Quaid who hastily caught up with her.

"What fantasies?" He touched her flushed cheek with his fingertips.

"We have to retrieve the scrolls now. No more talk." Zaira slipped between the rock facing and water as it plummeted over the canyon ridge.

"Another cave." Quaid switched his lantern on.

"Yes, but no more speckled spiders. The scrolls are in that wall over there." She pointed to a wall covered in painted figures of oddly proportioned shapes, their pin-sized heads squashed on top of bloated bodies. "Ancient drawings of some past civilization. We haven't been able to decipher the combination. Several stones need to be pushed in, but push in the wrong combination and death comes to the meddler."

Quaid studied the drawings. "What makes you think I can do any better with something like this?"

"Your mother was an archeologist. She taught you her findings, but then she was killed. We know she intended to raise you as an archeologist. She was world renown for her findings and had several published works. We've read all of her books to see if we could find a clue."

Frowning, Quaid ran his finger over the spiked hair of one of the figures. "I was so little."

"Yes, but they say you have her gift for ancient writings of pictographs like she did."

"Others died trying to solve the puzzle?" Quaid ran his fingers over a horned head resting on a human form.

"Yes, in various ways. I can tell you what combinations not to use."

"Then you must leave here while I attempt to—"

"I will stay by your side, husband."

"If I die, you can marry again—"

"We mate for life. If we lose our mate, we can never remarry. It is our way. So if you die, I choose to die with you."

"Then I won't test my theory."

"You must hurry, Quaid. The Rondovins placed the scrolls here. They'll know where we've headed. When the storm began, their craft landed at the top edge of the cliffs."

He frowned as he considered the mural again. "If the correct sequence is not attained?"

"Every stone must be pushed in correctly. But we won't know if it is the correct combination until the last is pushed in."

"And then?"

"Sometimes poisonous gases are released. Fireballs killed another of our men. Jagged spikes shot down from the roof of the cave on one occasion."

Quaid studied a curtain of rocks folding down from the ceiling. "What about standing behind those?" He pointed at the limestone formation dripping with groundwater.

"We've always had someone write the combinations down, when we've tried this in the past. The place behind the rocks is safe."

"Then you'll stand there." He pushed the bull's head. Seeing Zaira still standing nearby, he said, "As your husband, I insist."

She raised her brows as a glimmer of a smile touched her lips. "You'd have to have fulfilled me first." She folded her arms and tilted her head to the side. "Proceed."

He pushed a stone that pictured a woman whose breasts and stomach were unnaturally swollen. "How would the Rondovins have known of this place?"

"All we know is according to the plans found on the Rondovin officer, they did indeed use these caves to hide the documents."

"What would an ancient civilization have designed such a puzzle for?"

"We've considered that the Rondovins copied ancient paintings, then covered the wall with the mural for their own use only not in the proper sequence to throw anyone off who wished to tamper with the settings."

"They copy everything of other civilizations."

"Agreed." She frowned at his selection. "We have done this combination before. And the next is the small infant."

Nodding, he pushed the stone in.

She placed her hands on her hips. "This has not worked before."

He studied the painting further, then pushed a stone painted with the figure of a young boy with raised spear in hand.

"We have tried this sequence before."

"How can you reset the stones?"

"You can't. Once you've pushed the wrong set of stones, death follows. Then the stones reset themselves."

He raised his hand to a stone covered with the figure of a bull-like creature lying stiffly on his back while his legs stuck straight up in the air. A spear piercing his skull appeared broken in half. He pushed the stone in. It recessed and he pressed another stone of a man wearing a bull's head.

"We've already tried this sequence, Quaid," she said with exasperation.

"I know and it's the wrong sequence." He shoved a

stone where another pregnant lady was pictured.

"What are you doing?"

He reached up to compress the stone of another infant.

"Setting the stones incorrectly." He saw her turn her head suddenly toward the waterfall, and he knew before she said it...the Rondovins were close by.

She whispered, "The Rondovins."

He nodded, then pushed the stone of a fallen deer. Then he ran to her and grabbed her arm. He shoved her behind the curtain of rock. With his blaster, he shot at the cave wall, then as several pieces of rock fell from the wall, he grabbed one and readied it.

Her eyes grew big. "What in the world are you doing?"

"Doing what I do best," he whispered back as he hid with her in the shadows of the rock curtain.

A party of six Rondovins entered the cave. Quaid threw the rock at the last of the stones in the sequence. Before the Rondovins could turn their weapons on him, he ducked behind the curtain of rock. In the same instance, balls of fire shot from every direction. The room grew hot as a furnace. After the inferno quit, Quaid peeked around the corner. Six Rondovin piles of ash rested on the floor. "I didn't kill them," he said, as he saw her disapproving look. "The ancients did. If not them, the Rondovins killed their own when they set the trap in the first place, which I highly suspect to be the case."

He hurried to push in the stone decorated with the symbol of the moon in a sliver of its usual glory. Then he pushed the bull's head. He considered the painting further, then pushed a stone that pictured a horned creature mounting another without horns. The next he selected was of the sun as the rays stretched out from the ball. The impregnated woman was the next stone he pushed in and as it recessed, he pressed the infant's. The stones picturing the young boy, dead bull and boy wearing the bull's head were poked in sequence. Finally, he pushed in the painting of a pregnant lady. A grating sound resulted and across the cave a door opened. He ran into the next cave and stared at the round disk and the colored lines squiggling across its surface.

"You did it! This one I know." She hastened to align the twisting lines. "The Rondovins had it pictured on the paper." Each of the lines connected, and they heard a click. The disk popped open. Inside the safe, she found the scrolls and sighed deeply. "We must hurry and get these back to Father."

***

For over an hour, Zaira led Quaid through the canyon as it snaked its way through the meadow grasses. Then she took his hand and climbed out of the canyon where the land sloped more gently. When they reached the shelter of a forest of firs, she smiled. "Martius would be pleased to see this forest."

Feathered fir trees reached for the sky while needled pines scented the air. A slight breeze whooshed through the needles as Zaira ran her hand over the flat feather-like spray of the greenery of a juniper. Clusters of blue grape-like berries snuggled against the branches. Nestled underneath, white, pink and yellow flowers bloomed on dogwood.

Quaid stared at the sight. "What other wonders does Martius intend to create?"

"He hopes to bring birds and other wildlife to the planet. But he has to ensure they will be suitable to our world. We don't want to create any new problems."

"Wise decision." He touched a berry. "I don't know how many times some plant or animal is removed from one world and brought to another, with the intention it will help to solve a problem. And then another solution is sought when this organism causes a new dilemma."

"Yes, well, that's what Martius is considering first." She climbed over a tree trunk blown down in the recent storm. "How did you know the true sequence of the stones, by the way?"

"They wouldn't have done it in the light of day."

"You mean procreating?" She laughed. "We couple any time of day or night."

"Not the ancient civilizations. They were too busy

trying to survive. With the cloak of darkness and nothing else for them to do at night...well, it was as good a time as any."

"Well, I'm glad we don't have to fight for our survival." She stared at the needle-filtered sky and frowned. "The Rondovin crew must have discovered the ashes of their fallen warriors. The war bird is in pursuit of us again."

"They won't be able to detect us in this thick vegetation."

"No. You were brilliant back there. I would never have thought of trying such a thing. For a moment, I thought you were so disappointed in me, you were planning on ending your own life."

He pulled her to a stop. "Being married to you isn't as grave as all that." He kissed her lips and when she melted to his touch, he pulled away. "I just knew the Rondovins would catch us before long." He held her hand while they walked through the forest. "And it was the only solution I could come up with where I wouldn't have been accused of killing them."

"I have another confession to make, Quaid," Zaira said softly.

Quaid studied her eyes as she looked up at his with longing. "My father wished for me to marry Caryndian Bach."

"The Chief Magistrate?"

Zaira nodded.

"The Chief Magistrate," Quaid repeated as he rubbed his whiskered chin. How could things keep getting worse? It was rumored many otherworlders had disappeared at the hands of this man.

"Caryndian is liable to be pretty sore."

"How does your brother feel about this?"

"He never liked Caryndian. He's well-pleased I've mated with you."

"Even though we haven't—"

"He understands. He's been quite shy with the ladies, too. Except he hasn't lain with any before."

"He told you this?"

"I told you, I know all about him, as he does about me."

"If you are the same age, isn't it time for him to find a mate also?"

"Yes, but his mind has been on the greening of the planet. He'll choose a mate soon." She squeezed Quaid's hand. "The Rondovins just landed their ship. Their craft has to be somewhere in the meadow near the edge of the forest. If we become separated—"

"I won't leave your side."

"If we become separated," she repeated with a tone of urgency, "you must keep on a westerly path through the woods. A ship will be waiting for us beyond the forest if my brother has returned the other set of scrolls to our father by then."

"If not?"

"Continue west and when you come to a river, follow it until it makes a sharp bend to the southwest. You'll find the village of Kranobia. The scrolls will be returned to my father by a messenger."

"And you?"

"Wait for me there, and I will soon follow."

"I won't leave your side." He gripped her hand tightly, then quickened his pace in a westerly direction. He'd promised her brother he'd take care of her. But it wasn't just that. He wanted to keep her safe for his own personal reasons. There wasn't any way she could manage alone.

She leaned over and rested her head against his shoulder. He kissed her head, but his feelings were in turmoil. She was forcing him to rethink this marriage situation, but he wasn't giving in.

The two continued on for another hour, but when Rondovin boots tromped on the fallen branches nearby and their heavy drawl as they conversed back and forth shattered the tranquility, she pointed to a hole in the ground and whispered, "Climb in. When they walk past, we'll continue on our way."

"After you, Zaira." He waited for her to slip into the hole.

"You have the gun. If there's anything waiting down

there for us—"

"All right," he said, as the voices grew close. He poked his legs into the hole and looked up at Zaira. Her eyes showed concern as she hurried to lean over and kiss his lips. As soon as he slipped into the hole, his heart filled with dread as his boots connected with nothing but air. Down he dropped through a natural chute, clawing at the earth to stop his rapid descent. There was something about her words...she'd planned on being separated from him. Blasters pelted the air above him, mixed with screams and shouts in the forest above. He landed with a thump into a pile of soft dirt and stared at his surroundings. He was still in the forest, only several feet below where he had been. He heard caterwauling. What the hell was going on?

"Zaira!" he shouted.

His worst fears were realized. She wasn't joining him...not here.

***

Zaira threw off her clothes as fast as she could and shifted into her jaguar form, her body turning hot with the shift, her muscles stretching until she was a big cat and ready to take the men on. There were six of them, and with the cover of the vegetation, this was going to be much easier to manage. She'd fought the speckled spiders in the caves before, but never the Rondovins, so this was a new experience. They could be just as deadly.

She saw the men spread out, thankfully. They would never see what hit them. She leapt into a tree and saw the first of the men close by, lunged, and took him down. Before he could cry out, she bit him in the throat and ended his life. Then she went on the prowl for the next man. They were easy, no one expecting an attack from the trees. Or probably from anywhere. Not when her kind were pacifists. At least, many of her people were. But not her. And not her brother. And some of her friends felt the same way as they did. This was their land. Their new land. And they'd fight to keep it as theirs.

Then one of the men saw her and shot in her direction, only he hit the man behind her as she leapt into the tree. He yelled out in pain before he collapsed. Shouts through the forest caught her attention. She tried the same maneuver again, plotting to encourage Rondovins to fire upon their fellow crewmembers.

She, or the men themselves, had taken down all but one of the men when he saw her out of the corner of his eye and began shooting. Damn it. She thought she could finish him off without endangering herself. And she hadn't wanted Quaid to have to fight this many men. Not when they needed him to train her people to fight for themselves.

She circled around through the vegetation and lunged at the man from the ground, her leap a good twenty feet, though if she hadn't had so much vegetation in the way, she could have managed thirty-five feet.

He still shot off a laser pulse that whisked by her ear, right before she cried out in anger and made the killing blow.

**

Quaid raced along the bottom edge of the jagged cliff, but not finding any way to climb to the top, he dashed back to the chute he'd just fallen from. "Zaira!" he shouted again. There were no sounds now, and the silence made him fear the worst. "Zaira!" He ran along the bottom of the ravine in a westerly direction, then seeing a foothold, he shouldered his weapon and began the arduous climb.

When he finally reached the top, he ran as fast as his legs could carry him back to the chute. When he reached the place where he had first slipped into the hole, bodies of Rondovins were scattered about the forest floor. He studied the blast marks that had ripped into the men's bodies. *The Rondovins had fired on their own kind?* Then he examined two of the men's throats torn open. He stared at the carnage for a moment, then yelled, "Zaira!"

Other than the slight ruffling of pine needles in the breeze, no other sound met his ears, and Quaid sprinted west as she had advised. For three miles he ran, dodging branches, jumping over fallen tree trunks, and slugging through dense brush. When he reached the edge of the forest, he found no sign of her, or of the spaceship that was to meet them.

His heart sank. He promised he'd keep her safe and he'd lost her.

CHAPTER 11

With a heavy heart, Quaid hurried his pace to the west and walked for another hour. When he heard the sound of the river rushing south, he ran toward the water. The land dipped slightly, and he stopped atop his lofty perch, then spied a figure sipping the water. "Zaira!" he yelled. She stood and watched him. He raced down the hill and across the beach to her. He grabbed her arms and held them tight. "Why the devil didn't you follow me down the chute?"

Her darkened amber eyes appeared slightly dazed.

"What's wrong, Zaira?"

She sank to the beach, his hands on her arms the only thing keeping her from collapsing all the way.

"I haven't eaten for quite a while."

He held onto her and ran his hands through her dark hair. "At the village, they'll have food."

"I won't make it that far."

"If I carry you then."

She nodded and stretched her arms to him like a toddler who wanted to be carried. He lifted her in his arms, her eyes closing. "What's wrong, Zaira?" he whispered.

She didn't reply and he quickened his step as he walked along the stone-covered beach for many miles. She didn't seem to be injured, and he assumed her lack of sleep and food had exhausted her. Holding her close like this stirred his longings for her, but not just the noncommittal kind. When her breathing grew shallow, he kissed her forehead. "Ministry of Defense. Guess it couldn't be too bad a job."

The village of Kranobia came into view, and he hesitated. No children were playing in the tended green grass wavering slightly in the breeze, no villagers working in the new gardens they had created; not a sign of anyone.

The stone houses stood neatly in a double row along the perimeter. A large plot behind the first of the stone homes was filled with green yakims, blue wasoons, and purple yaroos, vegetables most prized from the Feronian home world. The garden gate swung open, creaking back and forth as if some thoughtless Xenonian had left it open in his haste.

Plots behind the other homes also were filled with

colorful fruits and vegetables of home worlds across the galaxies. Next to one of these, a basket filled with the afternoon's pickings lay on its side. Purple berries scattered beside it as they'd rolled away in their attempt to escape.

Some distance from the gardens, each of the families had constructed a circular storage building. Quaid studied these for signs of movement or sound. Instead, all he heard was a stream trickling nearby. The aroma of gregoron stew drifting from the first stone house, touched his nostrils and the sensation made his stomach rumble. *Food.*

Then the glint of sunlight off a metal object caught his eye. The curt yell of a Rondovin shattered the peace. Quaid dashed for the cover of a storage building, trying not to disturb Zaira's slumber. Crouching behind the building, he heard the distinctive Rondovin drawl in conversation nearby.

"Out here!" a Rondovin soldier shouted. "You too!"

Quaid peeked around the stone structure and saw a young girl being pulled by her mother. A black-uniformed Rondovin signaled to them with his blaster to join the rest of the villagers in the town square. Quaid raised a finger to his lips as the young girl stared at him. The mother seeing this, leaned down to her daughter and spoke. The two turned their backs to Quaid and hurried to obey the Rondovin guard.

Two Rondovin soldiers pulled a family of three Xenonians from the home nearest him. The soldiers corralled the Xenonians into the common square in the center of the village. Quaid dashed toward the first of the houses with Zaira. After charging in through the backdoor, he hastened into one of the bedrooms and lay her down.

He returned to the kitchen where stew bubbling away over a warmer caught his attention. Grabbing a plastic bowl, he hurried to fill it. He spied a spoon already resting in its place on the table. After snatching up the spoon, he hurried back to the bedroom with the stew. "Zaira, I have something for you to eat." He crouched beside the bed.

Her eyelids fluttered open, then she tried to sit. Grasping her arm, he helped her up. He sat on the edge of the bed and spooned some of the stew meat though her parted lips. She ate several bites. "Where is the family who resides here?"

"The Rondovins have forced all of the villagers into the square. After you've eaten, I'll see what I can do—"

"We must get the scrolls to my father."

"Then I must at least free the messenger who—"

"You will get yourself killed, or captured." She finished eating the stew.

"Get your strength back while I see what I can do."

Quaid set the scrolls next to Zaira. "I'll get you a

refill." He hurried back to the kitchen and filled her bowl with another generous portion of thick gravy stew chunked full of vegetables and boar meat. When he returned to her, he said, "You eat and rest. I'll be right back."

"Quaid—"

He leaned over and kissed her lips, then took a deep breath. "Stay here." He handed her the bowl of stew, then walked over to the bedroom window. He peered out, but saw no sign of any Rondovins loitering between the houses.

He hurried back to the commons area of the home and stared out the front door still hanging wide open. He darted out of the house, then ran across a grassy area to another home directly across from the first. Then he entered it and crossed the floor to the other side where he had a better view of the square.

Leaning next to the wall at the open doorway, he heard one of the soldiers yell, "Where are the ones who have taken the scrolls?"

"Hand them over to us, and we will let you go!" another growled.

The Xenonians remained silent, and Quaid slipped back out the front door. He considered what to do next and noticed the glint of metal again. He stared at the sight for a moment. Rondovin space shuttle! Dodging behind buildings, he dashed for the shuttle parked in the field beyond the cemetery. After climbing into the already open hatch, he shoved the button to close it. "First rule as a pilot, never leave your craft vulnerable to theft."

He smiled to think a Rondovin commander could have been so sloppy.

Five Rondovin soldiers guarded the prisoners as two others ranted and raved in front of the hostages. The one with gold stripes down his pants leg had to be the commander of the craft. Taking a deep breath, Quaid turned on the engine. The craft's engines roared. The Rondovin soldiers turned toward the ship. Quaid smiled.

For an instant, he figured they were trying to decide which Rondovin was starting up their shuttle. The Rondovins ran toward the craft. "Just an Orion pilot, fellows." In the confusion, the villagers scattered to the woods. Before Quaid could fire the phasers, a sleek black cat, five foot in length from head to tail, jumped twenty-two feet from the roof of one of the stone buildings. As soon as it leapt on the first of the Rondovins, the others turned to fire on the jaguar.

The cat dodged the laser blasts and jumped ten feet into the air before grabbing the throat of another Rondovin. Attempting to shoot the jaguar, one of the men fired at the cat, but she twisted around so that he shielded her from the blast. The man took the full brunt of the blast and she released him. Before the same shooter could take her out, she pounced on him too.

And he realized then, it was like the carnage he'd witnessed in the forest.

Quaid watched in awe as the jaguar's dark brown spots shined in the fading light, and her sleek body coiled for another attack. By now the remaining three Rondovins turned and fled the village. The jaguar took chase after one.

Quaid landed the craft. He dashed back to the house where Zaira was resting, but found only the scrolls lying on the bed. He grabbed the scrolls, then ran to the front door of the home. "Zaira!" he hollered out the doorway.

***

What was wrong with her? Zaira had never felt like this when she ran as a jaguar. Never felt drained of energy after a run. Was it because she wasn't fully mated? Everything was changing for her. She hoped if Quaid decided he could live with being mated to her, all of these changes would subside.

She cursed feeling so out of it. She'd only given a moment to think about her actions, knowing that sooner or later she would have to let Quaid in on the secret. That she could turn into a jaguar. That she was a killing machine when she needed to be. That she had a temper to go along with all that sweetness.

She sighed. It couldn't be helped. The Rondovins were getting ready to kill some of her people, and Quaid couldn't have taken them out and missed hitting her people at the same time.

Now she was feeling lethargic again. She hated feeling this way. She wanted to help her people in the worst way. She wanted Quaid to know that she could be a help, not a hindrance.

Quaid was frantically searching for her, and she knew even if he didn't believe he could commit to her, he felt something for her.

She returned to where she'd left her clothes, shifted, and dressed, then headed to the house he was searching.

"Here, Quaid." Zaira walked in through the backdoor, her movement annoyingly slow. "No need to shout. My hearing is quite sensitive, you know."

He ran to her and embraced her warmly. This was how she wanted it to be between them. The caring, loving, protective way in which he treated her. She wanted to embrace him back, but she didn't have the strength.

"Did you see what happened out there? I didn't know they had cats that big on Xenonia! Did you see what happened?" He sounded excited to have seen it, not adverse to it.

That gave her some hope, but the notion *she* would

be that big cat was probably a little much for him to handle right now.

"The messenger must take the scrolls to my father." She pulled away and sank into a plush chair in the commons of the home.

"You're still too weak, Zaira." He knelt on one knee in front of her. She loved how he acted toward her when he was like this, taking her hands in his, caressing them with his thumbs, the concern in his expression.

A black-haired man ran into the house, and Quaid stood. "I'm Quaid Lassiter and this is—"

"Zaira, Darrant sent me," the man said, bowing low. "I'm the messenger who will take the scrolls to your father, but your brother, he has not returned yet."

"And Drake?" she asked, concerned that he had not made it either.

"We haven't heard from the privateer yet."

"How do you know he's a messenger from your father?" Quaid asked her.

"Darrant sent him."

The messenger took the scrolls from them, bowed, and hurried out of the house.

Zaira stood, still weary, but she had to ignore her own lack of physical strength. She felt as though she'd run a marathon halfway around the planet. She was physically and emotionally drained. "They've encountered trouble. They should have been here by now. We had the longer trek to make. We must go in search of them at once, Quaid."

She knew this could only mean bad news. Her brother and Drake were in trouble. She only hoped they were still alive.

***

Quaid walked out of the house with Zaira, the absence of the villagers of Kranobia causing him concern.

Zaira took his hand. "They'll find refuge in Riverine. It will not be safe for them here once the Rondovins who escaped tell what happened at the village."

Her step was still slow. He took hold of her arm. "I'm not certain you'll make it, the way you seem so tired."

"I fear for my brother. He is not a warrior like you or Drake."

"We could take the Rondovin's craft—"

"We couldn't make it there by spacecraft."

"How far is it?" Quaid paused at the forest fringe.

"Not as far as the trek we had to make."

"Maybe you should go with the villagers to Riverine."

She waved her hand at the empty village. "Don't see any. I'd never make it on my own."

He considered the sun disappearing beneath the treetops, while Xenon's three moons' faint light illuminated their way. "I'm not sure you'll make it with me, Zaira."

He worried about her lethargy, concerned she was reacting similarly to when she'd been poisoned, except she was more alert.

"You'll never find your way to the location of the next scrolls. That's why I had my brother lead Drake and I had to remain with you."

Breathing a heavy sigh, Quaid said, "All right. I'll carry you then."

She cast him a small, tired smile. "You'd never be able to make it. I'll walk as far as I can."

Not wanting to force this issue for the moment because he thought maybe she knew she'd gain her strength back, he walked with her at her slower pace through the woods.

After they had walked for half an hour, he stopped briefly to allow her to catch her breath. She sat down on the forest floor, and Quaid crouched beside her. He touched her cheek. "Tell me what ails you, Zaira." He assumed she knew, but was afraid to tell him. "Do we need to find a healer?"

The sound of boots crunching through the woods made her touch her fingertip to his lips. "Shh," she whispered. "Hold me close, Quaid Lassiter." He sat beside her, then pulled her close against his chest as he embraced her tightly. "Your heartbeat pounds as fast as mine, Quaid." She snuggled her face against his chest further. He ran his left hand through her soft, silky hair and tightened his grip on the trigger mechanism of his blaster with his right.

"*Talcrasin!*" one of the Rondovins shouted to another in greeting only a few yards from where Quaid tightened his hold on Zaira.

"*Talcrasin! Se rar clasousin por Xenonians sal rast friovle scrolls. Du mas rast bren rouste. Forense bashon por lishen.*"

Zaira whispered against Quaid's ear, "They know we have the scrolls and are headed for the caves to retrieve the last of them."

"Uh," the other Rondovin grunted in a low-disagreeable manner.

"*Stren yan signature o Xenonians?*"

"*Nah. Nin signature o Xenonians.*"

A slap to the shoulder of the one ensued. "*Crasolian!*"

"*Ya, Crasolian!*"

The boots crunched in different directions away from Quaid and Zaira. Quaid finally took a breath and rubbed her shoulder. "They have Drake and Martius," Quaid further translated. He leaned over and kissed the top of her head. He knew he had to rescue them, but he was afraid of losing Zaira.

"They're going to use them as bait to catch us," she

whispered.

He helped her to her feet. "I'm sure Drake doesn't like being bait any more than Martius does. Guess we'll have to do something about it." He studied her eyes still shaded with sleep, but his comment made them sparkle briefly.

"Thank you, Quaid." She wrapped her arm around his. They began their slow trek south, her weight resting on his strength again. "We'll come to a canyon soon that we'll have to cross."

"A deep one?"

"Yes, and there's only one point to cross the ravine. It has a steel rope bridge."

"That doesn't sound good to me." He tried to pick up their pace, the worry nagging at him that she would never make it across. "Rather sounds like the perfect ambush site."

Nearing the location of the bridge, he slowed his step. Zaira listened for the sounds only she could hear. "Nothing."

They continued to the bridge. When they came into sight of it, Quaid frowned.

The swinging, braided-steel bridge spanned an eighth of a mile across the chasm, a sturdy wind blowing it sideways. Quaid whispered to Zaira, "Stay here in the shelter of the trees." He hurried over to the bridge and ran his fingers over the steel ropes secured to posts cemented into the ground. Not finding anything wrong with the rope, he signaled to Zaira.

The moons had risen farther into the nighttime sky. He studied her. He could tell she was making a valiant effort to appear as though she was perfectly fine, though her drooping eyelids and her slumped shoulders told another story. "Can you make it?"

She nodded, then took hold of the rope handrail. He seized her arm. "I'll carry you."

"No, I can make it." She started to make her way across the bridge. He waited a minute to allow her to get balance, then followed her. The bridge swung back and forth with each step they took. He reached her, grabbing her hand just as it slipped off the railing. He gripped her fingers tightly and waited for her to catch her breath. "What's wrong, Zaira?" He knew every second they stood on the bridge increased their chances of being caught. Any wrong move could send them both to their deaths to the rocks below.

"I'm just a little tired still." She squeezed his hand.

"You're the strongest woman I've ever known. Something else is the matter."

She leaned her head against his chest. "Can you carry me across the bridge?"

He frowned at her. "Zaira, what's wrong?"

"I can't make it. I'm sorry, Quaid. Can you carry me?"

"Yes." Like he'd wanted to do in the first place, despite how dangerous it would be.

He glanced down at the dizzying height as the chasm shot down 300 feet or more below them to a string of a river meandering along its way. White caps on the surface indicated the water swirled around the peaks of rocks. Not that the rocks would kill them. If they slipped from the bridge, the fall would do the deed.

Balancing himself, Quaid wrapped his arm around the bridge railing, then leaned down slightly. He reached out to wrap his free arm around Zaira and boosted her up by the rump, then rested her flat waist over his shoulder. Quaid squeezed her legs tightly against his chest, then made the treacherous trek as slowly as a dehydrated sand beetle crawled in the middle of the desert. He wanted to cross faster. He wanted to get off this bridge as soon as possible, but he knew the only way he'd make it was by taking one slow step at a time.

When they finally made it to the other side of the chasm, he laid her in the grass and considered her eyes as they had the same dazed look as before. He felt her brow, but not feeling it above a normal temperature, he took her hand and caressed it. "Will you be safe here, if I look for the scrolls on my own?"

She paced slowly back and forth.

"Believe me, Zaira, I wish nothing more but to keep

you with me, but I worry for your safety."

"Take me with you. I must guide you."

"All right." He cradled her in his arms again. She closed her eyes and he said, "Where to first?"

She motioned to the west and he frowned to see her movements so weak. Taking a deep breath, he walked for twenty minutes through a dense forest until he came to the side of a cliff. Seeing Zaira sleeping soundly, he kissed her cheek. "We're at a cliff, Zaira. Where to now?"

She stirred slightly and he repeated his question. She pointed to the cliff.

"We have to climb it?"

"No."

He studied the rock face closer, but not seeing any opening, he laid Zaira on the ground. With hands outstretched, he ran his fingers over the surface of the rock. Finding an unusually square hole in the wall, he took a deep breath and shoved his hand inside. Among the spun-candy feel of spider webs, he found a lever and pulled. A grating roar punctuated the air and an opening appeared in the cliff. He hastened to Zaira. "Is this it?"

She nodded.

"Will you stay here for me?"

"No."

He knelt down beside her and kissed her forehead. "How are you feeling?"

"More rested. I'll be fine, Quaid. Just help me to my feet, if you would."

He pulled her to her feet, but his brow furrowed as there was no spring to her movements, and he knew she was still too weak. He took her arm and led her into the cave. The moss-covered walls glistened from groundwater dripping into a pool nearby. Natural light filtered into the room from high above. Zaira pointed toward the left side of the cave.

He walked over to the wall. Zaira clung to his arm while he studied the strange markings. "Now what?"

She pointed to a rectangular tile with grooves cut around the sides on the floor. "Weight-release shelf."

"What—"

"We need the correct object that will weigh the right amount to open the door."

"And that is?"

She rubbed her brow. "There was a rock here." She pointed to the barren floor nearby. "I believe I might weigh the right amount though."

"Once we open the door—"

"Ready your blaster."

Zaira stepped onto the platform; Quaid readied his weapon. The rock door grumbled open, and he stared into the lamp-lit room. "Looks empty."

"Martius wouldn't have left the lamps burning."

Quaid walked into the room, then studied the walls.

"Don't see anything here."

"Another hidden entrance is there." She pointed at the wall opposite them. "A lever is there, but ready your weapon."

He pulled the lever. More grinding filled the air, but as soon as the door rolled open, he saw Drake and Martius gagged with their ankles and wrists bound. Both wild-eyed, they shook their heads at him.

"It's a trap, my brother tells me."

Quaid rushed into the room and pulled his dagger from his pants leg, then hurried to cut their bindings.

Drake yanked the gag from his mouth. "We haven't gotten the scrolls yet, Quaid."

Martius pulled his gag and hurried to join them. He pointed to a wall filled with drawers. "They have to be opened in the correct sequence. At least a thousand drawers are built into the wall and according to the Rondovin documents, eleven have to be pulled out in the proper order."

"Any clues?"

"Yes, but we haven't been able to decipher several of them."

"The Rondovins will be coming soon," Zaira warned through the open doorway.

"First clue?" Quaid studied the symbols inscribed on the drawers.

"Worst known enemy of the Rondovin people,"

Martius said from memory.

Drake scratched his beard. "We looked for a symbol of Orion, but couldn't find one on any of the drawers."

"No, not Orion." Quaid looked for a different symbol.

"If not Orion, the Caspians? We looked for them too," Drake responded.

"Old age. Where is the symbol for that?" Quaid said.

Martius reached up and pointed to a drawer nearly out of reach. Quaid pulled it open. "Next riddle?"

"The Rondovins' most sacred possession."

Quaid searched for the symbol he had in mind.

"We tried to figure all of the things they've stolen from other civilizations, but couldn't decide on what was their most sacred," Martius said.

Quaid smiled. "Their bodies."

Drake said, "Hadn't considered that."

Martius found the drawer and pulled it out. "Next riddle, what is the first thing given to a Rondovin child upon his birth?"

"Knowing Rondovins, a blaster," Drake said.

"A name?" Zaira asked.

"Sounds good to me." Quaid pulled out the drawer.

Martius cleared his throat. "Fourth clue, most favored pet of a Rondovin child?"

"An Orion slave," Quaid and Drake said in unison.

Martius pointed to a drawer nearer Drake, who hurried to pull it open. "Greatest Rondovin technological advancement?"

"They don't have any," grouched Drake as he folded his arms. "They've stolen everything from other worlds."

"Space net." Martius searched for the symbol.

"They didn't develop that." Quaid found the drawer and pulled it out.

"Yes, but they claim they did. The next clue, the most important item buried with a Rondovin."

"A blaster," Drake said.

Quaid rolled his eyes. "A carypsian coin. Gets them into their heaven more quickly, they believe."

Martius pointed to a drawer near Drake and while he pulled it out, Martius said, "Seventh question, who was their first leader?"

"Malasortia," Drake said, "but there's no symbol for him."

Quaid stared at the symbols. "Their war god." He pulled out the drawer.

Martius nodded. "Eighth one, their war cry?"

"Crah!" Zaira exclaimed.

Everyone looked over at her and she smiled. "I just read about that in a recent book about them."

Martius pulled out the drawer. "Ninth, the most important part of Rondovin education?"

"Physical training." Quaid pulled out the appropriate drawer.

"The planet lined up with their home world during the spring equinox in even years."

Quaid raised his brows as he stared at Martius. "We'll never get that one unless you know—"

"Shalander." Zaira beamed to see the men's looks of surprise. "Pays to read."

Drake found the drawer.

Martius said, "Final clue, we weren't certain of the translation but it was something like most important button in space."

Everyone quietly contemplated the answer, then Drake, grinned. "Refuse dump." He hurried to find the symbol, then pulled the door open.

A grinding noise followed and Zaira whispered, "Rondovin command ship of prey just flew overhead."

Drake grabbed the scrolls from a small shelf where the rock door had moved aside. "Let's get out of here then." He handed the documents to Martius.

Martius and Drake rushed out of the room, while Quaid grabbed Zaira in his arms. When the door shut behind them, the four ran into the forest. "The scrolls." Zaira nodded at her brother. He frowned to see her so incapacitated, but she glared back at him, and he responded with a nod.

"My brother will carry the remaining scrolls to

Father. We must act as a diversion."

Quaid and Drake shook Martius's hand in turn, then as he fled in a direction south of the bridge, Quaid said to Zaira, "Are you sure that we can't kill—"

"No killing, Quaid."

He turned his blaster on to stun, then faced Drake, who reluctantly did the same. "Surprised they didn't disarm you," Quaid said to him.

"They were in kind of a rush, and I imagine didn't think you'd get us out that quickly. They made some comment they were going to get reinforcements and set up quite a net for you."

"Where to, Zaira?" Quaid asked.

"We should cross the bridge to lead them away from Martius."

The three backtracked to the location of the bridge and watched as it swayed in the breeze as if ghosts walked across it in the dark.

"That would be suicide." Quaid studied the darkness across the chasm. "If they meet up with us while we're anywhere along the bridge, we'd never make it."

Zaira pointed at the other side of the bridge. "They're already speaking across the chasm, but their vision at night is very poor."

"Can you see them?"

"There are five."

"Piece of cake." Drake grabbed hold of the rope with one hand and readied his blaster with the other.

"If we do this, Zaira, you'll have to stay behind." This time, she sat on the grass and didn't object. Quaid knelt beside her and ran his hands through her silky hair. "Now I know something's wrong if you don't argue with me."

"I'll only endanger you. Goddess speed."

He kissed her lips with passion this time, and she kissed him back. He could sense her fragile touch. Hating to leave her, he kissed her forehead. "I'll be back."

CHAPTER 12

When Quaid looked up, Drake was already halfway across the bridge. He hurried to catch up. When the two were side-by-side, Drake nodded, indicating the distance was acceptable for shooting at the Rondovins. He gestured to the right, while Quaid nodded in agreement.

They balanced themselves and then blasted away. Then they counted the Rondovins as they dropped to the ground. Hurrying, they crossed the remaining length of bridge.

"All accounted for." Quaid rolled one of the Rondovins over with his boot. "I'll get, Zaira. Be ready for any further trouble."

He turned to cross the bridge and his heart nearly stopped. Zaira was attempting to cross it on her own, but she gripped the rope railing with such a tight hold, he knew she was still having difficulty. He slung his weapon over his shoulder and shouted, "Hold on, Zaira! I'm coming to get you."

He hurried across the bridge, trying in vain not to swing it too much as Zaira sank to her knees. When he finally reached her, he hoisted her over his shoulder again, then made the trek back across the bridge.

"What's wrong with her?" Drake helped ease her off his shoulder.

"She won't tell me." He stared at her closed eyes. She was sound asleep. "Come on. Let's get back to the way station and return her to her father."

"When did she begin to show symptoms like this?" Drake kept his weapon at the ready while Quaid cradled Zaira in his arms.

"She's got more energy than most men I know," Quaid said. "Then we became separated during an encounter with the Rondovins. When I found her again, she was lethargic, just like she is now. She said she was hungry. I fed her, and she seemed to perk up a bit, but then grew weak again. I don't know what's wrong with her. I could tell Martius knew something, but he wasn't saying."

"Martius mentioned to me you're going to be the new Minister of Defense. Guess that goes along with the marriage to Zaira."

"No," Quaid said, shifting Zaira's weight a bit in his

arms. "She told me the High Council had already decided to offer me the job. It was her idea to choose me as her mate. Her father knows nothing about it. Apparently, the Chief Magistrate had intended to make her his wife instead, with her father's blessing."

"Caryndian Bach?" Drake's eyes grew wide. "I wouldn't want to be in your shoes. Powerful man, powerful friends. Otherworlders have known to just vanish off this planet when they have conflicts with him."

"Martius likes me."

Drake laughed out loud. "So you're finally adjusting to the notion of being married, eh?"

Quaid studied Zaira's angel-like features as she slept comfortably in his arms. "I could do much worse." Quaid held her closer to his chest. "Much worse." Fact of the matter was he didn't want to think of life without her any longer. Before he could make it right with her, he had to speak with her father.

"I'll say." Drake studied Zaira's low-cut bodice. Quaid glanced at him. Drake smiled, then looked away. "Doesn't look like she's got a scratch on her."

"I know. That's what has got me so concerned. Did Martius show any similar signs of lethargy?"

"None that I recall. We were kind of caught off-guard by the Rondovins when we discovered the cave for the scrolls. They left us for bait, then removed the weight-bearing stone we had placed on the scale. I noticed you used Zaira to replace the stone. Good thing she was the proper weight."

"We were told there was no news of you at the village. She knew there was trouble, but if she could have communicated with her brother while he was in the cave, her weakness seemed to preclude that."

"He indicated to me you were nearby. We could hear the rock doors moving, and he said it was you and not the Rondovins."

Quaid glanced up at the stars as the tree branches stretched in front of them. "Are we heading in the right direction?"

Drake nodded. "This is the way." He faced Quaid. "Have you considered who you'd have on your staff? I understand you're going to be training pilots and organizing them into a defensive force."

Quaid smiled. "Are you volunteering for something?"

"Only if it pays enough!"

Quaid said, "I'll need another pilot to train and to help organize missions, but...all aircraft have to have the proper fire power, shields, and speed."

"I'd have to do a little practice on the shooting end of the deal, but sounds good to me."

"There are several Xenonian pilots who fly missions to bring back supplies to this place. Now with the planet producing its own food, they'll be out of a job. I believe I can recruit a few of my own Orion space force, if the pay's right. Certainly the challenge will hook 'em."

"Have you told the lady, yet?"

Quaid considered Zaira's pale cheeks as her dark hair framed them. "We haven't talked."

"Secret's safe with me. Martius asked about you."

"Oh?"

"He seemed concerned about something. He's really a likeable guy...a little introverted, doesn't really talk much, but he seemed to want to know something about you."

"Oh."

"Of course it made me curious, to say the least."

"What did he ask about?"

"How many women you'd been with."

Quaid jerked his head to look at Drake.

Drake grinned back at him and shrugged. "Told him I didn't know a thing about your personal life, just that you were seeing a girl for a while, but nothing ever came of it. That's all."

"Ahhh," Quaid groaned.

Drake laughed. "I didn't think you wanted me to tell him about the others."

"What others?"

"Come on, Quaid. There were three or four others, at least. Why there was that copilot on—"

Quaid gave him a look to shut-up.

Drake looked down at Zaira and smiled. "All right. Enough said. Martius didn't seem to be satisfied with my answer, somehow."

Quaid heard a noise and stopped in his steps. "You did use the maximum stun, didn't you?"

"Yep," Drake whispered back. "The Rondovins we hit back there should have a twenty-four hour nightie-night with another twenty-four hour major hangover."

More crunching of twigs followed and Drake readied his weapon.

A tall dark-haired woman dressed in a long, dark-blue gown appeared in the moonlight-filtered shadows of the trees. Drake frowned. "Catarina, you could have been killed."

"Are you headed for the way station?" She sidled up to Drake and took his arm in hers.

"That's the idea."

"Two Rondovin spacecraft landed there a short while ago." Catarina considered Zaira, then squeezed Drake's arm. "The scrolls are safe and sound. Martius was picked up by a Xenonian pilot who took him to Riverine. Word has been sent to the other worlds that the High Council is back in session. I came in search of you to lead you to Riverine." She touched Drake's red beard. "Wanna mate?"

Drake smiled. "Haven't had as good an offer in

years."

"Riverine is back to the west. It's surrounded by rivers. We'll try our luck there." Catarina looked over at Zaira. "She can sleep there, and you can get some rest too. You look a bit haggard, Quaid Lassiter."

"Long day. Flying missions isn't half as exhausting as the workout I've had the last couple of days." They headed west and Quaid asked, "Do you know what's wrong with Zaira?"

Catarina's eyes widened. "Don't you?"

"Well, no. She's had the stamina of three men, then suddenly she's been like this—as though she's come down with a sleeping sickness."

"Oh." Catarina didn't volunteer anything further.

Quaid glanced at Drake who shook his head in response.

The three looked skyward as a war bird fly over the tree tops. The ship clipped the pine trees. Needles showered down on the party.

Catarina said, "We knew there would be trouble once the greening of the planet took place, but not this soon."

"Blasted." Quaid couldn't have been more furious. "If the Rondovins are at the way station, they've undoubtedly confiscated the Exiter."

Drake turned to Catarina. "The Exiter is Quaid's war craft."

She frowned at Quaid. "That's all the matter is."

Quaid and Drake exchanged glances, then Drake squeezed her arm slightly. "You're talking about the love of his life."

She pointed to Zaira. "She's supposed to be that for you now."

"How can I train pilots if I don't have—"

"Carver Cole hid your ship."

"Where?"

"At the village where we're now headed. In fact, before Martius began the greening of the planet, all craft were to be docked at Riverine."

"The Rondovins will be sure to—"

"Safest place on Xenon. Martius had already constructed an indestructible shield over the city. Of course, 'til now, we hadn't bothered to use it."

"But your people in the outlying villages—"

"Scattered. There are places all over the region where our people can gather together in safety. Places hidden from sight. Only the capital city of Riverine is open to the sky and impervious to the Rondovin threat."

"How long before we get there?" Quaid shifted Zaira in his arms again.

Drake reached his hands out to him. "Let me spell you a while, Quaid."

Zaira stirred and Quaid stopped. "Zaira?"

She took a deep breath, then frowned. "Where are

we?"

"On our way to Riverine," Quaid said.

"I can walk the rest of the way."

Catarina studied Zaira's appearance. "It's another five miles. Are you sure—"

"I'll walk."

Quaid set Zaira on the ground and she began to walk toward the village with a sure but slow step as he held her arm.

"So what have I missed?" she asked.

"Two Ronodovin ships at the way station, a war bird passed over us a short while ago, and Catarina joined our party. That's about it," Drake said. "Oh, and Martius is safe at Riverine and the council is back in session."

"No more encounters with Rondovins on foot?"

"Not so far. Been pretty quiet actually," Drake said.

Zaira turned to Catarina. "It has started already, hasn't it?"

Catarina nodded.

Quaid waited for an explanation, but Zaira stopped suddenly, then signaled for everyone to crouch down. "Rondovins are in the woods nearby. I hear one"—She paused and listened further, raising her eyebrows for a moment, then continued—"relieving himself."

"Can you tell how many?" Quaid pulled his weapon from his shoulder.

Zaira listened further. "Three are conversing to the

west, two more to the southwest."

"Five?"

"And the sixth who has just zipped up his zipper directly south of us."

"Distance?"

"About two-hundred yards."

Drake turned to Quaid. "Same game plan?"

Quaid nodded. He said to Catarina, "You'll take care of Zaira?"

"Of course."

"Good." Quaid leaned over and kissed Zaira's lips then, hurried south first and Drake turned west.

***

The men disappeared into the forest and Catarina whispered to Zaira, "Have you not told your husband?"

"There's no need." Zaira could still envision Quaid's beautiful blue eyes studying her, worrying about her.

"He's concerned for your health. You should tell him what ails you."

"He wouldn't understand."

"Then you shouldn't have selected him to be your mate."

Zaira turned her head to the south and took a deep breath. "I had to save his life."

"What do you hear, Zaira?"

"Do you not hear it?"

"My hearing is not as strong as yours."

"A blast from a weapon."

Catarina nodded. "Ours or theirs?"

"The weapons sound the same. The Rondovins stole the Terran's technology."

"Oh."

The two women settled back down on the ground. "Are you afraid, Zaira?"

Zaira nodded. She was afraid all right. She knew her brother would soon take matters into his own hands if Quaid did not pleasure her. Then what a mess things would be.

"That he will learn the truth?"

"Yes," Zaira said so softly that Catarina had to strain to hear her word. Yes, she was afraid Quaid couldn't accept her for what she was...a changeling. It was one thing to know she could hold her breath under water for longer than a human could, but to be able to shift into a killer jaguar?

"Martius said you were afraid. He's really quite upset about it, you know."

"Yes."

Catarina reached over and patted Zaira's hand as a tear rolled down her cheek. "Quaid really cares for you, even if he's afraid to show it."

"You sense this, Catarina?" Zaira believed so, but that was only because he didn't know what she could do.

"Very much so. And you know I'm not one to fail in my perceptions. I could see the strain in his face as he carried you. His arms ached with your weight and yet he wouldn't release you, not once, even into his best friend's care. Drake told me it was the same when you were bitten by the speckled spider. He also told me how Quaid didn't wish for you to return to the caves for your own safety." Catarina smiled. "And I haven't told you this as I haven't seen you since the illegal mating party, but I thought Quaid was going to do one of the men injury who was hovering over you."

"He was?"

"Yes."

Zaira wrung her hands. "He won't couple with me." She looked to the west and frowned.

"You've been kind of busy. More shots fired?"

Zaira nodded.

Catarina listened. "Number?"

"Four."

Catarina scooted over and embraced her warmly. "He's afraid of losing you, Zaira. He'll come around...given time."

"He doesn't...know what I am, that I can shift into the jaguar, that I was the one who killed the Rondovins." Zaira groaned. "I can't stand these feelings I'm having. The ups and downs. The highs and lows. And this business with the shifting, being so tired I can barely focus on anything. I'm never like this. Ever."

"I know...I know. I'm feeling the emotional turmoil too. As soon as we get to Riverine, Drake and I will mate. I cannot wait any longer either. My mother never warned me how mating season would affect me when I came of age. Guess she was afraid I'd be alarmed."

Zaira touched a leaf that stirred with the breeze. "At least with Drake, you won't have to keep any secrets from him."

Catarina sighed deeply. "Nor do you with your husband."

"He won't understand, Catarina. He won't understand, and he'll reject me further." Zaira shuddered. He was the only one she'd ever selected for a mate and no one would ever be right for her again. If he didn't act soon though, Martius would take the matter out of their hands. And then, well then her life would come crashing to an end.

Catarina stared at Zaira for a moment, then squeezed her hand. "Your emotions are unstable again. You must calm yourself—"

Zaira jumped up. "I hear a Rondovin speaking in an angry tone." She paced back and forth. "They're in trouble. We must go at once—"

"But—"

She studied Catarina's face for a moment. Her friend wasn't ready to come of age. Not yet. And there was no way she could force it. "You are still not ready, are you?"

Tears filled Catarina's dark eyes as she ran her hand over her long skirts. "No, Zaira. I'm sorry, but I just cannot."

Zaira leaned down and hugged her. "You know what I must do."

Catarina nodded. "I'm so sorry...be safe, Zaira."

***

Quaid considered the young Rondovin's posture, shaking slightly while he aimed his blaster at Drake and him.

"Guess I sort of got us into this one," Drake whispered, rubbing the tender spot on the backside of his head already raised to a nice-sized lump.

"We've been in worst scrapes," Quaid replied in a low voice.

An older Rondovin reloaded his weapon nearby.

"So what do we do now?"

"Wait."

"For?"

"The right moment."

"Game plan?"

"Haven't quite got one, yet." Quaid turned to look in an easterly direction.

Drake looked that way, the young Rondovin glancing east also.

"What's wrong?" Drake peered into the sprinkle of moonlight filtering through the thick leaves of the forest.

"Heard something."

"What?" Drake asked.

"A low growl."

"Didn't hear a thing."

"Listen."

Quaid studied the leaves for movement and heard a twig snap. A Rondovin called out, "Talcrasin!"

"Approach," the older Rondovin said. "What news?"

"We found five of our crew stunned."

The older man glared at Quaid and Drake. Quaid shrugged a shoulder and smiled back at him.

"You're lucky we have orders to take any hostages that we can, alive. Otherwise..." He spit at the ground. He turned to the other man. "And the others?"

"Still searching for any who may have been with these two."

Drake's eyes narrowed slightly.

A shuffling in the leaves and another long, low growl caught Quaid's attention. This time, the Rondovin who had just arrived turned to stare into the woods.

"What's the matter?" the older man asked, joining the other.

"I felt I was being followed, but never saw anything.

Something's out there for certain though."

"But you saw nothing?"

"Only heard a throaty growl."

"Only Xenonians inhabit this planet," the older man said. "Nothing else."

"And a few speckled spiders," Quaid corrected the older man.

"Yeah, well, I know what I felt," the Rondovin said, ignoring Quaid.

Everyone peered at the forest for several minutes, then a laser blast fired several hundred yards away and the young boy dropped his weapon. The older man hit him in the shoulder. "Keep your wits about you."

The boy hurried to grab his weapon and pointed it at his hostages while the other man took a step toward the forest. "Talcrasin!" he shouted.

The man made no response. The stirring of the leaves as a breeze swirled about them was the only sound.

The men all stared in the direction of the weapon's blast, then turned their attention farther south as another blast fractured the quiet. Distant muffled shouts erupted, then silence.

"Check it out," the older man said to the other.

Quaid smiled to see the man's hesitation. "Give me a gun, and I'll check it out."

Drake nodded in agreement.

"Go!" the older man said to his crewman.

The man bolstered his weapon, then walked slowly into the leaves, vanishing within minutes from sight, but the sound of his boots treading on crinkly leaves and fallen twigs continued for another hundred yards.

The sound of the footfalls faded and the young Rondovin looked back over his shoulder at where his crew member had disappeared. Quaid poked at Drake and nodded at the young man.

Drake smiled.

A weapon's blast from 400 yards shattered the serenity, and the old man said, "We're all going to take a walk together. The two of you go first."

"Guess that means us," Quaid said to Drake. He turned back to the old man. "Don't think much of your treatment of prisoners. No telling what the Xenonians have unleashed in this world along with the greening of the planet."

"Shut up and just walk straight ahead."

Quaid said to Drake as they walked abreast, "If it's a jaguar like the one I encountered at the village of Kranobia, drop to the ground if he attacks. Cats like to chase their prey. She probably won't bite too hard, if we play dead."

Drake stared at Quaid. "What?"

"You heard me. The biggest, most beautiful, wild cat I've ever encountered close up. Her teeth were wicked though. Tore a Rondovin's throat clean through."

The older man poked Quaid with his blaster. "Shut up."

Quaid turned to him. "Listen, if we're going to be offered to that creature for dinner, I think I owe it to my friend to let him know what he's in for." The young boy dropped back with a slowed step.

"Keep moving!" the old man growled.

"Yes, siree." Quaid scratched his beard while he walked at a slow pace. "Meant to get a shave and a haircut before I sort of crashed into Xenon, but guess I won't be needing one any further." Drake studied the trees before him with renewed concern, while Quaid patted his arm. "Deep space kind of seems like a warrior's playground to this place right now." Then Quaid grabbed Drake's arm and pulled him to a stop.

"Move!" the old man said.

"Didn't you hear that growl behind us?" Quaid turned to face the old man.

"Move!"

Quaid looked at the trees high above some distance away, and Drake followed his gaze. The old man narrowed his eyes at them. "Oldest trick in the book. Now move!"

"All right, but don't say I didn't ever warn you." Quaid pulled Drake with him and said under his breath,

"He's going for the boy, who has dropped way behind us. If he gets the old man next, as soon as he strikes, run like hell."

"I thought you said—"

"Forget what I said. Did you see those fangs? That's one angry pussy."

The three continued to walk for another ten minutes when Quaid finally chanced to glance backwards. The old man glared at him, but it was the disappearance of the boy that satisfied Quaid. He whispered to Drake, "Boy's gone, but don't look back. Old man doesn't know it."

"What now?"

"He's a wiry old fellow and combat ready, but if we can convince him to look behind him for the boy, we might just get the upper hand."

"And then?"

"Stun him and find the women."

"Sounds like a plan."

Before Quaid could signal for Drake to turn around, the old man said, "Halt!"

Quaid and Drake both turned, but he never took his eyes off them nor his finger off the trigger mechanism on his weapon. "Jshloshm?" he called out.

"Boy has run off." Quaid folded his arms across his chest.

The old man gesticulated for Quaid and Drake to

maneuver on past him so he could look the way they had come with his hostages still in his sights. "Told you so." Quaid placed his hands on his hips. "Now what? The three of us aren't a match for the likes of this creature. Certainly not when two of us are unarmed."

"Unless that's what aggravates it so in the first place." Drake rubbed his chin. "Maybe you should let one of us hold your weapon for you and..."

The old man waved for Quaid and Drake to continue in front of him. They headed in the direction where one of the sounds of weapon blasts had been heard. They finally came across a tree where the bark was bared by laser blasts and found three Rondovins sprawled out in a cluster.

Quaid said, "Poor devils, didn't even know what hit them."

Drake frowned. "Or maybe they did."

Motioning to his hostages, the old man maneuvered them closer to the bodies. He glanced down to see his crew mates' necks torn wide open just as Quaid had described. "What is it?" the old man whispered, his eyes filled with terror.

"Black jaguar."

"The boy," the old man said, as he stared at the dead men.

"I told you the creature was waiting to pounce from the trees above. You wouldn't believe me."

The old man turned to look up at the trees. Without hesitation, Quaid lunged at him.

CHAPTER 13

Quaid shoved the Rondovin to the ground.

Drake scrambled to disarm him.

"We won't kill you either." Quaid studied the man's frightened face. "Just let you sleep for a while."

"But that cat will kill me."

"Maybe not."

Quaid signaled for Drake to pull the trigger, then as the sound of the blast reverberated through the woods, the old man slumped backwards. Quaid pulled one of the weapons free, still clutched in a dead Rondovin's hands. "Come on, Drake. Let's hope the women are still all right."

He prayed the jaguar was friendly to the inhabitants of this world, and knew that Quaid and Drake were here to help them.

***

For over an hour, the men backtracked to the location where the women had been. When they arrived, they found Catarina sitting in a heap of blue gowns, sobbing. Drake ran to embrace her as tears streaked down her face.

"Where's Zaira?" Quaid shouted at her.

"She...she...," she managed to get out, then broke into a fresh set of tears. She pointed in the direction Drake and Quaid had first ventured into the woods after the Rondovins. Quaid charged back into the forest.

"Wait up!" Drake hollered as he dragged Catarina with him. "We'll find her, Quaid, just wait for us!"

Quaid forged ahead through the area they had initially tread, then slowed his pace as he looked for clues. "Why did she come looking for us?" he asked Catarina, then turned his attention back to the ground.

She shuddered. Drake wrapped his arm around her and held her tight. "The women were frightened, Quaid. We'll find Zaira."

"I promised I'd keep her safe," Quaid said under his breath.

Forever, they searched the forest for signs of Zaira. They backtracked to where the woman had been again and Drake shouted, "Over here!"

Quaid brushed past him and stared at the sleeping figure of Zaira as her hair cascaded over her shoulders while the gold gown lay open, revealing her voluptuous breasts. Quaid rushed to her side and hurried to tie the gown at the bodice while Drake waited for him to give the okay.

"Zaira." Quaid tried to revive her.

"She needs to rest." Catarina wiped the tears from her cheeks.

"What's wrong with her?" Quaid lifted Zaira into his arms.

"I can't say," Catarina said.

"Back to Riverine?" Drake indicated a westerly direction.

"Surely there will be a healer there who can take care of her." Quaid quickened his pace.

The party of four made the trek to the edge of the forest as the river beat a path around the city of Riverine. Before they could move a muscle in that direction, Drake pointed to Rondovin movement a quarter of a mile downstream.

"Blasted." Quaid lay Zaira on the ground. He took a deep breath as he studied her sleep-filled features. "She hasn't stirred, not once."

"She's not ill, Quaid," Catarina said. "She just needs rest."

"It has nothing to do with the mating dilemma, does it?" Quaid looked at Catarina.

"Something to do with it."

He glanced down at Zaira, then frowned. "Nothing

can be done about it right this minute. Where to now?"

"We'll go to one of Martius's safe houses," Catarina said, then pointed back northeast.

***

The party walked for half an hour through a deciduous forest without any more Rondovin encounters. When the roar of water splashed ahead of them, Quaid frowned. "Sounds like a river ahead."

"Yes," Catarina said.

Furrowing his brow, Quaid didn't like it one bit. "We have to swim it?"

"No. There's a ferry in this direction. It'll take us across the Tristinian River."

A few minutes later, the pebbled beach stretched out to them. The three stared at the sight of a raft of sturdy steel sitting idly on the pebbles on the other side. "That's what we were to take to get across?" Drake looked up to see the cables on the ferry blasted clean through.

"Yes." Catarina's voice was masked with worry.

"Where else can we cross?" Quaid studied the frothing foam created by the water striking the boulders in the middle of the charging river.

"This is it, Quaid. The next safe house is a couple hours farther east. I fear with all of the Rondovin movement in the area, we'd never make it before someone catches us."

TERRY SPEAR

Drake folded his arms. "I'm pretty sure I could get across."

"I can." Catarina touched his arm.

"What about Zaira?" Quaid rested her on the beach.

"If we can rouse her, she can swim."

Quaid took a deep breath. "I don't think I can swim across that."

"We have no other choice, Quaid." Catarina turned her ear south and frowned. "I'm afraid we're about to have company. We must hurry."

Quaid crouched down to Zaira. "Zaira, wake up." He shook her gently, but she didn't stir. He turned to Catarina who motioned for him to try again. Quaid touched his fingers to her cheek, then kissed her lips. She tilted her chin up and puckered her lips slightly. He smiled and kissed her more firmly.

She responded with a tender pressure applied to his mouth, and Drake said, "We must go, Quaid."

"Zaira." Quaid helped her to sit. "We must cross the river. Can you swim?" Her eyes studied his lips, and he said again, "Zaira, we must cross the river."

She turned her head in the direction of the river, then looked back at the forest. "They're coming."

"Yes." Quaid helped her to her feet. She stood shakily and he assisted her to the edge of the water. "I don't know if she can make it."

222

"She can swim, Quaid. Just help her into the water. When she makes it to the other side, you can assist her further."

He walked into the river and the warm water tugged at his legs with a fierce grip. Catarina took Zaira's hand and led her into the deepening water, then dove under with her.

"Are you game, Quaid?"

"Guess I don't have any choice."

The sound of a Rondovin's voice made the two men dive into the water. Quaid came up for air. The two women already rested on the other side of the river while Drake reached the halfway point. Quaid was glad the woman had made it. Struggle as he might, he couldn't fight the torrent of water, washing him downstream. He could only make a little headway across the river.

He grabbed onto a moss-covered boulder a quarter of the way across. Thankfully, Drake ushered the two women to the safety of the forest nearby. Quaid's relief to see them safe was at once dashed as a laser blast slammed the rock he held onto with a fierce grip. Splinters of rock spewed in all directions. Without looking back, he released his death hold on the boulder, and the water dragged him downstream again.

Banging into another rock, he grabbed at it with his fingers, then hung on as he looked east to see the

TERRY SPEAR

Rondovins running in his direction. He took a deep breath of air and dove toward the beach with as much strength as he could muster. The river commanded him to move west, but Quaid fought against the elements. If things ever settled down for him, he vowed he was going to practice swimming daily.

His feet touched a rock beneath the surface finally, and he grabbed hold of the remainder as it jutted out of the river. He breathed in the air and rested as the boulder broke up the path of the water. Another blast made him shove away from the rock, and this time he managed to reach a point three quarters of the way across the river.

He surfaced, then stroked the water before being dashed into another boulder. His boots touched the pebble beach, and he scrambled out of the water. He bolted from the beach as shots rang out, striking the water behind him. He smiled. "Out of range." A flash sent stones flying nearby, and he sprinted faster. "Maybe not." When he reached the cover of the forest, the Rondovins shook their weapons at him and screamed obscenities over the roar of the river.

A twig snapped nearby. "Catarina!"

She ran toward him. "Come. Drake has taken Zaira to the hideout. She's giving him the directions."

With legs weary from swimming, Quaid rushed after Catarina. He mused at how fast she could run in her long wet gowns. Her breath never seemed to rise above a whisper as if she were taking a leisurely stroll in the woods. Just like Zaira normally would.

They soon caught sight of Zaira's gold gown as Drake cradled her in his arms. Crouching on the ground, he turned to face them. "Catarina," Drake whispered, "Zaira sort of fell asleep on me. I didn't know where to go next."

Quaid took Zaira from him while Catarina watched the clearing, listening for sounds. She waved for the men to follow her. When they reached Martius's underground shelter, Catarina lifted the hatch buried in grass. She stepped onto the stairs, leaned down, and pressed a button. The three hurried down the steps, then Drake shut the door behind them. A soft light filled the cavernous space. Quaid and Drake stared in awe at the polished ivory marble walls, veined with streaks of green surrounding the room.

"Hello?" Catarina called out, her voice echoing. There was no response. She pointed to a large space filled with cushions of golds, greens, pinks and whites for seating. "The commons. Used for group socializing when Xenonians alight here."

She walked across the common area, then pushed a button on a wall. The door slid open with a whoosh, and she walked into the room. "This is the bedchamber Zaira uses when she's in this region." She pointed to a small cabinet. "A change of clothes are in there for her, and a few personal items she may need."

Quaid still held Zaira securely in his arms.

Catarina pointed to the bed. "There's ample room for two." She pulled aside a green velvet-like coverlet freckled with pink, rose embroidery. "Her favorite side of the bed."

Quaid lay Zaira on the floor. "Her gowns are wet."

Catarina smiled. "Yes. We are all wet."

"But, she should be wearing something dry."

"You are her husband."

He straightened. "I wouldn't have a clue what—"

"All right, Quaid. I'll take care of her. You can carry her to her bed afterwards."

Quaid hurried out of the chambers and closed the door behind him. He frowned to see Drake grinning at him. "I would think you could figure out what to do with the lady."

"Not a word." Quaid walked into the kitchen. "Are you hungry? I haven't eaten since last night." He poked his head into a cooler and frowned. "Don't know what I'm looking for in here anyway. I couldn't cook even if I wanted to. Used to the food simulator on the craft fixing everything at a push of a button." A bowl of fruit sitting on the kitchen counter caught his eye and he pulled a purple fruit from a gold wicker bowl. After eating the peppermint-tasting fruit, Catarina gestured to him from the commons.

Quaid hastened to the bedchamber, then stared at the pink satin gown Zaira wore touching her ankles. He lifted her from the floor, then lay her on the mattress. Studying her serene features, he frowned. "You're sure she will be all right without the aid of a healer?"

"Yes, Quaid. Just let her sleep. You must get your rest too as I'm certain you have many defensive measures you need to plan for. There are other chambers that Drake and I can sleep in. Once we've rested, we can have a meal and contemplate what to do next."

Quaid pulled the coverlet over Zaira, then looked to see Drake rubbing Catarina's arm.

"I forgot, Quaid." Catarina pointed to a closet-like feature. "The necessarium. Part of it has a toilet and the other a shower. Just pull the lever inside the shower, and the water heats up to a perfectly predetermined temperature—courtesy of Martius."

"Nighty-night." Drake shut the door to the room. "Did your father say it was all right to—" Drake pulled Catarina away from the door.

"He approved of our mating."

Their footsteps fell away while Quaid pulled off his jacket, then rested it on the back of a chair. He plopped down on the leather seat, then pulled at the buckle on one of his boots.

A knocking at his door sounded, but before he could respond, the door slid open. Quaid jumped from his seat to see Catarina holding clothes in her arms that she offered to him.

"Martius has some clothes that you and Drake can wear. Then we can wash your own."

"Thanks, Catarina." Quaid took the garments.

"Pleasant dreams." She hurried out of the chambers.

He retook his seat on the chair, grabbed at the buckles on his boot. He never had expected to be living a nightmare on this peaceful planet.

***

The next afternoon, Zaira ripped open a package of freeze-dried asparagus and dumped the flat green spears into boiling water. She poked them with a fork for a second as the water filled their pores and turned them into plump edible spears.

Next, she poured potato flakes into a pan, added water, then stirred until the potatoes mixed into a satiny mashed potato mixture. In another pan, she added water to a powdered gravy and after the rich, brown, perfectly-textured gravy was ready, she pulled out a package of flash-dried steaks. After coating them with Orion herbs and spices, she grilled the steaks to a plump form with centers perfectly pink.

With the aroma of garlic and sucian permeating the

air, Drake and Catarina hurried out of their room. "Now this is truly the life." He leaned over to smell the steaks. "Don't get meals like this in space." He turned to Catarina. "You do cook like this too, don't you, Catarina?"

She folded her arms and smiled back at him. "And if I don't?"

"Well, we could visit Zaira often, I guess."

Zaira chuckled. "Catarina taught me all I know."

Catarina laughed out loud. "Right. But I do know several recipes of home-cooked meals you might like, Drake." She kissed his cheek, then hastened to pull silverware and napkins out of a drawer.

Quaid buttoned his blue shirt as he exited from his room.

Drake raised his brows at him. "Looks like you had rather a rough night of it."

Quaid rubbed his beard. "Are you sure Martius doesn't keep anything around here I could use to shave with?"

Zaira ignored him while she hurried to serve up the steaks.

Catarina grabbed glasses from the counter and filled them with water. After placing the glasses on the table, Catarina wiped her hands on her long yellow skirts, then joined Zaira at the kitchen counter. Zaira spooned out potatoes; Catarina forked asparagus onto each of the plates. After Zaira smothered each pile of potatoes with gravy, Catarina carried the plates to the table.

"Thanks for washing my garments." Quaid looked from one of the women to the other not sure exactly who to thank. Neither replied. Drake shrugged. Quaid was definitely in the doghouse, most likely because he didn't sleep with Zaira last night.

Quaid and Drake waited for the women to take their seats first. Quaid frowned as he had to sit across the table from Zaira at the farthest distance from her. He studied the black blouse she wore buttoned nearly to her chin. The sleeves stretched to her wrists. The blowsy shirt covered her beautiful curves.

"So, did everyone have pleasant dreams last night?" Drake carved his steak.

Catarina leaned back in her seat while stirring the gravy atop her potatoes. "I dreamt my backyard turned into a jungle while everyone around me had a forest for a backyard. I was quite angry for Martius for messing up my own yard!"

Quaid and Drake laughed, but Zaira remained quiet as she nibbled at her steak.

"Well, I dreamed I mated Catarina but before I could pleasure her, a Rondovin barged into our home and told me I couldn't marry her because I hadn't asked *his* permission yet!"

Quaid and Catarina laughed and noticed a slight smile appear on Zaira's lips.

"What about you, Quaid?" Catarina asked.

"Quaid had a nightmare." Zaira cut off a piece of steak. "He thought he was free, then when he woke, he found he was married to me. Kind of hard sleeping sitting upright, isn't it, Quaid?" Zaira took a deep breath. Catarina and Drake mouths dropped open slightly. "Eat up, folks." She cut up her asparagus. "Can't let this good food go to waste."

"Oh, no," Catarina said hastily. "Gosh you're such a great cook."

"I'll say." Drake dug into his potatoes coated in gravy.

"Zaira—"

"Not a word, Quaid," Zaira said, with a softness to her voice, shaded with hurt.

"I didn't want to disturb your sleep as tired as you were yesterday."

Zaira stood up from her chair, then smoothed out her long purple skirts. "I'll be right back."

Zaira left the safe house with her usual quick stride.

Quaid jumped up from his seat. "Zaira?" he called out to her. He hurried outside of the underground safe haven and saw no sign of her. "Zaira!" He walked a hundred yards in all directions. "Damnation, Zaira, it's not safe out here for you!"

CHAPTER 14

After returning to the house, Quaid retook his seat at the dining table and poked at his meat.

Drake watched the doorway. "Where's Zaira?"

"Taking a walk."

"It's not safe out there." Catarina touched the table with her fingers.

"Tell me something I don't know." Quaid continued to eat his meal while Drake and Catarina looked on.

"What happened?" Drake asked.

"Nothing."

"And that's the whole problem." Catarina poked at her asparagus. When she finished her meal, she took Zaira's half-eaten portion of food and wrapped it, then placed it in the cooling unit. "She should have finished her meal. I can tell she's lost some weight over the last few days."

Quaid finished his food, then looked up as Drake studied him. "What are you looking at?"

"I don't understand you, Quaid."

Quaid stood up from his chair. "I'm going to look for her."

Drake hurried to finish his last bite of steak. "I'll go with you." He turned to Catarina. "You stay put. Be back in a jiffy."

Catarina kissed Drake hard on the mouth. "Don't get lost."

"I won't." He pushed her dark curls behind her ears. "Boy, am I one lucky fellow." He kissed her again on the lips.

Quaid frowned. "Are you coming or what?"

"Sure." Drake hurried to get his blaster.

Quaid grabbed his, and the two left the safe house and moved into the sunlight.

"You've got to get a grip, Quaid," Drake scolded as they headed south. "She's the best thing you've ever had and—"

"I don't need a lecture."

"You need a head doctor. Okay, Quaid, I'm your best friend. You can tell me. Is it not working?"

"What?" Quaid stared back at him, not getting his drift.

"Hey, listen, I know some guys have problems with it. Not me of course, but other guys I know of."

"Shut up, Drake." Quaid studied the ground for signs of Zaira's passage anywhere nearby.

"No, really. They've got laser surgery for that sort of thing. Takes a couple of seconds, then you're a new man. Truly one of the most sought after technological advances known to mankind."

Quaid stopped to look at a branch torn slightly askew. "I don't have any problem with it."

"Well, I really didn't think so, but then again—"

"Shut up, Drake."

They walked in the dappled shade of the trees, then heard a voice spoken softly. "Zaira?" Quaid whispered. He took a deep breath. "I smell jasmine. She's near here."

They listened intently to hear her words, but except for the ripple of leaves, heard no further sound. "Which direction?" Drake asked.

"That way." Quaid waved his hand in a westerly direction.

"Just don't get us lost. I want to be able to return to the shelter—"

"Shh." The two men listened and Quaid frowned. "Listen," he whispered. "I can hear her voice spoken in a whisper somewhere over there."

Drake listened, then nodded. They walked with a slow pace, stopping every so often to listen.

"Ahhh," Zaira groaned.

"This direction," Quaid urged. "Zaira!" he shouted in a whisper. She struggled to drag her brother toward the shelter. "Is he...," he said as he reached down to feel for a pulse, then took a deep breath. "He's sleeping like you sleep."

She nodded as she glanced back at the woods. "They're coming."

Quaid caught sight of six charred bodies. He grabbed Martius's arm.

Drake and Quaid lifted Martius under the armpits, then grappled with his legs. In a mad dash, they ran with him toward the shelter in a seated position. Zaira followed at a slower pace behind. Quaid said, "Zaira, run ahead and get the door for us." She fell farther back. "You sure are stubborn," he said under his breath.

"As are you, Quaid."

The shouts of a Rondovin scout made Drake and Quaid sprint faster. Finally reaching the safe haven, Drake dropped Martius's leg to open the hatch. Without hesitation they eased him onto the steps. When Quaid looked back for Zaira, all he saw were the trees swaying in the wind.

Drake pulled at his arm. Quaid reluctantly shut the door. "We'll have to find her later. We can't risk having the Rondovins find this place. She knows that and has apparently shifted their attention from here so we could get her brother safely inside."

***

After they lay Martius in his own chamber, Catarina said, "Where's Zaira?"

"She misdirected the Rondovins away from us so that we could get Martius back to the shelter safely," Drake said.

Quaid said, "I've got to find Zaira."

"Wait, Quaid, let me see if I can hear anything first." Catarina hastened across the commons, then ran up to the top of the steps. She listened at the hatch. "There are at least six of them camped near our entrance. You will have to wait."

"But—"

"Catarina is right, Quaid." Drake grabbed Quaid's arm and headed for the kitchen. "Maybe, we can have something to drink."

"Sure. I'll fix something right away," Catarina said.

"But Zaira—"

"If we go out there now, all of us will be at risk." Catarina tossed herbs into water.

Drake patted Quaid's shoulder as he stared at the entrance to the shelter. "She just has to be all right, Drake."

"I know, Quaid. Come on. We'll have something to drink. Then, well we'll just have to wait and see."

Quaid and Drake returned to the kitchen. Catarina let out a sigh of relief, then poured the minty-flavored drinks into cups. Quaid fingered the handle on his cup. "I can't believe she'd leave here like she did."

"Undoubtedly, she sensed trouble for her brother. She's not stupid, Quaid," Catarina said.

"Why didn't she say anything to me?" He ran his hand through his hair.

"I believe she was a bit peeved with you." Drake slugged down the tea. He turned to Catarina. "Any more?"

After finishing his drink, Quaid stood, then walked over to where his blaster rested against the wall.

"Wait up!" Drake jumped from his seat. He grabbed his blaster, then turned to Catarina. She nodded, then Quaid and Drake ran up the steps.

"Be careful," she said to Drake.

"Aren't I always?" Drake winked at her, then Quaid tugged him out of the shelter.

They quickly entered the forest and Quaid hurried in the direction where they had found Martius.

"She wouldn't have returned here," Drake whispered, as he studied the piles of Rondovin ashes on the ground. "The Rondovins were behind us, and she must have slipped away somewhere in that direction." He waved his hand east.

Quaid nodded, then turned east. He walked for several minutes, then a scrap of purple fabric dangling on a tree limb caught his eye. "Zaira."

Drake beckoned him. As he joined him, Drake pointed to a spot of blood. They hurried to follow the trail. He poked his boot at another spot on the ground ten feet away. Quaid made a sweep around the area and found a drop of the red cells on a rubber plant's broad shiny leaf. Panicked, he lunged into the forest searching for more clues, then discovered a blood-soaked cloth. As he examined it, Drake met up with him. Drake scolded, "You shouldn't be rushing through here so...what's that?"

"It appears to be Rondovin kerchief-issue. It's not Zaira's." He stood and peered into the dense forest. "Zaira, where are you?" he asked under his breath.

"Come on, Quaid. We'll find her."

They began the slower-paced search again.

Quaid leaned over to study the crisp imprint of a Rondovin's metal-tipped boot when Drake cried out. Quaid turned to the spot he'd seen Drake searching only moments before, then stared in disbelief to see he'd vanished. "Drake?" Quaid whispered, hurrying to the location.

He walked around the area with a cautious step, then heard Drake whisper, "Quaid, down here."

Quaid dropped to his knees and stared into the hole. "What are you doing down there?"

"Get me out of here! No telling what's down here."

"Hold on, Drake. I'll find a vine to slip down to you."

"Hurry! I'm sure I heard something stirring about down here."

Drake fired his blaster and Quaid scrambled to his feet. "Be right back!" he yelled. He yanked his jacket off, then dropped it next to the hole to mark the spot. His gaze turned heavenward as he observed the vegetation in the area. The vines covered the cliffs near the waterfall, but there were none here. Dashing due east, he searched for any sign of a vine. After a futile attempt, he ran back to the hole. "Drake!" he shouted. "Drake! I couldn't find a vine. I'm going to return to—"

"Quaid, maybe you can tie some of your articles of clothing together and lower it down to me. Quaid?" He waited a few more seconds, then shouted, "Quaid!"

Quaid opened his mouth to speak. A blaster was shoved into his back. He watched silently as the Rondovins lowered a rope into the cave.

"You got one!" Quaid shouted. "Where did you ever..." Quaid shrugged at him as Drake's red hair crested the top of the hole. "Sorry, Drake. Guess our voices carried a bit too far in our panic."

***

"How do I seem to keep getting into messes like this with you?" Quaid squirmed against his bindings. He studied the ropes securing Drake's ankles and wrists.

"Guess it's just our adventurous way. By the way, Martius asked me what happened when you and Zaira got hitched while we were still searching for the other scrolls. He said that when he mentioned the arrangement to his father, Carver nearly exploded. Well, actually he did. He threw three dishes at the wall before his wife finally took hold of his hands and made him settle down."

"Oh?" Quaid took a deep breath. "Guess he's not too happy about my being his new son-in-law."

"I believe he was more afraid of how Caryndian Bach would handle the news."

"So what did you tell Martius?"

"The truth."

"Which was?"

Drake squirmed to get comfortable as he twisted his hands in an attempt to free them. "I told him how Zaira tried to protect us by marrying you before the male Xenonians crashed the party."

Quaid tilted his chin down slightly as he narrowed his eyes at Drake. *"And?"*

"Well, Martius was pretty quiet after that...mulling over the notion in his mind. I asked him what he was thinking, but he just rubbed that perpetually smooth chin of his. Did you know Xenonians grow no beards? You know what they say?" Drake smiled. "They're more evolved than us. Well, anyway, he just nodded, then said nothing more about the incident."

Quaid listened to a guard arguing with another.

"Why can't we kill whole salocom lot of them? Be end of this thing." The guard waved his hand at Quaid and Drake.

"Up to me, I'd agree, but you know how ralora wants it," the other said.

"Yeah, only they're never on planets we conquer. Instead, they sit back swilling shots of rancine."

The other Rondovin laughed. "Yeah, no drinking allowed." He pulled a flask from his jacket. "Want blast?"

Quaid watched as the guard looked back at them. "Sure, no ralora is gonna tell me I can't have slug of rancine when he isn't here."

"Where ralora?"

The Rondovin grinned broadly. "One of them put him to sleep, twenty-fours. Pounding head, no quit. More trouble to live with, but...sure gave us chuckle. Some Xenonian took out great ralora! Ha...ha!"

Quaid grimaced.

Drake smiled. "What they don't know won't hurt us."

Quaid kicked the dirt with his toe. "Yeah, and they won't be expecting what comes next."

"Oh?" Drake's eyebrows lifted. "Got a plan?"

Quaid wiggled his rump on the ground as he tried to get his arms locked in place behind his back, underneath the seat of his pants. "Working on it."

"What are you attempting to do?"

Quaid flattened his body. "If I can get my hands in front, I might be able to get hold of my dagger still sheathed in my leg's trouser pocket. Just kind of watch the guards and alert me if they look this way."

"Sure thing. They're still concentrating on that flask."

"Good, I'm making some progress."

"Hey," one of the guards said. "This not bad juice."

"Alcohol clean engine parts."

Quaid smiled as he twisted his feet through the loop his tied hands made. "Rot gut."

"They're still busy, Quaid. Just hope they don't get trigger happy once they've had enough of the stuff." He grinned at Quaid. "Hey, you did it!"

"Yeah." Quaid sat up, then leaned over as he reached for his pants pocket.

"Hold still, Quaid. They're coming over here."

The one Rondovin tilted the flask to his lips as the other kicked Quaid's boot with his own. "Not know Xenonian shoot like two you."

Quaid kept his hands in his lap as he hoped the guard wouldn't notice their changed position.

A sprinkle of perspiration dotted Drake's forehead as he tilted slightly on his side and tried to point to his leather flask. "Maybe you'd like to try a bit of Caspian delight."

The Rondovin stared at the flask for a moment, then his gaze focused on Drake's. "Xenonian forbidden drink."

"Well, we're what you might call a couple of outcasts," Drake said. "Surely you must have rogues like us on your home world."

Quaid wondered where Drake had gotten more of the stuff.

The Rondovin grinned broadly as he glanced at his friend who tilted a bit in his stance. He leaned over and untied the leather strap from Drake's belt loop, then removed the top to the flask. As the top dangled from a chain to the container, the guard lifted the drink to his broad flat nose. He pulled his face away from the container and coughed.

"Great stuff, eh?" Drake asked.

The guard covered the mouthpiece with his large lips as the other watched his friend in great anticipation. The guard tilted his head back. His eyes widened, and he quickly pulled the bottle from his mouth, coughing while his friend stared at him, his face shaded with concern.

"Great stuff," he whispered hoarsely and held the flask out to his friend. The Rondovin reached for the flask, but the other warned him, "Slow."

He raised the flask to his lips and took a swallow. The strong, bittersweet, peppermint-flavored mixture cleared out his nostrils and his eyes watered while he coughed in response. "Ah," he said with a deadened voice, "Caspian delight?"

"The best." Drake grinned at the guard.

The two men walked back to where they'd been conversing earlier and slumped down against the back of a pine. "Chemist copy?" the one said.

"Synsysizers...," the guard said slurring his word.

The guard turned to Drake. "Hey! Where you get this?"

"Some privateer took it off a Caspian supply ship en route to restock fighter pilots in the war effort."

The Rondovin stared at Drake for several minutes, then grunted and punched his buddy in the shoulder. "Hear? Cap..Caspie...Cap...those guys we been fighting...commander let them drink." He turned to Drake. "More?"

Drake's face scrunched up with thought.

Quaid frowned. The wrinkled red brow meant Drake was formulating a plan.

"Sure, but it's quite a walk from here."

Quaid groaned. Now what did he have in mind?

"Show...show us!" The guard attempted to stand, but crumpled back to the ground.

"Sure," Drake said, "but I might need a bit of help standing up."

The guard pushed on the top of his friend's head

while attempting to stand. Boots crunched in their direction, someone in charge, Quaid was afraid.

Quaid frowned. "Now there'll be trouble," he said to Drake.

The older Rondovin studied the hostages for a moment and satisfied they weren't going anywhere, he turned his wrath on the inebriated guards. After liberating them of Drake's flask, he slapped the guard across the face. "Reshel corysitan setyn!" For several minutes, he cursed a tirade of Rondovin dialogue as he waved his arms in the direction of the prisoners.

The one guard stared at him with glassy eyes, then leaned over and passed out. The other eyed the flask as the Rondovin waved it about in his anger. The officer finally pulled a blaster from its holster and pointed it at the guard's temple.

Not good.

Seemingly oblivious to his imminent extermination, the guard's eyes continued to lock onto the flask. The officer holstered his weapon. "Shelyndrean!" the man shouted.

The guard attempted to stand, but slipped back to this seat grinning. The officer's berating words bellowed across the campsite. The guard closed his eyes and leaned against his friend's reclining body.

"Gradors! Gradors!" the officer shouted.

Two men ran through the woods.

Quaid closed his eyes. "Got another plan? Looks like the old man is going to keep your ale, and the drunken guards are going to be replaced with fresh stock."

Drake sighed deeply. "Fresh out. Next one is yours."

"I'm working on it."

The officer paced back and forth, too angry even for words as the new guards waited for their instructions. "Grador Xenonians ras salen corder. Caryndian Bach wayls bushe dace morshaley."

"Did you catch that?"

"My Rondovin is a bit rusty. Caught most of the swear words earlier however. And then something about guard Xenonians I believe he said and their lives."

"With their lives."

"Oh. And Caryndian Bach wants to eat us."

Quaid smiled. "Your Rondovin is rusty. He wants to question us."

Drake chuckled. "Good, I didn't relish being Caryndian's supper. So what does it mean?"

"Caryndian Bach is in cahoots with the Rondovins, so it seems. I wondered how the information about the greening was leaked to the Rondovins so soon. Catarina did mention the war with the Rondovins had started awfully quickly."

The officer hurried away, tucking the flask into his jacket.

Quaid let out his breath in exasperation. "Bet you he'll never give the stuff up. You stole it from a cargo ship?"

"Stole the whole cargo ship, actually. Why should all that great mixture go to making the Caspians happy?"

"So who did you sell it to?"

"The Xenonians. You know you've got to love 'em. They're totally against drinking, totally. But they'll pay any amount to get their share of the stuff whenever they can. Got my flask refilled at the illegal mating camp after Tagaron drained my Orion ale."

Quaid chuckled.

"Come on, you're not against drinking spirits from time to time."

"Orion ale. I wouldn't drink Caspian spirits even if not doing so killed me."

Drake nodded.

The replacement guards' eyes remained fixed on them.

Drake squirmed in place. "Guess you'll have to wait until it gets dark to reach your knife. Their eyesight is poor at night, so Zaira said."

Quaid took a deep breath. "Imagine so." He leaned back against the tree. "In the meantime, think I'll get some rest."

Just as he closed his eyes, the sound of footsteps

made him reopen them. He looked up to see one of the guards looking him over, then the guard turned his attention to Drake. "Wonder what's up?"

The guard reached down and untied Quaid's hands. He pulled Quaid to stand, then retied his hands behind his back. After shoving him on the ground, he tied the rope to his ankles. He studied the artwork, smiled, kicked Quaid's boot, then sauntered back to where the other guard stood watching the hostages. Quaid bumped into Drake several times as he tried to sit, but without being able to use his hands to balance himself, his head fell into Drake's lap. "Sorry, Drake." He wiggled about to sit upright. "They could have at least helped me to sit."

"Probably afraid to get into the kind of trouble the other two will be in when they come to."

"Yeah well, might as well make the most of it and get a little sleep until we can come up with another plan."

For some time, they lay quietly on the cushioned woodland floor, then as Quaid drifted to sleep, a waft of jasmine floated on the breeze. He stirred slightly against his leafy green pillow.

The scent tickled his senses. He sighed deeply.

Zaira walked out of the underground lake, her gold gowns clinging to her shapely curves. The tips of her breasts poked against the cold, wet fabric. He rolled onto his side as she said, *"Your grandfather started the Great Galaxy War. He started the war...the war."*

The words seemed to echo off the walls of the cave. Quaid squirmed on his leafy bed. *"Only you can stop it...you are the key, Quaid. Pleasure me."* Her long polished nails fingered the pearl button in front of the buttonhole. *"In or out, Quaid,"* she whispered. *"The choice is yours."*

The breeze grew stronger, and Quaid shifted again on the forest floor. *"You are unworthy, Quaid."* Her amber eyes captivated him. *"Disappointed?"* she asked and he opened his lips to speak but couldn't. *"The words are there,"* she said, *"you just choose not to use them."*

He held her close while she slept soundly in his arms, and he wanted more of this. But he didn't want to leave her behind when he fought the rest of the world at war. What is wrong, Zaira? Her face faded from view and he stood in the cave of conifers. The magnificent firs stretched heavenward with their blue cones tucked about the tree like Christmas ornaments.

"The familial greeting," Drake whispered to Quaid as he watched Martius kiss Zaira on the mouth. Too familial for him.

Quaid rolled on his back, but the ropes cut into his wrists and he tossed onto his side again. *"Caryndian Bach is going to eat us,"* Drake said, then Zaira appeared in his place. *"Caryndian Bach wishes to marry me."* A *tear rolled down her cheek as she sat in the meadow. "I never thought you'd reject me like this, never thought, oh, Quaid, never to be touched by a man, to have my own set of twins...you are unworthy. Leave here at once."*

The scent of jasmine grew stronger.

Zaira, she's here somewhere near. Her fragrance scents the air. "Don't see what the problem is, Quaid. If it were me..."

It's not you. Can't you understand, Zaira? It's not you, it's me.

Quaid woke himself. He opened his eyes. The dark had returned. He squirmed to sit up. Two new guards had taken the others' place. Drake slept soundly still.

Quaid stared into the dark. Moon-streaked shadows wavered in the breeze, stretching pointed fingers across the forest floor. Then the scent of jasmine caught his attention again. It hadn't been a dream. He studied Drake. If he woke him, the guards would become suspicious. He frowned. If Zaira was here by herself, she was at terrible risk. What could she be thinking?

A low growl peeled through the dark, and the guards ended their conversation. Quaid suspected they had already received word of the deadly menace stalking the forests of Xenon, day or night. He poked at Drake with his shoulder.

Drake grunted. "Yes, yes, Catarina."

Quaid made a face at him.

Again, he pushed at Drake and this time Drake grumped, "What?"

Quaid whispered, "Jaguar is back."

"Jeez." Drake hastened to sit. "Why didn't you say so in the first place?"

"Got the guards pretty spooked. I'm afraid they might even run off and leave us here unguarded."

"Great, doesn't sound like much of a plan."

"Can you get your hands in front of you like I did? Now that they've tied my ankles along with my wrists, I can't do the same trick again twice."

Drake stretched out, then as a low growl carried on the breeze, he tried to shove his hands under his rump in a hurry. "No deal." Drake sat up. "Guess you have longer arms than I do, or you're just a bit more flexible."

Quaid studied the guards' backs as the men watched the woods. "I sure don't like this." Quaid tried to wriggle his hands out of the rope.

A Rondovin cried out some four hundred yards away, then silence followed. One of the guards muttered a prayer. Quaid whispered, "This doesn't look good."

The other guard poked his companion. "Shut up and stay alert."

A twig snapped nearby and everyone turned to see

a Rondovin walking toward them. "See anything?"

"No, sir, not a thing. Heard the black devil though."

"Keep an eye out." The officer turned to face the hostages and smiled. "Maybe we feed these two to the black devil."

The man hurried back to the campfire where five others hovered. Quaid raised his chin. "They could at least take us over nearer to the campfire, eh, boys? Cats don't get near fire."

The one guard looked at the other, then back at the campfire as the flames licked the night sky a couple of hundred yards away.

"Why can't we move the prisoners back there where the fire is?" the guard asked the other.

"The commander didn't authorize it."

"Why don't one of you fellows suggest it? He probably never even gave it any thought." Quaid smiled as the guard rubbed his chin in thought.

"If one of us leaves our post, the other guard said the commander would shoot the guard himself," the guard said to his companion.

The other nodded and readied his weapon as he stared into the darkness. Another cry in the distance made them both glance back at the fire.

"Looks pretty safe back there...and hot coffee or whatever it is you drink to keep you warm at night," Drake said. "Can't imagine they'd deny you a bit of comfort on a cool night like this with the black devil prowling about."

The one shouldered his weapon. "I'll ask if we can move to the campfire."

The other guard faced his hostages as his friend hurried to the fire. Angry words were spoken by the commander and a single blast resounded. The guard dropped to the ground dead. The remaining guard's already white face turned whiter as his black beady eyes widened.

CHAPTER 15

"Not good," Quaid said under his breath as boots tromped in their direction. The new guard joined the other.

"Idiot," the new guard said to his companion. "The commander said *no one* leaves their post."

Quaid glanced back at the fire to see the dead Rondovin guard being dragged away. "Well, one less to have to deal with," Quaid whispered.

Drake smiled. "Yes, now we only have to manage six more. Piece of cake."

The guard poked at the dirt with the metal edge of his rounded boot. "The Xenonians said the black devil won't go near the fire."

"Great, now look what you got me into. I ought to kill you myself." The new guard's eyes narrowed. "Only three of our men still sit at the fire. Where'd Chlrostinst go?"

The other guard frowned. "Guess he removed Flon's body."

"Yeah." The new guard continued to watch for any signs of trouble in the dark woods in front of them.

Quaid rested against the tree trunk while the guards studied the forest. Then footsteps approached, making him turn with the rest to see an officer join them. "One of you go look for Chlrotinst."

"Sir?" the new guard said.

"He took Flon's body away from the camp so it wouldn't stink up the place. But he hasn't come back. One of you can guard the hostages while the other searches for Chlrotinst."

"The job's all yours," the new guard said to the other.

The one grunted his displeasure, then hurried off into the woods in the direction the officer directed him. Quaid smiled at the officer as he considered their bindings, then walked back to the campfire.

Quaid wriggled his hands. "Guess this one outranks the other. You see the way the commander let it be this man's choice without directing it to be so?"

Drake nodded. "He's a junior officer."

"Brand spanking new, I'd venture to say."

Quaid twisted his wrists several times as he tried to

get his hands free. Drake studied his actions. "They use pretty good knot techniques."

"Stolen from us!"

The young officer smiled at them, then turned his attention back to the woods. A low growl rumbled nearby; he walked back toward Quaid.

"Shalr! Shalr!" the guard shouted.

The three remaining men ran to join them, then the commander said, "What's the matter?"

"I heard it growling just over there, no more than thirty feet from here."

The commander waved his weapon for the men to spread out and search for the black devil. The commander stayed only a couple of yards away from where they sat.

"Fearless leader," Quaid whispered to Drake.

The woods were silent for several minutes, then a blast shot out and the commander readied his weapon, pointing it in the direction of the sound.

"Craaaaaaah!" a Rondovin screamed out and again there was silence.

Three blasts were fired in sequence, and then no more shots were heard.

"Talacrasin!" the commander shouted once the sounds had died away.

He walked backwards toward the fire. Quaid glanced back to see the terrified look on the man's face.

"Hey, sir!" Quaid shouted. "Don't leave us here like this!"

The commander paced before the fire. Drake and Quaid watched him, while they tried to get free of their ropes. "Maybe, Drake, you can crawl over me and slip your hand into my pocket and get my knife."

"And then what? Dig a hole in your flesh? With my hands tied behind my back, I couldn't cut a thing that I'd intended to."

Quaid studied the forest. "I don't relish being ripped apart by a jaguar, Drake."

"I told you once he might not go after unarmed beings."

"True." Quaid took a deep breath, then looked back at the fire. "Damnation!" His worst fears were realized. The cat rested its paws on the commander's chest. There was nobody left to protect them and bound as they were, they had no way to escape. He'd gotten out of plenty of tight squeezes before, but this was the worst.

"Is he dead?" Drake whispered as he stared at the lifeless body.

"Or fainted dead away. Can't tell."

Beads of perspiration dotted their foreheads despite the cool breeze swirling about them as the jaguar looked in their direction. Then with a couple of bounds, the cat zigzagged across the spongy floor, heading directly for Quaid. "Sit really still," Quaid whispered.

The sleek black cat strolled over and licked Quaid's fuzzy cheek. He barely breathed as he knew it would be his last breath. The cat turned its attention to his trousers.

Drake whispered, "Collect your wits."

The cat poked its muzzle at Quaid's pocket and tried to grip the zipper with its teeth, but couldn't manage. With a heavy paw and claws retracted, she pawed at the pocket. He studied her large amber eyes as she met his gaze, and then she bolted into the woods. The jaguar couldn't be Zaira. But...she was a changeling and the cat's eyes looks so much like hers...

Before Quaid or Drake could speak, Zaira walked out of the woods toward them, her long, silky hair draping over her shoulders, her body naked. Both men sat speechless as they stared at her peach skin in the soft moonlight. In modesty, she covered herself as much as she could with her hands, and then she crouched beside Quaid. She tugged at the zipper to his pocket, then pulled his dagger out.

"Zaira, you're the jaguar?" Quaid asked.

Drake's mouth dropped.

As if in slow motion, Zaira nodded and cut the ropes from Quaid's ankles, then crawled over to saw the ropes from his wrists. He yanked the ropes free, pulled off his jacket, and covered her with it. While she pulled the sleeves over her arms, Quaid cut through Drake's ropes. He sheathed his dagger, then hastened to retrieve a blaster near the campfire while Drake ran for another.

Quaid returned to where she was crouched in place. "Come on, Zaira." He grabbed her arm and ran with her away from the Rondovin campsite, then noticed his jacket reached only high thigh. He frowned at the sight. He turned to see Drake looking too. "Keep your mind on business, Drake."

"Sure thing."

"Where are your clothes, Zaira?" Her light speedy step slowed. "Your clothes?" Quaid pulled her to a stop as her eyes glazed over. "Damn, Drake." He swept Zaira up in his arms, and she appeared to fall asleep again. "It's the change that seems to make her so lethargic, if she's the one who saved her people at the village."

"She sure saved our butts back there." Drake studied Zaira's legs.

"See if you can find any sign of her clothes on the way back to Martius's workshop."

"Man, I knew she had great lung capacity, but wow, those teeth of hers," Drake whispered.

"I can't believe she was the jaguar stalking us earlier on."

"She wasn't stalking us...she was protecting us."

"I'd forgotten she was a changeling. Now I know

TERRY SPEAR

why she wouldn't tell me what she could change into."

"You got to admit, she's sure got great legs."

"Heck, I wonder what else she can become."

Drake grinned.

"It's not funny. You're not married to the woman."

"Ah, come on, Quaid. She saved us back there. Admit it. I'd have given anything to have recorded the look on your face when she licked it. If I hadn't been so scared the jaguar would take a bite next, I would've laughed when I saw the petrified look on your face."

"I can just see it. Right in the middle of pleasuring her, she turns into a jaguar."

Drake punched Quaid in the shoulder as he stifled a chuckle. "You're going to make me laugh out loud. Not a safe thing to do out here."

"Or I say the wrong thing and here come those saber tooth tiger fangs."

"Quaid, you love the lady. Admit it."

"Jeez, Drake, what did I get myself into?"

"Disappointed?" Zaira whispered, her eyelids fluttering slightly.

Quaid and Drake stared at Zaira's sleep-filled face. Quaid looked over at Drake. "Now you've really gone and done it," Drake whispered.

***

Nearing the entrance to the hideaway, the sound of Rondovin conversation nearby made Quaid and Drake crouch closer to the ground. Drake readied his weapon, but Quaid whispered, "They're too near the entrance. If we put them to sleep there, we'll never be able to leave the safety of the shelter if we have to. We've got to sneak past them."

"They're a bit south. We'll continue toward the entrance and if it looks viable, we dash into the shelter."

"It's a plan."

Drake helped Quaid to stand and glanced down inadvertently at Zaira's legs, making Quaid scowl at him.

"Sorry, Quaid." Drake sighed. "Just can't pass up a great pair of legs, but don't tell Catarina I said so."

When they finally reached the safe house surrounded by the dense forest, they crouched and listened for any sounds of Rondovins. Finally, Quaid motioned with his head to try for the entrance. Drake took off running.

After opening the hatch, he waved to Quaid. Running more slowly, Quaid carried Zaira to the opening, then squeezed in past Drake. Drake closed the door as Quaid reached the landing at the bottom of the steps.

"Phew," Quaid said, "thought we were gonners there for a..." He quit speaking when he saw Zaira's brother with Catarina. "Martius, Catarina." He bowed his head in greeting to them.

Drake hurried on past Quaid and whisked Catarina

to the bedchamber they had claimed for their own. Martius reached his arms out to Zaira. "Thanks, Martius, but I've got her." Quaid carried her to their room. After laying her in the bed, he covered her with a coverlet. Turning, he saw Martius watching him from the open doorway.

"Disappointed?" he asked.

Quaid frowned to hear Zaira's word spoken so often to him in private. He hurried him out of the room and closed the door. "Somebody could have told me."

Martius walked into the common area. He sat on one of the pillows scattered about for seating. Quaid followed him, then waited for a response from Martius.

"From all Zaira has told me, you could not handle the truth."

"Those men back there were toasted. Did you do that?"

Martius nodded.

"With a flame thrower? What? I thought Xenonians were not allowed to kill."

"Special circumstances warrant special rules."

Quaid stared at Martius, not sure of his meaning.

Martius stiffened his back. "A changeling in its wild state cannot be held accountable to human laws."

"So you can kill anyone and get away with it?"

"We do not kill for pleasure. For protection, yes. Before the Rondovins invaded our peaceful planet, the changelings had no reason to resort to such tactics. In truth, we normally only change our form to please the populace in special celebrations or to please ourselves."

Quaid studied Martius for a moment. "The changelings, you said. There are more of you?"

Martius glanced back at the chambers where Drake and Catarina resided.

Quaid chuckled as he considered the door to the bedchamber. Then he grew serious. "Catarina has never been tired like Zaira. How is that possible?"

"Catarina has been reluctant to change."

"Would she become a jaguar like Zaira?"

Martius nodded.

"But if you used a flame thrower—"

"Fire, yes."

"Not a flame thrower?"

Martius said, "No."

"A jaguar doesn't breathe fire."

A smile spread across Martius's somber face.

"Nothing breathes fire." Quaid squirmed on his cushion a bit.

"Have you never read about the dragons of old? Every civilization had stories about the ancient ones."

"I'm not into fairy tales." Quaid rubbed his beard. "Zaira says you have no razor. Are you certain?"

"No need."

Taking a deep breath and exhaling with

exasperation, Quaid said, "Another matter needs to be discussed. Caryndian Bach is in cahoots with the Rondovins."

Martius stood. "The accusations you make label Caryndian Bach as a traitor—punishable by death. Can you prove this?"

Quaid rose to his feet. "I don't have any signed confession, if that's what you mean, but both Drake and I heard the Rondovins discussing how we were going to be turned over to Caryndian Bach for questioning."

Martius stared at the floor.

Quaid added, "Why did the Rondovins arrive on the planet so quickly after the greening occurred? Even Catarina thought it was odd."

Martius's gaze caught Quaid's for a moment, then he studied the floor again.

"Martius, does he know of your safe houses and can he lower the shield over Riverine?"

This time Martius's eyes widened. "No, no, I'm not sure why, but I decided only the other changelings would know of the safe houses."

"Caryndian is not a changeling?"

"No." Martius sat down hard on a pillow.

Quaid resituated himself on a cushion too.

"Without proof, nothing can be done."

"I was afraid of this, but somehow we need to get the word to your father and other members of the High

Council—"

"We cannot without proof," Martius reiterated. "Not a word of this must be breathed."

Quaid stared back at Martius. "But—"

"If the accusations cannot be proven, you could be sentenced to death for perpetuating the lie."

Shaking his head, Quaid said, "Okay, if proof is what you need, I'll have to get it...somehow."

"About Zaira..."

Quaid studied Martius's serious face. "What about her?"

"I understand you haven't...pleasured her."

"I haven't had permission from your father yet to even have married her."

"That is not what Zaira tells me your reluctance has been all along."

Now Quaid studied the floor.

"She says you are unworthy." Martius stood.

Quaid looked up at him. He wasn't sure what to say. Yes, he felt unworthy of her love. He couldn't help feeling as though he would leave her with child and she would live a life alone. His business of fighting meant his lifespan would be shortened considerably. He still hadn't come to grips with the fact that the woman wasn't all just well, human, either.

"I have business to take care of. Tomorrow morning I shall return. Rest well."

"But it's dangerous—"

"Tomorrow, Quaid Lassiter."

Quaid stood and Martius disappeared up the stairs and through the hatch. He glanced back to the room where Zaira slept. Giggles erupted from Drake's room. Quaid raised his brows. Drake didn't know what he had gotten himself into either.

***

Later that afternoon, Quaid refreshed from a shower, studied the pale blue trousers and shirt Martius had loaned him. No pockets for a dagger. Quaid reconfigured the straps of the dagger's sheath to strap around his thigh, then looked into a mirror to see the color of his blue eyes rejuvenated again. He ran his hand over his dark beard. *I look like a wild man, not a fighter pilot, prince of Orion.* A rustling of covers made him turn to see Zaira watching him.

"Sorry if I disturbed your sleep, Zaira." He turned back to the mirror and fumbled with the leather ties on his shirt. "You might not be used to buttons, but this sort of fastener never took hold on Orion."

"Used to be the standard of dress on Orion." Zaira slipped his jacket off her shoulders. She dropped it on the bed, then pulled her covers aside. Quaid watched her step into the shower. The whooshing of the water pelted the translucent glass and Zaira. She ran her hands through her dark hair to wet the long strands.

He took a deep breath as she squirted soap onto her hair. Her long fingers spread the soap through her silky tresses, then she massaged it until it was a thick lather turning her hair violet. After she folded the curls on the top of her head like a Japanese doll in ancient times, she poured more soap onto her hands. He chided himself as he watched her slip her hands over her breasts. *Turn away, Quaid,* he told himself. She ran her hands between her legs, and he heard Drake's boisterous voice, then turned his attention to his shirt ties again. Exasperated with the fasteners, he walked over to the door to their room and hit the button.

"Good morning," Drake said to Quaid as he walked into the commons. Drake squeezed Catarina to his chest.

"Catarina, do you think you might tie these for me? I've made a mess of them," Quaid said.

"Where's Zaira?" Catarina considered the doorway to the bedchamber.

"Showering."

Catarina walked over to Quaid. When she tied the ties properly, Zaira left the room, freshly clothed in green gowns. Quaid stared at the cowl neck that rose three-quarters of the way up her neck. Her long sleeves rested at the wrist and her skirt brushed the floor, the bodice, heavily embroidered.

"Everyone have a pleasant sleep?" Before anyone

could respond, Zaira brushed past Quaid and headed into the kitchen.

"Where's Martius?" Drake looked at the doorway to Martius's room.

Quaid shrugged. "He left for Riverine late last night."

"Kind of a dangerous notion, wasn't it?" Drake asked.

Quaid sat at the kitchen counter, then tapped his hands on the countertop. "He said he had business."

Zaira nodded.

"What kind of business, Zaira?" Drake asked.

She poked at mushrooms sautéing in the pan. "Important business."

Quaid raised his eyebrows to Drake as they exchanged looks. Drake sat beside Quaid as Catarina and Zaira prepared the meal. "Catarina and I have decided to live in Riverine for the time being, until things settle down a bit."

Catarina smiled.

Quaid stared at the woven basket of fruit sitting on the center of the counter, then pulled out a green apple. For several minutes he fingered the polished apple, then finally looked up to see everyone watching him. Catarina and Zaira continued with their meal preparations.

Quaid turned to Drake. "Listen, Drake, we have

rather a situation with this..."

He turned to see the women both listening to him, and he took Drake's arm and led him into the common room. "I spoke with Martius last night about Caryndian Bach. Martius said unless we have proof Caryndian is a traitor, we can't speak a word of it. Otherwise, our libelous actions could get us the death penalty."

Drake said, "That's not good."

The two sat down on cushions beside each other, then Quaid said, "I believe Caryndian was the reason the Rondovins arrived so quickly when the greening of the planet began."

"The shields to Riverine—"

"Martius said Caryndian doesn't know how to..." Quaid glanced up to see Catarina carrying utensils to the table. He cleared his throat, then waited until she returned to the kitchen. "He can't withdraw the shields. And luckily he doesn't know about the safe houses. Only some of the changelings know about—"

Drake's eyes widened. "There are more?"

Quaid sighed deeply. *Sorry, Drake. I don't keep secrets from you normally, but this one is between you and Catarina.* "Yes, Martius says there are several."

"Wow." Drake smiled at the notion.

"But about Caryndian, we have to find a way to get proof—"

Drake and Quaid turned as Catarina studied them

from the kitchen. "What's up?" Drake asked.

"The meal will take a while to cook. May I have a word with you, Drake?"

Drake frowned. "We'll have to make some plans, Quaid." He smiled at Catarina. "Yes, Ma'am." He jumped to his feet, then hastened to Catarina's side. She walked him back to their bedchamber while Quaid studied the serious expression on her face.

He turned his attention to the kitchen, but not hearing any sound in there, he stood, then strode across the commons. Not finding Zaira in the kitchen, he glanced at their bedchamber.

No sense in getting into another argument. He grabbed up the apple and bit into the sweet spicy fruit. When he had finished the seedless fruit, he walked over to see what culinary delights bubbled away in the pots. Quaid turned to see Zaira watching him. Once her eyes caught hold of his, she lowered her gaze to the floor.

"Catarina had business to discuss with Drake." She pulled the pan of mushrooms out of the cooler.

Drake walked into the kitchen with Catarina, her arm wrapped around his securely again.

"Food almost ready?" Drake tilted his nose up to breathe in the scents of the meal they would soon enjoy.

"Seems that it'll be a while longer. Maybe we can discuss this other matter further."

Drake kissed Catarina on the lips and smiled at her. "You sure are beautiful."

Quaid returned to the commons where Drake hurried to join him. "You won't believe what Catarina just told me."

"Oh?"

"Yeah, seems she's a changeling like Zaira."

"Oh. About Caryndian Bach—"

"Isn't that something?" Drake grinned from ear to ear.

"That's something." Quaid frowned at Drake. "About Caryndian—"

"Okay, what's the plan?"

CHAPTER 16

An hour later, the foursome sat to eat the meal, and Drake poked at the mushrooms. "I've never eaten anything quite like this. Sure is good."

"Good for you too." Zaira lifted a rib to her lips.

"Gregorion boar never tasted this good." Drake reached for another off the common server.

"You sure can eat." Catarina studied Drake's enthusiasm for their cooking.

"Just a growing boy." Drake patted his firm chest.

Quaid stared at the dappled brown and pink spots on his mushroom, turned green and yellow with cooking.

Drake poked at him. "What's wrong, Quaid?"

Quaid looked up at him. "What?"

"You've barely eaten any of your food."

Quaid glanced at Zaira, but she avoided his look. He

saw Catarina studying his behavior and he turned back to his food. "Sorry, everything is as delectable as before, but my mind is on something else."

Zaira slammed her fork on the table. Before Quaid could react, she jumped up from her seat and stormed off to the commons. The three looked back to see her collapse on a cushion with her back to them.

"What did I say now?" Quaid was genuinely perplexed with her behavior.

"Her emotions are unstable during mating season, Quaid, unless she's pleasured by her mate." Catarina pulled another rib from the platter.

Quaid poked at his mushroom with his fork, then stood. He faced Zaira, then took a deep breath. With a long stride, he quickly arrived at the commons, then stood before her. As he crouched in front of her, she stared at her fingers as they touched the green ribbons on her bodice.

"I'm sorry, Zaira, if I've upset you about something."

"Leave me alone, Quaid."

Quaid sat beside her and reached for her hand, but she yanked it away.

"It is not safe for me to leave this place at the moment. Rondovins are searching for us just above the hatch, but if you touch me again, I will leave here just the same."

"Catarina says you have lost weight. At least return to the table and eat. I will stay here in the commons, if you prefer."

Her eyes darkened as she glared at him. "If you do not leave me at once, I cannot be responsible for my actions."

His mouth dropped open and he rose. "I'm sorry, Zaira." He walked into their bedchamber and closed the door.

***

Early the next morning, Martius pulled the door open to Quaid's bedchamber. "Come, Quaid Lassiter, you have work to do."

Quaid considered Zaira's sleep-cloaked features. He nodded to Martius. Standing, Quaid stretched the sleep from his muscles. Martius's dark brown eyes narrowed as he considered Quaid's naked figure. Quaid frowned back at him. "Can you give me a moment to dress, Martius?"

Martius bowed slightly just like Carver Cole had done the day Quaid had ionic propulsion failure when he first arrived on Xenon. Quaid knew something perturbed him, but wasn't sure what this time. He grabbed up his freshly washed shirt.

Martius studied Zaira.

"Do you mind?" Quaid asked.

Martius pushed the button to the door. As it slid

closed, Quaid continued to dress. After he slipped his jacket over his shoulders, he leaned over to kiss Zaira's lips. To his surprise, she opened her eyes.

"Goodbye, Quaid," she said, her voice cloaked in sadness. She rolled over onto her side and pulled the covers over her head.

Quaid stared at her for a moment, then turned to the door as he considered Martius's behavior further. "Something's definitely up." He walked over to the door and punched the button beside it.

Quaid walked into the commons. He studied Martius's grave demeanor. "So what's this all about, Martius?"

"You are to go to the Screshinan."

"Court? I don't understand. How will we get to Riverine safely?"

"The transport awaits you, courtesy of Caryndian Bach." Martius pointed to the hatch.

Quaid hesitated. "Caryndian Bach."

"Once you told me he was dealing with the Rondovins, I knew I could enlist his support to get you safely to court."

"For?"

"At the moment, this is in his best interest."

Quaid climbed up the stairs. "Does Zaira—"

"She knows."

Sighing deeply, Quaid walked into the woods and

looked up to see a hovercraft waiting with steps extended. "Maybe I should let Drake—"

"Here I come!" Drake said as Catarina clung to his arm.

Quaid turned to see Martius waiting for him. "Should we leave Zaira alone like this?"

"She'll be along shortly."

After climbing into the shuttle, Quaid saw Drake and Catarina take seats in the back where they had more privacy.

Quaid sat in front, then looked out the window. To see the planet cloaked in green finery from the vantage point from the sky, made him smile. "Your work here has truly been genius."

"Thank you."

Quaid studied Martius as he stared out the window. A dark shadow clouded his face. "What's wrong?"

"Nothing is wrong, Quaid Lassiter."

Quaid leaned back in his chair. He wouldn't get anywhere with this conversation. Leaning into the window, he peered at the dense vegetation, looking for Rondovin troop movements. As the silver-domed buildings of Riverine suddenly appeared, Quaid admired it. This place sure was an improvement over the way station. He studied a larger gold-domed building situated in the center and assumed it was the court housing all of the ministers and the High Council members' offices.

"We are at Screshinan," the captain announced a few seconds later.

Martius led the party from the shuttle into the gold-domed building. He walked into a small chamber. "You must wait here while the court gathers." Then he left the room, leaving Quaid alone.

Quaid paced across the marble floor, clicking the shiny stone with his boots.

The sound of heavy boots approaching the chambers made him pause. Drake rushed into the room. "Boy, do you know how to draw a crowd!"

"What's going on, Drake?"

"You're being confirmed as Minister of Defense."

"Martius seems to be angry with me, but I can't find out what the matter is."

"Don't know." Drake shrugged.

They both turned as Catarina hurried into the room. She shoved gowns into Quaid's chest. "Wear these, Quaid Lassiter." Before he could say a word, she brushed past Drake and hastened out of the room.

Quaid and Drake stared after her. Quaid unfolded the gowns. "Something's not right. Even Zaira wouldn't speak to me this morning when I tried to give her a kiss."

"I don't know, Quaid. Everybody else seems pretty excited about you being named defense minister. Kind of elevated my position a bit, being your best friend and all." He helped Quaid to dress in the gowns. Stepping back to see the white gowns embroidered in gold, he grinned. "Looks pretty swift."

Martius walked into the room. "It is time, Quaid Lassiter."

He motioned for the two men to follow him, then as Quaid walked behind him, he leaned over to Drake. "Have you ever noticed Xenonians often say both your names when they're angry with you?"

They entered into a circular room with seats situated all around the coliseum-like building. Xenonians cheered.

"I wish Zaira were here with me." Quaid studied the myriads of dark-eyed faces gawking back at him. He realized that no matter what he did here, he always thought of her, of her safety, and though he'd screwed up big-time with her feelings, he wanted to make it right somehow. He wanted to ask her father for permission to mate her. He wanted to make love to her.

"Up there." Drake pointed to a specially draped balcony where members of the High Council and their families sat.

Quaid smiled to see Zaira standing in a short, sleeveless black dress, looking just as beautiful as the first time he'd seen her. From the distance he stood from her, he couldn't tell if she was smiling or not. What he could see is she stood still, watching him without a wave of her hand or any acknowledgment of him on her part.

"Zaira's mad at me."

"How can you tell from this distance?"

"I can tell."

Martius led Quaid and Drake upstairs to a stage where Caryndian Bach rested his arms on a podium.

Caryndian Bach, a middle-aged, fierce-looking man with a scar cutting across his brow, giving him a perpetual scowl, tensed. His white gowns swept the floor like Quaid's, and he held onto the podium with an aggressive grip. To Quaid, the magistrate seemed out of place among the peaceful Xenonians. The man bowed first to Martius, then to Quaid. Martius left the stage. Caryndian turned to the audience, raised his hands in the air with palms uplifted, and the crowds grew silent.

"In this day of Mercury of the fifth, two-hundred and one, we do proclaim Quaid Lassiter to be our Minister of Defense for as long as he shall live or as long as he desires to hold said post. So says the unanimous vote of the High Council of Xenon."

"So they say!" shouted an enthusiastic audience.

Caryndian leaned over and placed a gold medallion over Quaid's neck. He raised Quaid's arm in a salute to the people.

"Here, here!" shouted the crowd.

Caryndian signaled to Drake, who stepped closer.

The magistrate said, "Quaid Lassiter has chosen Drake Jorgenson as Secretary of Defense."

The crowds cheered.

"Following the next set of proceedings, our Secretary of Defense will select our pilots who will train in the first missions, with final approval from the Minister of Defense," Caryndian added. He placed a medallion over Drake's head, then held his arm up to the crowd in triumphant.

Cheers resounded, then Caryndian turned to Drake. "You may be seated. You will be called on as necessary."

Catarina hurried to guide Drake to a seat next to hers in the front row. Caryndian turned to Quaid and said for all to hear, "Now to a grave matter that must be righted. Evidence and witness reports indicate our Minister of Defense has been wronged by one of our fellow citizens."

The Xenonians sat in reverent silence as Caryndian continued. "It is with a grievous air that I do proceed."

Everyone clapped to encourage Caryndian to continue with the difficult proceedings. Zaira still stood in the balcony as she rubbed her eyes with a white cloth. *What is going on, Zaira?*

"Marriage to another, one of our most sacred rites of passage, has been violated."

Quaid stared at Caryndian. What was he up to now?

"When Quaid Lassiter first arrived here, he was an

outsider. By helping to return the scrolls to us, he became one of us with all of the rights and privileges of our citizens. However, before this happened, he was coerced into marrying our own beloved Zaira Cole, daughter of Carver Cole, President of the High Council."

"No, it isn't so." Quaid's head pounded; his hands grew clammy.

Caryndian turned to Quaid. "The wronged party will have his turn to speak presently."

Zaira collapsed on her chair as her mother reached over to pat her shoulder. Quaid looked down to see Drake shake his head with a confused expression on his face. When he caught sight of Martius, the man nodded slightly.

Caryndian continued, "Would Zaira Cole please take the stand?"

Zaira made her way down a long winding staircase, then hurried to take her place on the stage opposite the podium where Caryndian now stood.

"Zaira, I—" Quaid said.

"Would you please state your case, Zaira?" Caryndian interrupted.

"I had every intention of marrying Quaid Lassiter when he arrived here on Xenon. It was I who rewired his ionic propulsion drive, which caused it to malfunction prior to his arrival here."

Quaid couldn't believe his ears. She lied. Caryndian

forced her to lie.

"At the forbidden mating party, I warned Quaid if he didn't take my ring, he and Drake would have been in serious trouble. He didn't know by wearing my ring, he would be married to me for the rest of our lives. His culture doesn't live in such a way. Divorce..."—a hushed rush of words ensued—"Well, Orions don't believe in marriage for life."

The blood rushed to Quaid's face. His whole body warmed as his knees weakened. He couldn't believe her words. He could change. He would...for her, he would.

Zaira took a deep breath. "For many days following this, Quaid refused to believe we were married and insisted on having word with my father, Carver Cole, to straighten out the mess, as he called it."

I just have to have your father's permission, Zaira. I just have to ask.

"Because of Quaid's reluctance to recognize me as his wife, we were never properly mated. He is an honorable man, and I've dishonored him terribly. I ask forgiveness of the peoples of Xenon and of Quaid Lassiter for the irreparable harm I've done."

"It's not true, Zaira." Quaid's words were drowned out by the crowd as they clapped their approval. "You haven't harmed me. I've hurt you."

"Thank you, Zaira." Caryndian gestured to Carver Cole, who strolled across the stage as he glared at Quaid while Zaira hurried to pass by her father.

Zaira returned to the stairs, while Carver stood at the podium. "I beg forgiveness for my daughter's indiscretions. Her marriage to Quaid Lassiter was not approved by me, her father, as it should have been, considering the position she holds in our society. I only beg you to consider that she is my only daughter and has helped to retrieve the scrolls that set us free. Thank you."

You are not convinced I should not marry your daughter, Carver Cole. This is Caryndian Bach's doing.

Shouts from many as they stood, indicated the crowd was pleased to no end at the words of their president.

As everyone settled down, Lynonia took the stand. "Zaira was not quite in her right state, I must admit, when she encouraged Quaid Lassiter to take the ring. She'd been bitten by a speckled spider and was still recovering when she proposed to our Minister of Defense." The woman raised her brows as she considered Quaid's appearance. "Still, when he discovered they were married, he refused to lie with her that night."

Hushed sentiments swept through the court.

"It's not all Zaira's fault. Our Quaid Lassiter is quite a handsome figure of a man. Who wouldn't be interested in having him for a mate?"

Feminine voices chanted, "Quaid Lassiter, Quaid Lassiter."

Drake laughed.

Quaid glared at Caryndian. The whole thing was a travesty of justice...a courtroom filled with monkeys, all dancing to his tune.

Lynonia smiled. "Then too, Zaira was concerned Quaid wouldn't agree to be our Minister of Defense. With his marriage to her, she figured he'd be more willing to take the position. This is all I have to say."

The females in the court stood on their seats as they whistled and cheered.

Quaid straightened his back. He wouldn't be bamboozled by Caryndian Bach. Zaira was his mate and he'd prove it to her.

Lynonia took her seat and Martius stepped onto the stage. He cleared his throat as he avoided looking at Quaid. "I became concerned when I spoke with my father about his consent to Zaira's marriage, and learned my father knew nothing of the matter. Zaira herself told me Quaid didn't consider her his wife and refused to pleasure her."

There was complete silence and Martius cleared his throat again. "At first I thought he was just shy."

Quaid's face heated. *Did all of Xenon have to hear this? And it wasn't true!*

"Then as they were together for several days, and

284

still he couldn't find the moment to unite with her, I insisted on Zaira telling me what the matter was. She explained Quaid didn't understand our ways and she had misled him, which resulted in his marrying her." He glanced up at Zaira. "Please forgive me, my dear sister. It is the only measure I could think of that would break this commitment that shall never bring you pleasure. With the marriage's dissolution, you can once again find a suitable mate."

She nodded and the crowd grew wild with adoration.

Quaid clenched his fists. He wouldn't give her up. *Not ever.*

Martius left the stage and Caryndian signaled to Drake. Drake refused to speak.

Caryndian said, "No one is forced to speak here. Do you not wish to speak on Zaira or Quaid's behalf?"

Drake jumped up on the stage and received a standing ovation. Frowning, he stepped up to the podium. "I have never seen a man and a woman who care more about each other—"

"You must get to the point," Caryndian interrupted.

Drake began again, "Quaid wasn't aware he was marrying Zaira, when he took her ring. That's true, but—"

"That's fine." Caryndian took Drake's arm and led him off the stage.

The audience cheered as Quaid watched Drake shake his head to him. "I'm sorry, Quaid!" Drake shouted. "I'm afraid you're being space shuttled on this one."

Caryndian glanced down at Catarina, but she refused to testify. Drake turned to speak to her. She said, "No, I won't."

Caryndian hit a metal object with a rounded wand. The room grew quiet. "We shall now go into the sentencing phase."

"I didn't get to speak!" Quaid exclaimed, his voice darkened in anger.

"Did you understand our ways when Zaira wed you?"

"No, but—"

Caryndian raised his hands in triumphant and the crowds stood on their seats and cheered with their hands raised.

He placed his hands on the podium, causing everyone to sit. A deathly silence blanketed the room. "For the crime of marrying an outsider who had no knowledge of our customs, Zaira Cole, you are found guilty."

The room remained silent as Quaid glowered at Caryndian Bach. *You won't get your way on this, Caryndian. If it's the last thing I do, I'll make it up to Zaira, but you won't win.*

"For this crime you shall be incarcerated at the penal colony at Vaschon for six months. Upon your return here, you will marry a mate of your father's choice." He banged the metal disk with the wand again. As the Xenonians filed quickly out of the auditorium, Quaid bolted across the stage to reach Zaira. Two guards whisked her out the side door well ahead of the crowd.

"Zaira!" Quaid shouted. The crowds shoved him back.

"Perhaps you will consider me instead." Lynonia touched his shoulder. "Zaira will have no trouble finding a mate among her suitors. Several have already presented their wishes to Carver Cole. He only has to make a selection for her."

"I love you, Zaira!" Quaid shoved against the unyielding crowds.

"You will have many suitors as well. Only now that you know our customs, you will be able to choose more carefully. I hope you will consider me at the top of your list."

Quaid finally broke through the mob and darted across the courtyard, where he caught sight of Zaira being hustled into a spacecraft. "Zaira!" he shouted.

She turned to look at him for a second, then was shoved into the craft by her guards.

"Zaira!" he shouted. He raced to the ship within

seconds only to reach it just as the hatch closed securely. He struck his fists on the hatch with a clunk. Without another moment to lose, he turned and dashed across the platform, where the Exiter waited for him in the nearby hangar.

"Wait up!" Drake hollered, dragging Catarina behind him.

"I don't have time for any nonsense." Quaid climbed into his craft. Drake closed the door to the hatch behind them.

Drake indicated one of the passenger's seats. "Strap yourself in over there, Catarina."

Quaid glanced at her as he started the engines. "Was this all of your idea too?"

"Caryndian Bach's. I knew if I said anything in court, he'd twist my words to suit his interests. He already got Carver to agree to Zaira's marriage to him. He just needed to get you out of the way...only since you are new and extremely popular...and a necessary Minister of Defense, he just couldn't get rid of you in his usual way."

"And Martius? What does he get out of it?" Quaid took his craft up, then punched in coordinates to lock onto the prison ship's heading.

"He wished for his sister to be happy, Quaid. That's all. She was unhappy that you would not fulfill your obligations to her as her husband."

"We've been rather busy of late."

"There were times in between."

Quaid took a deep breath. "Had I—"

"The two of you could never have been separated."

Quaid stared at the pitch-black sky and frowned. "I thought when I returned to this, I would feel at home, but now I realize being with Zaira is what makes me truly feel at home." He turned to Drake. "Take the controls for a moment." He unbelted himself, then started to yank off his long white robes. After he freed them from his body, he noticed Catarina's mouth agape. "What's wrong?"

"I just thought you wouldn't have had anything on underneath them. You're supposed take your other clothes off when you put your robes on."

"Nobody told me the rules." Quaid dropped into his seat.

"What are you going to do, Quaid? You can't just storm onto the planet and steal her from a prison," Drake said.

He raised his brows as he tilted his head slightly to the side.

"Or maybe you can. So what's the plan?"

"Haven't got one yet."

"What if *I* were to switch places with Zaira?" Catarina said.

The two men shook their heads.

"Well, when they found out I wasn't Zaira they'd have to return me home. By then you could see if Carver would allow you to mate Zaira, again."

"No," Quaid and Drake said in unison.

She folded her arms across her lap as she glared back at them. "You have to save Zaira, Quaid. You know when she's returned to Xenon, she'll be mated to Caryndian Bach. He hasn't married in all of these years because he's waited for Zaira to come of age. The old corsias is twenty years older than her! And she despises him!"

"Why did she do it, Catarina?"

When Catarina said nothing in response, Quaid looked back at her to see her running her fingers over her gowns. "Her appearance as a changeling and the things she did, repulsed you."

"She said that?" Quaid stared through his viewing window, relieved to see the gap shortening between the prison ship and his own.

"Yes."

"I was just surprised is all."

"Shocked, is the way she put it."

"Well, both Drake and I were. We just never figured it out."

"And you avoided looking at her for most of the rest of the day."

"I tried to speak on the subject later, but she

refused to talk to me."

"That's because she had words with Martius...just before he collapsed in the woods. He's the one who came up with the perfect solution."

Quaid scowled. "Perfect solution. He may be a genius when it comes to technological advancements, but when it comes to matters of the heart—"

"You have all the correct moves, right?" Catarina asked.

Drake turned to frown at her. "Whose side are you on, Catarina?"

"Zaira's. She's in love with this man even if he's unworthy of her affections."

Quaid rubbed his chin. "I've got to get a shave one of these days." He used the touch-screen on the communication panel. Lights flashed on the panel. A long buzz resulted. "Damnation!" He glanced back at Catarina. "Sorry, I'm not used to having a woman on board my ship."

"That's okay, Quaid, if it helps Zaira."

"Catarina's really an agreeable sort." Drake leaned back in his seat.

Quaid ran his hand over a panel. The lights flashed in sequence. "Computer."

"Yes, Captain?"

"Locate the Black Crow Squadron."

A second passed in silence.

"Fourth Quadrant, eastern most section two."

"Computer, send the following message, Code 1 Priority. Divert ships to Vaschon to act as backup. Cpt. Quaid Lassiter, Exiter, Defense Minister, Xenon. Code 1 Priority."

"Message sent, Captain."

Quaid smiled to see the prison ship flying in a path directly ahead of them. "I wonder if Zaira can see us."

"Possibly, if she's in the tail section of the craft," Drake said.

A light flashed cherry against the communication panel and Quaid touched the screen. "Cpt. Lassiter."

"Lt. Farthing here, sir. We understand you wish for us to divert our current mission from Xenon to Vaschon."

"Affirmative."

"The mission? Some of the guys assume we're freeing rebel pilots at the prison to serve our cause."

"Something grander. We're saving the Xenonian daughter of the president of the High Council's life from a fate worse than death."

"A woman?"

"A damsel in distress."

"Yes, sir! Lt. Farthing, out."

Drake grinned at Quaid. Quaid frowned back. He touched the screen. "What?" he said to Drake.

"They'll have a good chuckle over this one."

"Good, they're due a chuckle. Computer."

"Captain?"

"Hail the prison ship."

"Yes, Captain."

The communication button lighted up. Quaid cleared his throat. "This is Quaid Lassiter, Defense Minister of Xenon. You must stop at once."

"Captain Pelly of Louella Prison Ship. What is your reasoning?"

Quaid turned to Catarina, who whispered, "Xenon prisoner, Zaira Cole, was mistakenly removed from planet without prior approval of the president of the High Council."

Quaid repeated Catarina's words to Captain Pelly.

There was some silence as a computer spoke in the background.

"Uhh," Cpt. Pelly said, "uh, it appears the paperwork is all here signed, with proper authorization."

"He's new." Quaid considered what to say next. "But is it signed off by the Defense Minister of Xenon?"

There was another long pause, then Cpt. Pelly said, "No, no, sir. There's nothing here signed off by such an individual."

"You must turn the prisoner over to me at once. I will return her to Xenon where the paperwork will be reviewed and—"

"Sir, uh, can't you just have the paperwork shipped with the next craft or flash it over by particle manipulator—"

"The particle manipulator is out of order. Would it be proper to hold a prisoner who wasn't officially recognized as a prisoner?"

"Well, uh…" There was another pause as the computer directed Cpt. Pelly when he asked it for advice again. "This is highly irregular," Cpt. Pelly said to Quaid.

"Mere oversight, Cpt. Pelly. The Xenonians have only just now appointed me to the High Council as Defense Minister. All prisoner movements and exchanges must be approved by my office."

"May I ask, sir, why in your high position, you are chasing us down?"

Quaid took a deep breath as he frowned at the impudence of the young officer. "Do you mind asking me another question?"

"Sir?"

"Of all the arrogance! Do you know who you are addressing, Cpt. Pelly?"

Drake leaned back in his chair. He locked his hands behind his head and grinned. "You tell him, Quaid."

"Cpt. Lassiter of the Exiter with over 496 kills to my name, son of Luke Lassiter, grandson of Reser Lassiter, ruler of Orion, finder of the lost scrolls of Orion, and Defense Minister of Xenon. Not to mention, a recent addition to the house of Acropolis." Quaid looked at Drake as he chuckled in response.

"I think you were just dropped from the house of Acropolis," Drake said. They saw Catarina's mouth agape. Drake frowned. "What?"

"I didn't know Quaid Lassiter was the prince of Orion."

"Yeah, well now you know," Drake said, smiling.

There was silence, then another button lighted up on the communication's panel. "Cpt. Lassiter."

"Sir, Lt. Farthing. We're gaining on your location, but have sighted Rondovin war birds to the southeast of your position. It looks like we're in for a fight, sir."

"Damn," Quaid muttered under his breath. "Not now."

CHAPTER 17

"All right, Lt. Farthing. Attack formation, Blue. Follow defensive maneuvers. Tight form. I'm in the middle of negotiations to free prisoner from prison ship. Out," Quaid said.

Cpt. Pelly buzzed Quaid.

He answered. "Cpt. Pelly?"

"Sir, uh, sorry, sir, just got confirmation on your credentials."

Quaid's brow furrowed. "Rondovin war birds are headed in our direction. Make the exchange at once."

"Can't, sir. I radioed ahead and the prison commandant said we must make the exchange at headquarters. I just transport prisoners. It's up to the…"

Quaid clicked Cpt. Pelly's voice off. "Quaking in his own boots. Can't take the risk."

"Probably doesn't know how to make a mid-space

exchange," Drake said.

Quaid sighed deeply. He clicked the button and the young man said, "...as he knows best as he's been—"

"Cpt. Pelly, Rondovin war birds will be at our location within the half hour. You might want to raise your shields. Out." Quaid considered the blips on his screen inching their way nearer to his ship. "Looks as though this is going to be a rough one." He turned to Catarina. "There's a bedchamber in the back. You might want to strap yourself into one of the beds and shut the door. Language might get a little rough up here."

Catarina said, "I'll stay here with my husband, Quaid."

"You've never even been in space before, Catarina. And fighting ship to ship isn't the most pleasant of ways to make your first trip," Drake said as he unstrapped himself. He walked over to Catarina and kissed her cheek. "I'll take you back to one of the rooms."

"If we live through this, I want to tell the other ladies what life with my husband is like."

"Hopefully, it'll be more pleasant than this." He kissed her lips firmly, then returned to his chair. "Okay, Quaid, what do you want me to do?"

"You said you needed a little gunnery practice. Here's your chance." He pushed a button raising his shields. "Now you'll see the need for higher-powered shields and more powerful weapons' systems."

His communication's button lighted up. "Cpt. Lassiter."

"Sir, Lt. Farthing. Rondovin war birds headed this way. Contact imminent, ten minutes. Tight formation, shields in place. Any other orders?"

"If the war birds attack the prison ship, I want all ships to break formation and protect her. Cpt. Lassiter, out."

"Affirmative. Lt. Farthing, out."

Quaid puzzled over another matter for a moment, then turned to Catarina. "Zaira said she tampered with my spacecraft, but she couldn't have. I hadn't been on Xenon in six months—"

"She was afraid just saying she had convinced you to marry her wouldn't have been enough to have convicted her. In the end, Caryndian never even considered the business with the ship."

"Zaira was unconscious when we took her to the Xenonian mating party. She was only trying to save our necks."

"True, but since there is no way to get out of a mating, both parties have to know what they are getting themselves into. Everyone could sympathize with your feelings in the matter."

Quaid stared out in the blackness only lighted by the prison ship ahead of them and the lights of his own craft. "But I love her."

"How can she know this if you do not show her fully?"

"I had to get her father's approval. And to begin with, I couldn't accept being married...to anyone. In the beginning." He turned back to stare out the window, then a red light flashing deep in space caught his eye. He faced Drake. "Here they come. Lesson number one."

Catarina squirmed in her seat. "Hailing them and asking for a peaceful solution, I guess is out of the question."

Drake and Quaid exchanged glances with brows raised. "No," the men said at the same time.

"No wonder our people left Orion long ago."

Bang! A volley struck the ship, causing it to shake with the impact. "Hit it!" Quaid pointed at the weapons' control panel. "Blue button, Rondovin ship cruncher."

Drake smiled. "Sounds like a winner."

As the green streaks of light crashed into the offending Rondovin command ship of prey, Quaid grinned. "Knocked out their shields."

"So they're vulnerable to your firepower," Catarina said. "Can't you let them go home and—"

"They're like a dog with a bone. They won't give up, Catarina," Drake said as he waited for further instructions from Quaid.

"The red panel. It'll do enough damage to either make them cease and desist or...not. Aim at their weapon systems in any event, first."

Drake ran his hand over the panel while Quaid monitored the screen.

A blue streak of light created sparks of red-flamed explosions on the Rondovin ship, sending the craft across the galaxy. "One down." Quaid studied the prison ship through his window as the ship idled in the middle of the firefight.

Suddenly, sparks of white light hit the prison ship, causing it to flounder briefly. Quaid pointed to the two-o'clock position. "Rondovin warship, soon to be annihilated."

Drake reached for the blue button and glanced back at Quaid. Quaid nodded. Drake punched the button and green streaks flashed across the black space illuminated only by the ships' lights in the vicinity and the colorful flash of fireworks displayed by the fighting ships. "They didn't know who they were messing with when they took us on," Quaid said.

The ship that had attacked the prison ship dropped out of formation with red streaks of flames trailing it like a kite's red tails blowing in a stiff breeze, then disappeared from sight.

"They're breaking up." Quaid punched his communication button. "How did everyone do, Lt. Farthing?"

"Lt. Farthing here, sir. Got two, Sorenson took out

three, RS hit two, Sweet took a hit, but not badly, Penderson had two kills, Griffen, Micel, Rassinio, Lapris, and Roux all took out one. The Rondovins have tucked tail and have scattered. Did you want us to pursue?"

"No, we need to stick to the prison ship. Keep your eyes focused in case they reform and attack again."

"Yes, sir. Lt. Farthing, out."

Quaid smiled at Catarina as she still held her breath. "All over for the moment."

"I thought you said they were like a dog with a bone."

Drake chuckled. "They must have realized once we took out their command ship, this was Quaid's crack Black Crow Squadron. Rarely does anyone knowingly attack his squadron...not without a bigger force than they had."

**

Several hours later, the squadron arrived at Vaschon and Quaid studied the gray buildings clustered in groupings. Different crimes warranted different confinement facilities, and he considered a building set off from the rest filled with gardens.

Drake nodded. "That's the prison for the upper classes. Zaira would be staying there. They say it's really a rather high-classed social club."

"Zaira's coming home with me. You stay here. We may need to leave in a hurry. I sent the plans over to Lt.

Farthing via the particle manipulator in the event we need to take more rash measures."

Drake smiled. "It's not out of order?" He chuckled. "Never knew you to tell a lie before, but I was surprised it wouldn't be working. You usually keep your ship tip top."

"Yeah, well, it's not something I really wished to do, but I'd do anything to get Zaira back."

The rest of Quaid's crew refueled and inspected their crafts for damage, while Quaid hurried out of the Exiter and headed straight for the commandant's office. He soon arrived at the colonel's office and knocked at the doorjamb as the door stood open.

Colonel Sorenson stood, bowed to Quaid, then reached his hand out to him. "I'm honored, sir, to meet you in person. I've read all about your exploits in the Great Galaxy War, and I even have a son who serves under you."

"Ah, Lt. Sorenson. Hadn't made the connection. Fine young pilot." Quaid shook Col. Sorenson's hand with a firm grip.

"Yes, well rather an upstart I'm afraid. You've written him up twice."

Quaid smiled. "As I recall, he started a brawl with a Caspian at a pub on a neutral planet. Can't say as I blame him terribly. But we were all to have a little R & R. Instead, I spent several hours trying to get half of my fighter pilots freed from the local jail."

"And the other time?"

Clearing his throat, Quaid said, "Case of mistaken identity. When we were visiting Feronia for repairs, someone called Mason a Caspian spy and before anyone could clear up the matter, he knocked the fellow out. Kid's got a natural right hook."

Col. Sorenson shook his head. "Hot head."

"About the lady, sir..."

The commandant gestured to a chair while he sat behind his desk. "Pleasantries aside...time for business. My son asked to join your forces at Xenon. I wish for you to deny his request."

Quaid studied the man's gray hair and wrinkles carving ridges beneath his gray eyes. "But sir," Quaid said, "your son is one of my best fighter pilots. He was supposed to help me train Xenonian pilots in the art of defense and—"

"His mother and I want him home."

Quaid observed the man's no-nonsense expression. "Or else?"

"I've spoken with Carver Cole. He laughed when I told him his Minister of Defense had come for the prisoner, due to a mistake in the paperwork."

Twisting his mouth in annoyance, Quaid looked down at the commandant's desk. Red, purple, blue, green, yellow, and gray paperclips sat neatly in a tray, each layered one color upon its matching color. Zig-zags of the rainbow exploded across the commandant's computer monitor as it sat idly awaiting his attention. Otherwise, the desk was waxed to a glossy shine, but nothing else marred its surface. Paintings hung on the wall behind the commander, each displaying orange, yellow, blue or purple sunsets of different worlds. Every gold frame matched every other and each hung perfectly in place.

"Been here long?" Quaid asked.

"Long enough," the commandant said, this time as he resituated himself on his cushioned high-backed chair.

"What made you come here?"

"Failing eyesight. Couldn't fly anymore."

"But you flew for?"

"Forty-odd years."

"Ah." Quaid lifted a gray paper clip from the tray. "Xenon was just like this paperclip...gray and unappealing. Except for the important repair way-station located strategically in the galaxy, no one ever cared about the desert planet." Quaid snatched up a green paperclip, then rested it on top of the gray. "Then one day a young scientist...a true genius, discovered a way to turn that gray desert planet into a lush, green, vegetated paradise."

Quaid's considered the colonel as he could see he

held the older man's attention. Quaid leaned back in his chair and locked his fingers together on his lap. "The scientist was called mad, until he succeeded in doing what everybody said couldn't be done. Now he is the new Minister of Science. Unfortunately with the greening of the planet, the Rondovins have taken an interest in controlling Xenon.

"It is young men, like Martius Cole and your son, who prove they can make a difference. The Xenonians are a peaceful people. They cannot succeed without our help. While your son is able, give him this chance to show how he can shine. What would you have him do, if he didn't continue to serve as a Black Crow fighter pilot?"

A glimmer of a smile curved the old commandant's lips. "You are a true politician, sir. Yet at the risk of losing the woman you love, you chance angering me."

"True, I want more than anything in the world to take Zaira Cole home with me and to marry her again, only with her father's permission this time. But I believe I have your son's interest at heart as well when I say I would be proud to continue to serve with him."

Col. Sorenson leaned back in his chair, took a deep breath and exhaled with resignation. "All right, if my son truly wants to continue to serve you—"

"And Zaira?"

Col. Sorenson stared at the green and gray

paperclips sitting on the middle of his desk still, then reached over and lifted the green one. He placed it back on top of its matching colored clip. He fingered the gray one for a moment. "Sometimes matches are made in heaven, even when the two are as different as they can be." He set the gray clip on top of the green one in the container, then looked up at Quaid. "You've made your point...at least with me. No man would go to the lengths you have gone if you didn't love the woman as much as you do."

The colonel rested his arms on his desk. "You're very much like your father...likeable, level-headed, and extremely fast thinking in a crisis. My son worships you and I can now see why. You're a positive influence on a hot-headed kid."

Col. Sorenson stood. Quaid rose from his chair. "Cpt. Lassiter." The colonel offered his hand again. "You may have pulled off this fiasco with Zaira Cole here, but you still will have to deal with Caryndian Bach when you return to Xenon."

"Thank you, sir. I'm afraid I'll have to deal with her father too."

The colonel smiled broadly. "Carver Cole hasn't much of a sense of humor, I admit. Rarely saw him ever smile and when he did it was in such short supply, if you didn't catch it early on, it would disappear before you even caught notice of it. More than that, I have never, in my ten years of working here, ever heard him laugh."

"You think that's a good sign then?"

The colonel chuckled. "The best. I believe he was truly pleased you and his daughter would unite as one."

"But Caryndian Bach?"

"Watch out for that one. He'll be lying in wait for you upon your return...no doubt."

"I want to thank you again," Quaid said. "You've made me a very happy man."

"I believe the young lady had some part in that. You'll find her two doors down the hall on the left." The commandant signaled to the left side of his open doorway. The colonel bowed and Quaid mirrored his respect. "Be safe and try to keep my son safe too."

"I will try, sir."

Quaid hurried to the doorway, then walked into the hall. With nearly a panic to his step, he hastened to the appropriate door before the commandant could change his mind. He knocked on the door, but stepped back as Catarina answered it. "Where's—"

"I asked to see her and they brought me to this holding room." She moved aside.

Quaid saw Zaira. Her tearful eyes studied his expression. "Zaira," he said under his breath. She stood wringing her hands. He stalked to her, pulling her into his arms, and embraced her warmly. "You've been released to my care." He kissed the tear off her cheek.

"Don't cry. We're returning home."

He led her into the hall, and she said, "To mate with Caryndian Bach."

"Not on your life. You're the only one for me, and I'll have it no other way."

"Why are we walking so fast, Quaid?" she asked, as he pulled her at a quickened pace. "You aren't breaking me out of here, are you?" She glanced back to see if guards had been alerted yet, but only saw Catarina running to keep up with them.

Quaid smiled. "No, the commandant released you. He had a word with your father." Zaira frowned. Quaid pulled her to a stop, then lifted her chin and kissed her lips. "He laughed when he found out I had chased the prison ship all the way here and had tried to use my position as the new Minister of Defense to get you released." He pulled her toward the ship again.

"You did?"

"Sure enough. And I brought my own fleet of fighter pilots in case I had to lay siege to the place."

"No wonder the commandant gave me up."

Quaid smiled. "He couldn't stand seeing a lovesick pilot in such agony."

As they boarded the spacecraft, Quaid said, "Once I get the Exiter space borne, she's all yours, Drake. I have some unfinished business with the lady."

Zaira's eyes widened. "We can't, Quaid."

Quaid hurried to belt her into her seat while Catarina locked her belt into place. "Catarina said if we'd taken care of business before this, none of the rest of this would ever have happened."

"Before, yes. But by court edict now, I must have my father's consent."

"We'll talk about it once we're in the air." Quaid hastened to take his seat and as soon as he strapped himself in, he punched in the coordinates for Xenon.

The craft shook as the engines came into play and soon after they were airborne, Quaid said, "Computer, hail Lt. Farthing for me."

One of the communication buttons lighted up. Quaid touched the screen. "Lt. Farthing, destination Xenon. Keep a sharp lookout for Rondovin war birds."

"Yes sir! Lt. Farthing out."

"Computer, get me Lt. Sorenson."

When the button turned red, he pushed it and said, "Lt. Sorenson, you're good to go!"

"Yahoo!" the lieutenant yelled out, making everyone aboard the Exiter laugh.

"Lt. Sorenson, guess that means you're pleased. Hope you had a word with your parents before we left."

"Yes, sir. Spent some good time with my mother; said goodbye to my dad. He was never much for words when it came to me."

"Great to have you back."

"Thank you, sir. Lt. Sorenson, out."

"Computer."

"Yes, Captain."

"Get me Carver Cole."

The panel lighted. "This is Cpt. Lassiter, may I speak with Carver Cole, please?" Static filtered back. He frowned. "I'll have to try that again when we get a little closer to Xenon. Could be storms are causing the interference. Computer, any messages?"

"Three. Two for Carylian Siding, one for laser facial tucks."

Drake frowned. "Beats me how those sales hackers can reach folks in deep space the way they do."

"Take the helm, Drake. I wish a word alone with my mate-to-be."

Catarina moved into Quaid's seat and smiled at Zaira. "I told you so, Zaira."

"So you did." Zaira took Quaid's hand. "But only talk, Quaid," she said as they headed for a room.

CHAPTER 18

Quaid escorted Zaira as they walked down the passageway to the quarters. "You know, Zaira, when I close my eyes your deep amber eyes beckon me. I smell the scent of your jasmine lingering in the air, and feel your soft fingertips on my scruffy beard. The sweet taste of your lips, the flavor of brown sugar, tantalizes me. And your words, whether spoken in anger or spoken softly with desire, touch me like no other."

He pushed the button to the door, and Zaira studied his fingers interlocked around hers. "But I'm a changeling and from time to time—"

"And a most ravishing one at that. How could a man ever get so lucky?"

Zaira frowned at him as he closed the door behind them. "You haven't been drinking Orion ale, have you?"

"Nary a drop. I'm as sober as a Xenonian living on

your dry planet when Drake hasn't sneaked liquor into the place." Quaid pulled her close and kissed one cheek with a tender touch, then the other. "I'm in love with you, Zaira, like I've never been before with any other woman. Marry me, and I'll do my best to please you for the rest of our lives."

"Aren't you afraid I'll grow saber-tooth fangs and bite you when I'm angry?" She couldn't believe Quaid's change of heart. She still wasn't sure she could trust him if she should turn, and he was afraid to see what she could do.

"It's a risk I'm willing to take." He brushed her dark hair away from her cheek and leaned over and kissed her. "I love you just the way you are...whatever the form." He glanced down at her black dress and turned her around and looked for the buttons.

"What are you doing?" Zaira asked, really believing they were only going to talk. That he was going to ask her father's permission first.

"How do you get this thing off?"

She smiled. "We can only talk."

"You told me once how you grow too hot if you wear too many clothes. I'm trying to make you more comfortable."

She smiled a little. "Martius told me he thought maybe the trial would be called off once he saw you climb out of our bed naked. When he read my thoughts, he realized you still had not pleasured me and it was time to end the relationship."

"Gravest mistake I ever made." Quaid rested his hands on her waist. "I wanted to do this right. I wanted to ask your father first, but I'm not chancing it. How do I get you out of this dress? There are no fasteners."

"It just slides off."

He studied the contour of her breasts beneath the stretchy fabric. "Good." He pulled Zaira to the bed, then lay her back down. "If you will not aid me, I shall have to work alone." He removed her shoes.

"I cannot help you, Quaid. We must wait. Caryndian will want to kill you, you know."

"That's a hazard of the kind of job I do." Quaid jerked off his shirt and tossed it on the floor.

She ran her hands over his legs, trying to remember all the books she'd read where men and women pleasured each other and what they had done at this juncture. She could smell his lusty pheromones interested in her just as much as hers craved feeling him inside her. But he couldn't smell them like she could. Even so, he seemed to be just as turned on by her as she was by him. So maybe his kind could still smell the heightened interest, but it just didn't register for them, and he wouldn't realize what was creating the craving.

She moved her hand to his trousers and stroked his erection through his pants.

He groaned and quickly sat beside her so he could remove his boots and socks. She ran her hand over his smooth, muscular arm and leaned down to kiss the mark of the royal house of Orion. "You are beautiful."

"You are the one who is beautiful." He stood and removed his trousers and boxer briefs, his voice rough with need.

She stared at the sight of his arousal, so proud and ready, dark short curly hairs framing it. She reached out to touch him, and he moved her hand to grasp him and then slide her fingers down the length of it. It felt rigid and yet velvety and she smiled.

He pulled her into his arms, and kissed her then, not sweetly like before, but like a man who was claiming her for his own. She pressed her mouth against his, her body reacting to his as much as his was reacting to hers. Her nipples felt taut against his bare chest, his hand sliding up her dress and lifting her leg around his. She anchored her leg around his, feeling the eroticism of his fingers sliding up her dress until he found her short curls and he stopped.

His mouth curved against hers. "You aren't wearing anything under the dress? I hope that meant you believed I would come to rescue you."

"I wasn't sure. Martius said you would. But I wasn't sure."

"No one will ever take you from me again." He

kissed her deeply this time, his tongue stroking hers, and she felt as though she would melt right through the ship's hull.

Her breath was unsteady, her heart beating spastically as she kissed him back, her leg rubbing against his, her hand in his hair, holding him close as she barely breathed, loving his touch, loving him.

"I love you," he said, his lips parting from hers, his eyes darkened to midnight. "I shouted it before the whole noisy gathering."

"I heard."

"Over all that noise?"

She smiled. "I told you. I have very sensitive hearing, but I also have selective hearing. When I heard you call out to me that you loved me..." She sighed. "I could only hope you would do something about it. And knowing something of your history, I knew you always go after what you want. I just hoped that might mean me."

"God, Zaira, I was such a fool. I knew it then, standing before the magistrate and the circus he put on." Quaid pulled her leg higher and kissed her again.

She felt sexy and loved like she'd never felt before. She had hoped from the first time she'd seen him, he would be hers and make her fantasy come true. And this was just as she had dreamed.

His hand slid between her legs, and he began

stroking her. No matter how much she'd read about this between couples, she never imagined how this could really feel. The way he was kissing her, stroking her, his free hand cupping the back of her head as he had his wicked way with her.

But she was kissing him just as much, her tongue stroking his, her hands combing through his hair, her body tight with need. She kept waiting for him to remove her gown, but he didn't. Instead, he continued to stroke her until she felt as though she'd fly away to another galaxy. The climax hit her, waves of pleasure rocking her, and she cried out. He quickly covered her mouth with his, kissing her, leaning her back against the bed, sliding her dress up her body in a slow and sensuous way until he pulled it over her head and tossed it aside.

For a moment, he stared at her body. "Exquisite. Art." Then he began kissing her all over again. Only this time, he began licking and suckling each of her breasts, making her beg him to finish her off before she couldn't take any more.

Boneless, she licked the shell of his ear and nibbled on it. She was ready for him to join with her, the final act of mating.

Quaid couldn't believe he was mating Zaira, a national treasure if there was any on Xenon. He couldn't believe she had chosen him over anyone else she could have had on the planet. He couldn't believe he was truly doing this when he had sworn he would never marry anyone ever.

But he wouldn't give her up for the world.

He knew he said he'd wait and get her father's permission first, but he had tried already and there was no way in hell he was going to take her home before he had mated her and could tell the world she was his when they arrived.

"This might be a little uncomfortable," he warned, cognizant that she was a maid and had never been with a man before. He didn't want to ruin her first time.

"I am ready. Make love to me. Mate me. Be mine so I can be yours."

He pressed the tip of his erection slowly inside her, and broke the membrane that changed her forever from virgin to mate. He pushed deeper, allowing her to stretch and surround him with her slick heat. She breathed in and breathed out as if she was trying to relax or work through the discomfort.

Her hands slid over his bare buttocks and he couldn't hold back any longer and pushed all the way in. He paused and she smiled up at him. "You. Are. Beautiful."

He smiled at her and kissed her mouth, his tongue tangling with hers and began to thrust his cock inside her, unable to stop the inevitable. He would give her time to heal and then he was pleasuring her as much as she would love him to.

She smelled of jasmine and of musk, of her special sweet and spicy scent. She tasted sweet and tangy, and she was velvety softness to his hardness. He still couldn't believe she had brought his spacecraft to Xenon so that he would help her to protect her people. He couldn't believe she had spied him one day, and had wanted this between them ever since seeing him that day. No one had ever been that interested in him.

She was a fantasy in the flesh, and she was his.

He was thrusting hard, ready to come, when he realized they hadn't used any kind of protection. But he couldn't pull out now. He couldn't hurt her with the knowledge he didn't want children right away, maybe never. He wanted to get to know her, to love her, and to enjoy this time between them first.

One time without protection wouldn't hurt anything. Statistically speaking, he knew the chances they'd make a baby without using protection would be infinitesimal.

And then he came, satisfaction filling him that she was fully and duly his. In a million light years, he would never have thought he'd want to make such a claim.

She wrapped her arms around him and hugged him to her body. "I love you," she whispered, tears in her eyes. "Prince of Orion. I love you."

"Zaira," he said, sighed, and rolled onto his back and pulled her into his arms. She rested her head on his chest and ran her fingers over his skin. He kissed the top of her head, wrapped his arms around her, and embraced her warmly. "I couldn't have asked for a better mate." Quaid squeezed her tightly, then ran his fingers over her back, tracing the contours.

"Nor could I have." Zaira kissed his chest.

"You don't regret not having waited?"

"No." She shook her head and her hair tickled his chin.

He took a deep breath. "Nor do I. I need to return to the helm before we arrive at Xenon."

"Yes," she said softly.

"Do you need any help with your dress?"

She rolled off him. Glancing down at his legs, she smiled, then kissed his cheek. "Go captain your ship. I'll join you in a moment."

He studied her breasts for a moment half hidden by her dark hair, then leaned over and kissed each with a tender touch. "More later." He kissed her mouth firmly. She kissed him back. He ran his hand through her hair. "Got to go. We should be in Xenonian airspace momentarily."

He tugged on his boxer briefs, then his trousers. After zipping them, he watched Zaira pull her dress over her head, the rest of her beautiful body on full display. He grabbed his shirt and buttoned the buttons. He was ready to make love to her all night through, but only when she was ready again.

She slid her dress down over her breasts, the nipples pressing against the black fabric. "You are a sight." He ran his hands over her firm breasts again, kissed her cheek, then hurried to the door. He glanced back at her. "I was...curious about something, Zaira."

"Yes?"

"You said when we first met that you didn't wish to marry anyone."

"When a woman tells a man she's interested in she doesn't wish to marry, the man often decides he wishes to marry her."

Quaid chuckled. "I will never understand women as long as I live. We need to be buckled in soon."

"Yes." She continued to pull her dress down.

He looked at the distance she still had to go with the fabric. "A wondrous sight." Then he pushed the button for the door and hurried out into the hall as the door whooshed open. Before it closed shut, he turned to her. "I love you, Zaira."

She smiled back at him. "As I do you."

Then the door closed, and Quaid hastened to his seat while Catarina switched to one of the other chairs. She studied Quaid for a moment, then her eyes drifted back to the hallway that housed the bedchamber.

Drake watched Quaid for a moment as he touched the screen. "So?"

Quaid smiled. "Still works."

Drake laughed. "Hell, I'm glad to hear it."

Zaira stepped onto the bridge. Catarina jumped up from her seat, her eyes widening and she let out a slight gasp. Quaid and Drake turned to see Catarina hurry over to Zaira, then hug her warmly. "Congratulations," she whispered.

Zaira kissed her cheek. "Thank you, Catarina."

Quaid furrowed his brow as he tried to tell what had changed about Zaira. Catarina continued to stare at Zaira, but then she returned to her seat while Zaira sat down on her own.

Drake shrugged. "Must be a woman thing," he said under his breath to Quaid. "Losing their virginity. You know."

Zaira was looking out the window. Catarina reached over and patted her hand, and Zaira looked up to see Quaid studying her. Then he saw what had changed about her. Her eyes were no longer amber, but emerald green.

Turning back to stare out his window, Quaid considered the implications. *Catarina's eyes have remained brown, but she's certainly been pleasured by Drake already.* Quaid looked back at Zaira, but her gaze focused on the window beside her. Catarina, however, watched his actions with interest.

He took a deep breath and considered the dark space in front of them. Zaira was a changeling. But so was Catarina. Carver Cole would realize at once that Quaid had pleasured her without his permission.

"Computer," Quaid said with an anxious rush to his voice.

"Cpt. Lassiter."

"Get me Carver Cole." Quaid sighed deeply. "This is Cpt. Lassiter of the Exiter. May I speak to Carver Cole?" There was a garbled response and Quaid frowned. "Messages aren't getting through." He considered the planet that grew as he neared its inner atmosphere. "Computer, atmospheric condition on Xenon."

"Storms plague southern hemisphere. Northern hemisphere clear."

Quaid stared out the window. "Carver is in the Northern hemisphere. Storms aren't causing the static."

Drake said, "Sounds like the Rondovins are wreaking havoc with the communication's systems on the planet."

"Computer, Rondovin activity on the planet."

There was some silence, then the computer said, "Three dozen war birds located at coordinates delta five, alpha seven. Troop strength of 5,000, coordinates echo six, tango three. Scout ships scattered throughout the northern hemisphere. Six-thousand soldiers, coordinates, foxtrot seven, zulu twelve..."

Wrinkling his brow, Quaid said, "Doesn't sound good."

"Cpt. Lassiter, I must interrupt previous request for data to inform you, Caspian war birds spotted and closing on your location."

"Computer, get me Lt. Farthing."

"Lt. Farthing here, sir."

"Caspian war birds approaching. Raise shields and ready for evasive action."

"Sir?"

"Do it! Cpt. Lassiter, out."

"Yes, sir. Lt. Farthing, out."

"Lt. Sorenson here, sir. You can't mean to tuck tail and run, sir. I mean—"

"Lt. Sorenson."

"Yes, sir."

"Our mission here at Xenon is to defend, not affect offensive maneuvers."

"Yes, sir."

"Cpt. Lassiter, out."

"Lt. Sorenson, out."

Drake chuckled. "He's a hard case."

"Computer, hail Caspian command ship."

"This is Cpt. Pfelsman, of the Caspian Rejuvenator, Cpt. Quaid Lassiter of the Exiter and Minister of Defense of Xenon. What do you wish?"

"Cooperation in a concerted effort against the Rondovins."

A long pause ensued and Quaid fingered the communication's button as he considered making a stronger appeal.

"What will you have us do?" the Caspian commander finally responded.

"Three dozen Rondovin war birds are situated at coordinates: delta five, alpha seven. If we could make a coordinated effort, my ships will take out the western most region, while yours head for the eastern portion of the plains. If we can get them while they're still on the ground, the better off we'll be."

"You have initiated a plan to end the Great Galaxy War, Cpt. Lassiter, I understand."

"Yes, Cpt. Pfelsman. I've already requested that all Orion forces halt hostilities in the war. Those who ally with us have also ceased operations."

"Good. We will join you. Barashon," the commander said.

"Barashon," Quaid said, then shut off communications.

"Can we trust them?" Drake squirmed in his seat slightly.

"What I worry about is can we trust Lt. Sorenson?" Quaid touched the button, then pushed it. "Lt.

Sorenson."

"Sir."

"The Caspians are joining us against the Rondovins."

"Yes, sir!"

***

As they neared Xenon, Quaid turned back to see Zaira's eyes grow big. "Take the helm," he said to Drake, then jumped out of his seat. "Zaira, you can wait back in my chambers until we finish with this mess."

She looked over at Catarina who smiled back at her. "The last conflict they were involved in was quite spectacular."

Quaid took Zaira's hand in his. "You don't have to be up here—"

"I'll stay with my husband." Her left hand gripped the armrest of her chair.

"But, Zaira..."

She glanced out the window to see Lt. Farthing's craft sailing beside them, positioned as their right wing ship. Quaid leaned over and kissed her cheek. "Close your eyes if it bothers you too much." She gave him a strained smile, her eyes shadowed in fear. He touched her hair, then returned to his seat. "Okay, Drake, since the crafts will be earthbound with no shields raised, you'll only need to target them with number two cannons." Pointing his finger at the button, he said, "It's the green one. Target the ion propulsion drive. Keep 'em from getting airborne."

Drake fingered the button. "Piece of cake." He glanced back at Catarina who puckered her lips and whispered a kiss to him. Grinning, he turned back to the controls. "Just tell me when."

As the ships swooped into the blue-blanketed atmosphere of Xenon, Quaid dove the Exiter toward one of the command ships of prey. Several of the Black Crow pilots maneuvered in the same manner as they targeted the command ships in a methodical way. Fireballs erupted from seven idle craft as laser fire slammed into the engine components. Blasts of debris shot into the atmosphere while Quaid turned the ship upward in a wide arc. When the Exiter returned to the scene of the parked crafts, he aimed for the next Rondovin command ship in his line of sight. What appeared like miniature-sized Rondovins dashed about the grassy field in a panic as some tried to reach the unmanned craft.

Zaira took a deep breath. "I suppose you can't use some kind of stun mechanism on the ships."

Quaid said, "Drake fire the cannons at the command ship."

As the Rondovin ship lifted off the ground, the missiles dove beneath the hull and Quaid swore. His attention remained on the Rondovin ship attempting to flee their wrath. "Blue button," he said, glancing at Drake. "Undoubtedly they've raised their shields."

Streaks of light flared through the sky when the cannon targeted the Rondovin ship, Quaid frowned to see the projectile had no effect on the craft. "The ship must be protected by a new type of shield stolen undoubtedly from some other world." When the ship fired upon them in retaliation, the blast shook the Exiter and Zaira screamed out in surprise. "Can't penetrate our shields." He twisted his mouth in thought. "Haven't tried this in a while. Everyone hold tight." He turned the craft sharply skyward, then wheeled back toward the Rondovin war bird.

With contact imminent, Drake said, "Didn't know you played chicken, Quaid."

"Only in my youth," he said, as the edge of his craft approached the hull of the Rondovins' ship. "Not sure this will work with this bunch."

"Did you want me to do anything?"

"Just hold tight."

"You can't be meaning to run into their craft with yours." Zaira was holding tight to the arms of the chair.

"Hadn't intended to." Quaid pointed at the canyons the Rondovins approached.

"You aren't going to run them into the cliffs—"

"Make them set down, rather. Once they're sitting on the ground, the shields no longer work. They stole our shield technology before we worked out the bugs."

"But this ship has a more advance shield system that—" Drake said.

Quaid narrowed his eyes. "Hadn't considered that."

The Rondovin ship tried to lift over the wall of the rugged canyon. Quaid pinned them in from up above.

"They're turning east down the canyon," Drake said.

Quaid nodded. "They won't cooperate." He lowered his vehicle, nearly resting it on top of the Rondovin's craft. A bang resounded. "Whoops, a little too close."

"They're diving."

"That's what I like to see."

The Rondovin bird swooped near the base of the canyon while Quaid snuggled next to their roof like a parasite attached to its prey. The canyon snaked along the once desert plain.

Zaira pointed in the direction dead ahead. "It twists sharply to the left just ahead."

"Can't see that it does, Zaira." Quaid stared at the canyon stretching straight for several more miles.

"The rock formations are green at that point instead of red. It gives the optical illusion that the canyon continues through the vegetation, but it turns sharply right."

"Emeralds?" He studied the shimmering green

lights sparkling in the sun.

"You must lift this thing, Quaid!" Zaira dug her fingernails into the armrests. "Now!"

CHAPTER 19

"We'll lose them for sure if we let go of them now." Quaid took a deep breath, then lifted the Exiter over the edge of the cliff, scraping the edge of the green crystals. A ball of fire exploded over the top of the canyon. Quaid turned his craft around and flew back over the site. "Glad you hadn't retired to my chamber, Zaira." He studied the scattered remnants of the craft, then headed back to the main area of battle.

"Maybe I can be your navigator."

He smiled.

When they arrived at the scene, fires still raged throughout the metal-warped skeletons of Rondovin spacecraft.

The communication panel lighted up. "Cpt. Lassiter."

"Lt. Farthing, sir. All of our ships are accounted for.

The Caspians have headed for Riverine. Only three Rondovin ships reached the sky, except for the one you tackled. Feronian pilots took off after them and were able to stop their exodus."

"Good, Lt. Farthing. Have everyone pilot their crafts to Riverine. Meeting in an hour. Cpt. Lassiter, out."

Zaira took a deep breath.

Quaid smiled. "Are you all right?"

"Yes, Quaid. Only now we have to see my father."

Quaid took a deep breath this time as he considered her emerald eyes.

Drake raise his brows at him.

"Not a word, Drake. Not one word."

After parking his vehicle in the hangar at Riverine, Drake and Catarina hurried off to her home, while Zaira led Quaid to her father's estates. They entered the flower gardens, and she reached for Quaid's hand. Tea-scented roses tantalized the visitors as they wound their way along the curving stone path. They walked beneath a wrought-iron trellis jasmine vines climbing all over it. Zaira squeezed his hand. He leaned over and kissed her upturned lips.

They paused for a moment more as they deepened the kiss, then he stiffened his back as he considered the silver dome of Carver's home. "Your hand is sweaty." She lifted it to her lips and kissed it. "My father shouldn't be too angry with you over me. You've made such progress with the Rondovin threat, helped to bring the scrolls to the High Council, and—"

"Pleasured his daughter without his permission when the court edict is in place." Quaid studied the dome looming nearby and breathed a heavy sigh. "I tried to communicate with him, Zaira. You know I did. I just couldn't get through."

She tugged at him. "Come on, Quaid. Remember, there's no killing allowed on Xenon, and he needs you as his defense minister."

Quaid walked her toward the house again. The glass reflected their images and he touched his bearded cheek. "Are you certain I shouldn't have shaved first? Everyone on Xenon is so clean-shaven. Well, I mean, they can't even grow beards. Don't you think I look a bit like a barbarian?"

She snuggled her head against his arm. "I like the look, my husband. People's differences make them interesting. Not their sameness."

He stopped and pulled Zaira close. "I don't know why I ever hesitated in the first place to mate with you. Maybe we should return to the Exiter and…"

Laughing, Zaira said, "He won't bite as hard as the spiders. Come on, Quaid. Let's get this over with, and then I'll show you my estates." She waved to the south.

Quaid looked in that direction and frowned to see a smaller silver dome-building next door. "Not right next door to your father's place."

"That way they can keep an eye on me. And you too now." She smiled and tugged him to the entrance of her father's house. The glass slid open and Quaid stared in awe at the lavish furnishings. Shimmering gold and blue satin-cushioned chairs clustered together in the commons. Drapes of blues and golds intertwined with ropes of gold holding them back against the all-glass walls. Strips of metal connecting the glass, arched toward the top of the dome and in the center, a gold medallion embossed with the figure of a woman in long, flowing gowns stood on a pedestal. Her long dark hair reached her hips while her slender fingers held the scrolls up to the heavens in an act of triumph. "Seal of the office of the President of the High Council," Zaira said.

"Zenith?"

She nodded.

A carpet centered in the middle of the commons was woven predominately in gold and blues, shaded from light to dark. He studied the picture created in the silk threads of a dragon flying across the blue sky with its wings outstretched in all of their glory. "Martius?"

"Ah-huh." She wrapped her arm through his and led him into her father's office. Zaira curtsied to her father, then clasped her hands together as she waited for him to greet her. He studied her eyes for a moment, then nodded and turned to Quaid. "I see you have pleasured my daughter." Carver's thin lips indicated no emotion.

"Sir, I tried to contact you—"

"Rondovins had tied up the communication channels out here."

"Yes, and I tried several times—"

"Take a seat."

"Yes, sir." Quaid sat in a high-backed chair Carver motioned to. Zaira had taken a seat across the room. She folded her hands on her lap in resignation.

"I take it you have some plans in mind for our defensive measures after your little jaunt across the galaxy?"

"Sir, I do, but I need to speak with you about Zaira, first."

"Zaira is fine."

Zaira watched him with a solemn expression on her face. He faced Carver. "With all due respect, sir, I must ask your permission to mate Zaira."

Carver sat in his chair as his eyebrows rose a bit while his lips hinted at amusement. He turned to Zaira who smiled broadly at him. "Seems my daughter has failed to confide my wishes to you. I gave her permission to marry you once Commander Sorenson called me to say you were intending to release her from prison at all costs with your Black Crow Squadron sitting in the wings."

Zaira smiled back at him.

Quaid took a deep breath. "Ah, it was a slight oversight on her part, I'm sure." He smiled at her. He would get even. "As to the defensive measures, the Black Crow Squadron pilots are instituting training missions with Xenonian pilots as we speak and the Caspians have agreed to help with the effort. Only three of the Rondovin ships were able to get airborne, but Feronian fighters, allied with Orion, arrived to knock them out of orbit. Seems that bringing the Great Galaxy War to a screeching halt has left some fighter pilots begging for another chance to play war games."

"I knew the council had found the right man for the job when we voted for you to be our Minister of Defense." Carver observed Zaira, then he smiled and stood. "Good, then I'll let you get on with business."

Quaid strode across the floor to shake Carver's hand, then turned and walked over to Zaira. He helped her up from her seat, frowned at her, then held her arm as he headed for the door.

"Be safe," Carver said.

"And you," Quaid said.

Zaira bowed her head slightly to her father, then Quaid pulled her through the doorway.

He walked at a quickened pace, and she glanced up to see his set chin. "You were unworthy, Quaid. You had to prove how much you truly wished to have me as your mate."

He walked several more steps before he burst out laughing. She stared up at him with confusion. "What is wrong?"

He leaned down and kissed her lips. "I thought your father was going to have me barbecued for mating his daughter without his permission, when all along he had already given you the authorization." He wrapped his arm around her shoulders as they walked side-by-side. "You knew then that I was coming to take you home?"

"No. My father only said he gave me permission to marry you. Not the reason why."

Quaid raised a brow.

"Are you angry with me?"

"I never get mad. I just get even."

"Oh?"

Quaid laughed again and his hearty laughter rang through the corridors. She smiled as she leaned against his shoulder. "I love you too, Quaid."

***

Two days later, Quaid hunched over the glass table across from Drake situated in Zaira's kitchen. He glanced out the window at Carver's silver dome looming heavenward next door. Drake grinned. "How does it feel to be living beside your father-in-law's estates in Riverine?"

Quaid chuckled as he took a deep breath of the roses scenting the air while minty-chocolate coffee bubbled away on a warmer nearby. The lilting of pipe flutes and harp-like string instruments played softly in the background, but the two men remained silent as they considered their next move.

"I can't believe Caryndian Bach didn't say anything to you about you mating Zaira," Drake said.

"He's biding his time." Quaid didn't believe for a minute that the magistrate had given up on Zaira.

Zaira resettled on a plump purple pillow in the commons, then moved a purple checker across a board. Catarina frowned at the tactic as she rested her chin on her hands. She leaned over and shifted a yellow checker to her chosen spot. Zaira smiled as she jumped Catarina's checker with her own, then removed the yellow chip to rest with the remaining captured legion of soldiers.

Drake drummed his fingers in a rhythmic pattern as he copied the plunking of the hallowin strings, then sighed deeply.

"I don't know." Quaid fingered the handle to his coffee cup as the fragrance of mint-chocolate rose from the steamy liquid. "I'd had the whole plan worked out in my mind until I learned Caryndian Bach had risked his own safety to save three women."

"A ruse, no doubt," Drake said. "Consider this, the

women had been cut off from their escape route. How did Caryndian get word of this so quickly? And how was he able to sneak through enemy lines without a scratch to any of them, not to mention evading capture?"

Quaid nodded. "From what I've heard, it's not in his character at all to have done such a thing."

"Of course he has no idea we know about his collusion with the Rondovins, but he may have done the deed, just in case any suspicion had been aroused. Particularly as several have voiced concern that the Rondovins arrived so shortly after the greening of the planet."

"But we have no proof." Quaid sipped his coffee. Setting his cup down on the polished table, he licked the minty flavor from his lips.

Catarina moved her yellow checker. "Aha, got you this time, Zaira!"

Zaira nodded, then lifted her chip and pounced once, twice, thrice. As she collected the conquered yellow chips, Catarina groaned. "Ahhh, Zaira, I should know not to play this game with you."

Drake tapped his finger on the table. "I've never known you to be without a plan, Quaid."

"Okay, maybe we're looking at this all wrong. Why would Caryndian Bach risk his position as high magistrate to help the Rondovins?"

"Maybe," Zaira said, "Caryndian Bach has been

offered a higher position...president of the High Council, perhaps?"

Quaid and Drake stared at Zaira. Quaid lifted his cup of coffee. "Stick to your game, Zaira. You're not to be listening to our slanderous conversation—you promised."

Zaira smiled as Catarina jumped one of her pieces with her checker. "Good, I've at least got two." She glanced at Zaira's collection of eight captured yellow checkers.

"Nobody would agree to Caryndian's being president of the High Council," Drake said, as he considered Zaira's notion.

"Of course not. The Rondovins wouldn't agree to a High Council, period," Quaid said.

Zaira moved a checker to a new square and Catarina studied the move for a moment, then looked up at her. "What did you do that for?"

Zaira smiled. "I like to win."

Quaid finished his drink. "Got any more coffee, Zaira?"

"For the calming effect?" Zaira watched Catarina make her move. As soon as her fingertips released her yellow checker, Zaira jumped four of her checkers. "I win."

"Okay, three out of five."

"Sure." Zaira jumped up from her pillow and walked

to the kitchen. She ran her hand over Quaid's shoulder. "You wanted something from me?"

"More of that coffee, if you don't mind."

"What will you do for me, if I get you another cup?"

Quaid wrinkled his brow. "Zaira, we're having a rather important discussion here."

Zaira raised her brows as she folded her arms across her chest. Jasmine scented the air around him as she studied him with her beautiful green eyes. They twinkled in the soft light and he rose leaned over, smiled, and kissed her. "Coffee, Zaira."

Zaira walked over to the warmer.

Drake smiled a little at him as if he knew Quaid wasn't getting away with anything concerning the lady.

"How could the Rondovins have gotten to him?" Quaid asked him.

"Why would he have gone against his own people?" Drake drummed his fingers in a new beat this time.

"Does it matter?" Zaira set the fresh cup of coffee before Quaid.

Quaid looked up at her. "Of course it matters. If we knew why he did it, we may have some clue as to how."

"He's not Xenonian." Zaira returned to the commons and dropped to her purple cushion.

"What?"

"He's not a Xenonian. Like you, he was made a citizen, but he's not truly a Xenonian by birth."

Quaid scratched his head. "He's not a Rondovin. His facial features are too dissimilar."

"Wait a minute," Drake said. "Remember the sales message you had on the Exiter when we were trying to rescue a damsel in distress? You know, the one about laser surgery?" Drake leaned back in his chair. "Why I've seen them transform a skinny-lipped Feronian woman into a perfectly sexy, full-lipped Xenonian woman. And I've seen pictures taken of a Caspian's large-nose shaved down to a button-sized Feronian nose, though I could never fathom why anyone would wish such a thing." He ran his finger along his Roman-shaped nose with pride.

"I don't know," Quaid said, as he considered the idea. "Sounds a little far-fetched to me. How can we ever prove that sort of thing?"

Zaira moved her checker piece, then studied Catarina's placement of her yellow checker.

"We need to search his quarters for evidence," Drake said.

"Can't," Zaira said. "Illegal search."

"Whose side are you on, Zaira?" Quaid asked with annoyance.

"Don't believe that coffee is having a calming effect on you, Quaid." Zaira moved her purple checker.

Drake tapped his fingers again. "I don't know, Quaid. We've been mulling this thing over for two days with no closer solution to the problem. We've got spies out just waiting for communications between Caryndian and his Rondovin cohorts, but nothing has come of it."

"What if we were to set a trap for him? Send a message to him as though we were Rondovins and wait for him to respond?"

"My Rondovin is rather rusty."

"Entrapment." Zaira jumped her checker over Catarina's and captured her first piece.

"Play your game, Zaira," Quaid said.

Zaira smiled.

"I honestly don't see what you're getting at, Zaira." Catarina rubbed her forehead. "You can't possibly get me from there."

"Not likely," Zaira said.

Catarina moved her checker tentatively while Zaira readied her posture as though she were ready to pounce. Catarina looked up at her and grinned. "You're making me nervous."

"That's my purpose." Zaira glanced to see the two men studying her. "What?"

Quaid and Drake exchanged looks. "We could make him nervous," Quaid said. "What if we…" He paused as Zaira and Catarina watched him. "Your game, Zaira." He rose from the table. "Want to go for a walk with me, Drake?"

"Sounds like a plan to me, Quaid."

***

Early the next morning, Quaid pulled on his flight jacket and leaned over to kiss Zaira as she appeared to be sleeping. She reached up and grabbed his shoulders. "Be careful, my love."

He kissed her soundly against the mouth. "I'll return soon, Zaira. Just got to take care of a little business."

"Caryndian has got a lot of friends, Quaid."

He nodded and squeezed her tightly, then kissed her forehead. "I'll be back shortly."

The door closed behind him to his bedchamber, and Catarina clung to Drake's arm. His eyes grew wide as Catarina's eyes had the same green cast now to them that Zaira's had. She smiled back at him.

Drake embraced her warmly as he kissed her hard on the mouth, then whispered into her ear, "Keep it warm for me."

"Always, Drake."

Quaid pushed the button to the door. "I'll try to keep him safe."

"And he, you," Catarina said.

"She's a shifter?" Quaid asked.

The door shut behind them and Quaid and Drake hurried to the hangar that sheltered the Exiter. "Yeah. Just like Zaira. Glad you stayed with us last night." Quaid looked over at Drake.

"Yeah, well, we appreciated you inviting us. Nothing worse than having no water in the place and nobody to fix it until tomorrow."

"Sir!" a young man shouted. Lt. Sorenson ran across the compound to join them. "I understand you're on a super-secret mission. Can I come too?"

"If it's so super-secret, how come you know about it?"

The lieutenant's ears turned slightly red. "Well, I sort of eavesdropped on you and Cpt. Jorgenson, beg your pardon, sir, yesterday, when you were walking in Carver Cole's private gardens."

Quaid regarded Drake who mirrored his look of concern. "What were you doing there?" Quaid asked the lieutenant.

"Carver Cole had me...well, he was concerned someone else might hear what you had to say. He knew right away you wished to keep your conversation secret from your mates to keep them safe from harm. But he was concerned someone loyal to you-know-who"—Lt. Sorenson's gaze darted around the spacious landing strip for any sign of Caryndian or his friends—"might have sneaked into his gardens to hear what you had to say. I was to protect you at all costs. Shoot to kill, were the orders given me by the president of the council himself."

"Zaira or Martius must have told Carver what we

heard the Rondovins say then. He must believe that we speak the truth," Quaid said to Drake.

"Aye, sir," Lt. Sorenson said. "Can I come with you?"

"Come on, Lieutenant." Quaid slapped him on the shoulder.

Drake frowned. "Are you certain? Don't you think we can handle this ourselves? I thought we were to hit the communications—"

"The Black Crow Squadron will create a diversion. Rondovin troops settled in around Kranobia Village will be where we make our move."

"But you said—"

"Get Lt. Farthing for me, Lt. Sorenson."

"Yes, sir!" Lt. Sorenson did a skip in the air, then dashed off to the Black Crow Squadron fighter pilot quarters nearby.

"What about help from the Caspians?"

"They're busy with the southern hemisphere where Rondovin ships continue to try to land supplies for their stranded troops. The Caspians have got their mission books full for the moment."

"And the Feronians?"

"Got them working on gathering up a Corp of Rondovins trekking through the western canyons."

"Guess that leaves just us."

The pilots of the squadron dashed out of their quarters with exuberance. Quaid smiled to see them pull on jackets or button shirts while their jackets were tucked securely under their arms. "Good crew. Go ahead and board."

The men saluted him while running past him, and Quaid saluted back. But the view of white robes sweeping the ground as the magistrate walked in their direction made Quaid groan inwardly at the unwelcome sight. He poked Drake's arm. "Here comes real trouble."

"Greetings, Cpt. Quaid Lassiter!" Caryndian Bach shouted as he strode across the compound. Quaid watched for any indication that Caryndian walked with a Rondovin stride, but not seeing any, concentrated on his build. He was certainly taller than an average Rondovin. Quaid's eyes drifted down to Caryndian's shoes. Definitely had some height to them. He looked back up and considered the man's neck. Hard to tell. He wore a high-necked collar that flared out from the center. Traditional magistrate garb.

As the man reached Quaid, he bowed slightly. Quaid and Drake greeted him in the same manner.

"I see you have a mission planned this morning."

"Kind of an impromptu affair."

Carynidan smiled. "Secret mission?"

"Not very. Don't think our hitting the Rondovins at Kranobia should come as a surprise to anyone."

Quaid noticed a definite lift in Caryndian's gray brows.

"Certainly, last major stronghold of the Rondovins," Caryndian said. "Well, be safe."

"I intend to be." Quaid bowed his head to Caryndian. The magistrate did the same, then turned and hastened back to his offices. As he grew diminutive in appearance, Quaid grabbed Drake's arm and hurried to the ship.

"Don't understand you," Drake said, "one bit. Why did you give our plans away?"

Quaid smiled. "I told you. My squadron will act as a diversion. They've just been waiting for me to give the go ahead. Caryndian will know Kranobia Village is the only major concentration of the enemy left for our forces to strike."

"He'll send word to them now—"

"They don't have the defensive measures to repel the attack."

Quaid ran up the steps into his craft and smiled at the squadron. "I think you all probably know where we're headed."

The young men all nodded.

"I've already discussed the plan of formation. You know what to do, so let's do it."

The men hurried out of the craft, and Quaid said, "A word with you, Lt. Sorenson, and your copilot."

"Yes, sir!"

When the Exiter was clear of Black Crow crew,

Quaid shut the hatch. "Take a seat, gentlemen." He studied Lt. Sorenson's copilot, Lt. Brown. "You've been flying with us for over a year now."

"Yes, sir," the man said with enthusiasm. His eager green eyes searched Quaid's for a clue as to their mission.

"Can you pilot in Lt. Sorenson's place?"

"But, sir...," Lt. Sorenson objected.

Quaid's pointed look at him made Lt. Sorenson relax. Quaid turned back to Lt. Brown. "Lieutenant?"

"Well, yes, sir." The young officer glanced to see Lt. Sorenson's disheartened expression.

"Good. I'll have a Xenonian pilot fly as your copilot."

"Sir?"

"Right, well, do a good job, Lieutenant. We'll all be counting on you."

Lt. Brown stood, then looked back at Lt. Sorenson.

"See yah," Lt. Sorenson said, his voice shadowed with defeat.

Lt. Brown hurried out of the Exiter, and Drake closed the hatch. "What's up, Quaid?"

"Lt. Sorenson is going to fly the Exiter after he leaves us off, farther west."

Lt. Sorenson stood up from his seat as if he'd been drugged. "But, sir, nobody, but nobody flies the Exiter except for you yourself."

Drake cleared his throat. "And me."

The lieutenant glanced at Drake, then back to Quaid. "You can't mean it, sir."

"You can do it, Lieutenant." Quaid sat at the controls. "You have to. The Rondovins will never suspect what hit them when we destroy their communication's center. They'll still believe we're flying a mission over Kranobia. Lt. Farthing is lead craft. That means you have to take my place."

Drake and the lieutenant belted themselves in.

"I couldn't risk having another crewman accompany you as copilot. Somebody might get a tad suspicious." Quaid set the controls in place. "I've already told Lt. Farthing I'll be slipping away from the squadron for a slight detour, otherwise, everyone will be thinking I'm still at the helm when it returns to Kranobia."

"Sir, thank you, sir."

Quaid smiled. "Show the colonel what stuff you're really made of, Mason." He took the craft up.

Lt. Sorenson cleared his throat. Quaid and Drake glanced back at him and he smiled. "I kind of wondered about your chicken maneuver in the canyons."

Quaid said, "Not something I would relish doing again."

"Don't you think you ought to incorporate the maneuver in the manual on offensive tactics, sir?"

"Don't think so, Lieutenant. Strictly going by the

book, I wouldn't risk such a thing."

"But *you* did, sir."

Quaid raised his brows at the boy.

The lieutenant nodded. "I guess with as many kills as you've had, you're entitled."

"More foolhardy, Mason. Don't want to get you or the others killed trying such a stunt."

"Yeah." Drake reached over and slapped Quaid on the back. "He only takes his best friends on such a maneuver." Drake studied the weapons' systems panel. "So, Quaid, where are we going and what exactly are we doing? You said we'd hit their communication's—"

"Speckled spider caves. Thought we might make sure they're still cleared out."

"That's where they've got the communication's center hooked up?"

"That's the place. But I couldn't think of a way to get in there until now."

"And that is?"

Quaid just smiled at him.

CHAPTER 20

An hour later, Quaid peered into the dark hole situated near the hill covered by jungle. He glanced back at Drake who whispered, "After you."

"Still afraid of cobwebs?" Quaid slipped into the narrow entrance until his feet connected with natural stairs that extended to the base of the cave.

"Only of the critters that weave them."

Taking a deep breath, Quaid said, "Keeping these lights to low at candlewick illumination is sure to be safer, but I can barely see anything in here in the gloom." He lowered the lantern to where the halberd poked out of the mud. The metal object had vanished, and he raised his lantern to look in the direction of the rock shelf. Resting on the flat piece of granite, the halberd glittered as the candlelight reflected off its shiny surface. "Somebody's been here."

"No one else would have reset the booby trap but the Rondovins."

Quaid nodded, then walked toward the first of the tunnels. He shuddered as he started down the long passageway.

"Kind of gives you the creeps, doesn't it?" Drake waved his blaster to clear the fine mesh of webs hanging from the ceiling.

"Means nobody's been through here in a while."

"Except for spiders. Are you sure this is where the Rondovins set up their center?"

"Yeah, one of the Xenonians said they saw about thirty Rondovins carrying the equipment into the caves. The only problem was, they didn't know which of the caves they stashed the gear."

They entered the main cave. Quaid tilted his nose up and sniffed the air. "Jasmine. Zaira. Damnation, that woman can't be here."

"Sorry, Quaid, can't smell a thing. Lead the way."

Quaid hurried toward the left most tunnel. He paused, then hastened through the narrow passage. Bats feeding on a dead body flew up in a flurry on the path ahead of them. "What is it?" Drake crouched down to get a better look in the dim light.

"Speckled spider...remains."

The glowing light revealed Martius's workshop as it framed the doorway in the next cave beckoning them and without thought for safety, Quaid dashed across the cave toward the door. He hit the button. The rock ground open, but the room appeared empty. Drake hurried after him and shut the door. "What now?"

Quaid strode through to the bedchamber and Drake cleared his throat. "Think I'll just take a seat over here." He turned away from the view of the door. As the door slid open with a whoosh, Quaid's mouth dropped open. "Zaira, what the devil are you and Catarina doing here!"

Drake bolted across the room to the doorway and bumped into Quaid's shoulder. "Catarina!"

"She's just going to sleep for a while, Drake, but you might like a word with her before you leave."

Drake sat down next to Catarina and took her hand in his and kissed it. "Catarina—"

She touched her finger to his lips. "Xenonian women stay by their mates, Drake. I couldn't let you have all of the fun."

"But—"

Catarina closed her eyes and Zaira said, "She'll sleep now. We need to do what needs to be done, and we can come back for her in a little while."

"I can't leave her," Drake said.

"I need your help," Quaid said. "Zaira will stay with Catarina."

Zaira smiled as she took hold of Quaid's arm and

squeezed lightly. "You'll need my help, Quaid. Let's go."

Her ice blue blouse was buttoned only halfway. Reaching down, he buttoned several more as Drake looked back at them. "Looked like you might have needed some help there, Zaira," Quaid said.

Her lips lifted slightly in a smile. "Thought you liked the look."

Taking a deep breath, Quaid said, "I do. I just don't want others to get that much of a look."

She chuckled.

Drake kissed Catarina's lips, then walked out of the room. "She killed the spider, I take it?" His brow wrinkled with concern.

"Yes, she had to, Drake." Zaira picked up a waterproof pouch. "She knew I had to lead you back through the underwater cave. Of course there's another way...the one the Rondovins use because they cannot swim. But that one is heavily guarded and we'd never make it that way."

"She told me she'd never changed—"

"That's true. She wasn't ready. Now she is."

"How the devil did you know to come here?" Quaid asked.

"You talk in your sleep, Quaid Lassiter." She reached up and kissed his cheek.

"Talking in my sleep?" Quaid let out his breath. "Can I take the pack for you, Zaira?"

"You need all of your strength to swim through the tunnel," Zaira said.

"I'll take it." Drake grabbed the pack. He lifted it and groaned. "Wow, what's in this thing?"

"A few special Martius-designed charges. He said it won't destroy the caverns, but it'll destroy any communication device known to humankind."

"He's quite a genius." Quaid led Zaira out of the workshop. He glanced down at her short blue shorts. "I kind of imagined you'd be my stay-at-home kind of girl."

Zaira took Quaid's arm and rubbed her head against his shoulder as her black hair curled over his jacket. "That's not what you truly want in a woman," she whispered in his ear.

***

Half an hour later, Drake surfaced beyond the tunnel first with lantern extinguished, then readied his weapon. Zaira had locked her lips with Quaid on the way out of the water cave and kissed him when she saw Drake waiting for them. Quaid caressed Zaira's breast as he leaned her against the rock ledge. Drake cleared his throat. She smiled at Quaid. She would make him love the water one way or another. Already he wasn't as nervous about it and that was a good sign.

"Wanted to do that before." Quaid nibbled Zaira's ear.

She nuzzled her cheek against his. "Never would

have gotten the scrolls at that rate."

He lifted her onto the rock floor. "You're right about that." He took a deep breath as he studied her breasts, the water-soaked silk clinging to them. "Business first," he whispered, touching the pearl button on her blouse. "Pleasure next."

They had come a long way since that first time in the caves. She had no regrets. Quaid hurried to climb out of the water as Zaira wrung the water from her hair. Then she walked to the cave entrance. "Back to the right."

"Where we were trapped before?"

She nodded. "They won't expect us to come this way. The hall shouldn't be guarded. But there'll undoubtedly be communications' officers there."

Quaid said, "The edict was approved that the killing of forces during wartime is acceptable."

Zaira said, "Stun."

Quaid and Drake set their weapons to stun. "Just like a Xenonian." Drake led the way.

Nearing the conference room, they heard three Rondovins conversing. Zaira stepped back into the shadows of the hall as Drake and Quaid maneuvered closer. Quaid made a motion with his fingers and Drake nodded once. The two walked into the entryway and fired three blasts. Thumps ensued as the men fell to the floor, fast asleep. Zaira dashed into the room and grabbed the pack from Drake. "Two more are coming to see what the noise was all about." She set the charges against the communication lines.

Drake and Quaid hurried out of the room and stood in the dark shadows, waiting to ambush the Rondovins. Two strode into view. Quaid signaled to wait. The one Rondovin told the other to enter the room, but before he could take another step in that direction, Quaid and Drake fired on the two men. They slumped to the ground. Zaira darted out of the room. "The charges will go off in two seconds with a poof. But Martius believes there might be as many as four more rooms of communication equipment."

"Which way, Zaira?"

"Straight ahead."

Drake reached up and turned off the light to a lantern hanging on the wall to lower the Rondovins' visibility. He pointed to another farther down and Quaid hurried to switch that one off too. Zaira whispered in the hall's well-lighted passage, now half-shadowed in darkness, "Take a left at this next hall."

"Any Rondovins?" Quaid whispered back.

"Yes," Zaira said, "but I can't tell how many."

Quaid and Drake readied their weapons, then turned off two more lanterns before they reached the next room. They both took a deep breath, then walked into the entryway and fired at everything that stood.

Drake chuckled to see only one Rondovin sleeping on the floor.

"Sorry," Zaira said, "he must have been talking to himself."

"Or communicating on that." Quaid pointed with his blaster at the communicator still gripped in the man's hand.

Zaira hurried to set the charges while Quaid and Drake returned to the hall and knocked out a couple of more lights. Hearing footsteps, they turned to see a Rondovin officer approach. "What the...," the man said. Quaid hit him before he could utter another word.

"Nap time." Drake pulled the officer into the room with the other.

"Ready, Zaira?" Quaid asked.

She nodded and set the timer. "Two seconds."

"Where to next?"

Zaira studied the three paths they could take from the room, then pointed left. Boisterous laughter filled the hall ahead of them and a man said, "Cayrnidian Bach is genius. When word reaches troops at Kranobia to move, Quaid Lassiter will find no one to fight at all."

Several men laughed.

Quaid smiled.

A metal cup slammed down on a table. "Comrade Caryndian has to find a way to drop the shield to Riverine!"

"He's working on it."

Quaid motioned to Drake, who nodded, then both of them closed in on the room. They quickly walked into the entryway. The Rondovins' jaws dropped. Drake and Quaid sprayed the Rondovins and the men sank to the floor.

"It's some kind of break room. No communication's devices here." Zaira grabbed one of the men's radios, then poked a few buttons. Smiling, she set it on the table. "Dead."

"Then Martius's devices *are* working!" Quaid said.

Zaira nodded. "He truly is a genius. Another room is down the hall from this, third corridor on the right."

Quaid and Drake hurried toward the next corridor, pausing to see that no one occupied the hall, then signaled to Zaira to follow them. When they reached the third corridor, they spied two men speaking outside of the entrance to the doorway.

"If we shoot them where they stand, the others will be alerted."

"It is the last room, Quaid," Zaira said. "We must set the charges in there."

"If they're able to set off an alarm, we might not ever make it out of here alive, Zaira." Quaid took her arm and pulled her aside. "Show me how to set the charges. You return to Catarina."

"No, Quaid. I stay with you. Remember?"

"I hope Catarina isn't as stubborn as my mate," he said to Drake.

Drake smiled. "Slightly."

"Okay, well, same plan as before, you hit the—"

"Hey!" a Rondovin tried to yank his gun off his shoulder while he spilled a hot drink on his uniform. Drake whipped around to blast him while Quaid targeted the two down the hall.

Two more burst out of the room. Drake and Quaid hit them. Zaira waited. Quaid grabbed the officer's empty cup, then walking as softly as they could, they approached the room.

They both stopped just short of the entryway, then Quaid tossed the cup into the room. As soon as blasts fired on the cup, Drake and Quaid charged the door and fired on the three Rondovins still in the room. Quaid beckoned Zaira, who hurried into the room. She set the charges while Quaid studied a flashing light. "What's this?"

Drake glanced at it. "Internal warning system. Silent alarm has been sounded."

After setting the charges, the three dashed out of the room and headed straight for the tunnel leading back to the underground lake. Quaid glanced back to see Zaira keeping up with them. Then as they reached the lake, the men both shouldered their weapons while Zaira drew the empty pack over her shoulders.

Drake dove into the lake.

Quaid and Zaira paused.

"They're not following us," Quaid said.

"Maybe you already hit all of them that were there."

"Maybe."

"Are you ready?"

"Never."

Zaira took his hand and dove under the water and swam with him until he needed her help. When they reached the other end of the tunnel, Drake gestured to the other side of the lake. The three observed six Rondovins searching for signs of the intruders. Quaid waved his blaster at the halberd.

Drake nodded.

"You cannot kill them," Zaira whispered as she touched Quaid's arm.

"Not in the plans," Quaid said.

They waited for the men to relocate to the right spot, all but two and while Quaid aimed at the sword, Drake aimed at one of the two Rondovins near the stairs. "Now," Quaid whispered and within seconds the blast knocked the halberd from its resting place while Drake's blast knocked the Rondovin from his feet. Four fireballs shot out from the canons blinding the Rondovins with light. Quaid and Drake fired away until all six were sleeping on the cave floor. "Just had to distract them, Zaira, is all."

She sighed deeply. "Sorry, for having doubted you."

He kissed her cheek. "No, problem."

They swam across the lake, then hesitated at the shore. "Hear anything, Zaira?" Quaid asked.

"No, I don't."

They all hurried to climb out of the water.

Drake rested his finger on the trigger mechanism of his blaster and headed for the tunnel.

After running through the passage, he waited for Quaid and Zaira. "Nothing," she said.

They dashed toward the left-most tunnel and ran through that all of the way to the end. When they peered into the cave, the light from the workshop glowed softly. Zaira nodded. "I hear metal-edged boots coming this way."

"Rondovins." Quaid grabbed Zaira's hand and darted across the cavern as Drake ran behind them. When they hit the button, the door whooshed open and the three ducked into the room. As soon as the door closed, a blast of white light struck the rock facing of the door, then it sealed shut.

Quaid and Drake readied their weapons at the door.

"They can't get in," Zaira said. "The buttons will not work with the Rondovin's touch. Martius designed them that way."

Quaid lowered his weapon. "Genius."

"Drake," a voice from the bedchamber weakly called.

"Go see what Catarina needs," Quaid said.

"If you need me, just holler." Drake hurried off to the room.

"How long can we hold out here?" Quaid asked Zaira.

"A month. Water's good forever, but food for four will only last us a month."

"Don't intend to be Minister of Defense holed up here for that long." Quaid rested his blaster on the table. "Not another bedchamber hidden away in Martius's workshop, is there?"

"Don't need one." Zaira smiled.

"I kind of thought—"

"I'm not sleepy, are you?"

Quaid chuckled. "Not at all, I kind of thought—"

"Don't need a bed then." She patted the table.

He laughed. "All right."

He slipped her pearl buttons through the wet button holes, and Zaira struggled with Quaid's shirt buttons. He pushed her blouse from her shoulders and kissed her warm, wet skin with reverence.

Whoosh! The door opened behind him, and he turned to see Lieutenants' Sorenson and Farthing standing in the open entryway. "Uh, sir, uh, captured the Rondovins, sir," Lt. Farthing stammered.

Zaira hid behind Quaid and she started to button her blouse.

"Five-thousand, eight-hundred and fifty Rondovins were rounded up at Kranobia. Another 150 scattered into the forest, but the Xenonians are trying to capture those."

He motioned behind him and said, "These we'll take from here."

"Ship's safe and sound," Lt. Sorenson's face showed his pride. "She's awaiting your command."

"Job well done," Quaid said.

"It was all your doing, sir," Lt. Farthing said. "At first, they were making a pretty good coordinated offensive, then all of a sudden, there was total mayhem. Had to have been when you knocked out their communications' system."

"Anything else, sir?" Lt. Sorenson asked.

"I'd say it's time for a little R and R."

"Yes sir!" Lt. Sorenson said.

Quaid wrinkled his brow at him.

"I'll absolutely be on my best behavior."

"See that you are, Lt. Sorenson."

"Yes, sir," the young man said, beaming.

"Rendezvous at my ministry chambers in seventy-two hours."

As the pilots returned to their ships with their

Rondovin prisoners, Quaid studied the floor.

"What's wrong, Quaid?"

"Caryndian Bach."

"I had a notion about him."

"Oh?"

"My library might have some clue."

Quaid strode to the bedchamber and tapped on the door. "What?" Drake said grouchily.

"Going to get a cup of coffee with Zaira. Want to join us?" Silence. Quaid laughed. "All right. We'll come back for the two of you in an hour or so."

Quaid led Zaira outside of the caves. "I still can't get used to seeing all of this greenery on the planet."

"You think you can't. How do you think I feel when a desert planet is all I've ever known? I've never seen the Xenonian people happier. Except of course for this business with the Rondovins."

***

Quaid sat down at his controls and Zaira sat beside him. She studied his fingers as they caressed the control panel. She reached over and touched his hand. "I didn't know there would be another woman in your life."

"Sorry, I forgot to mention her." He took the ship up and they sailed across the clear blue sky toward the way station.

Zaira said, "I have to confess something else to you, Quaid." He looked over at her as she cast her eyes downwards. "About the drive—"

"I've been wondering about that."

"Well, Father knew you'd need a new one—"

"How did he know I'd have the failure right when I did?"

Zaira looked up at him, then down at her hands as they fingered one of the buttons on her shirt. "Don't get mad, Quaid."

"All right, Zaira, what happened?"

"You'll get mad." She looked over at him.

"Sabotage?"

"The High Council was afraid you wouldn't come to defend us. They thought it was the only way you'd stay...and help."

"I could have been killed."

"I know, Quaid. My heart nearly stopped when I heard your engines screech so." A tear cascaded down her cheek, and she brushed it away hurriedly.

"So you did—"

"No, not me. Martius. He set the timing device just right, then shipped it to a friend of his on Orion. The woman installed the device to coincide with your trip near here. My father had already installed a navigational diversion emitter to switch your destination from the Feronian home world to Xenon."

"Who was the woman who installed the timing device?"

"A female copilot." Zaira studied Quaid's response. His brows furrowed. "Who?"

"Pelly Schoran."

Zaira twisted her mouth to see his ears turn slightly red.

"She wasn't a friend of Martius."

Zaira shook her head slowly.

"How did you find out so much about me?"

"The Council wanted both you and the Exiter. They knew how important your craft was to you. Otherwise, they had considered shanghaiing you. They figured if they had taken you in that manner, you wouldn't have helped us. It had to be your own idea...only we had to make sure you couldn't leave once we got you here."

"You nearly got me killed."

Another tear rolled down Zaira's cheek. "I know, Quaid," she whispered. "And it nearly killed me. You can't imagine how I had to pull myself together before you arrived at the shop."

Quaid took Zaira's hand and pulled her from her seat. "You certainly did a good job of pulling yourself together." He sat her on his lap. "*Now* I understand why your father was so shaken when I exited the ship." He kissed her wet cheek. "So then he replaced the drive while I was seeing you and took off for Riverine in the Exiter to keep it from falling into the hands of the Rondovins." She nodded. He pressed her head against his chest. "Desperate causes require desperate measures." He kissed the top of her head.

"I'm sorry, Quaid. I've wanted to tell you all along. Martius really likes you and he feels just awful about it."

"I'll have a word with him."

"You won't be too hard on him, will you?"

"Not if you fix me some of that chocolate-flavored coffee of yours that has such a calming effect." As they approached the way station, Quaid stared to see the desert landscape. "What happened?"

"Martius and I didn't get to this section. Sort of got sidetracked when the Rondovins arrived."

They landed and Quaid grabbed his blaster, then opened the hatch. He climbed down the steps, then reached his hand out to Zaira. She grabbed his hand and he walked with a sure but slow step toward the shop. "Let me go in first, Zaira."

He yanked the door open, the bell jingling, then peered in. Seeing the place clear, he strode across the room to the office. Finding no one in there, he turned to see Zaira studying her bookstore. "Looks like they didn't touch the place." He walked into the coffee shop and laid his blaster on one of the café tables.

"The Rondovins despise coffee and they despise reading. I just hoped they wouldn't destroy it based on that." She pointed to a jar of chocolate coffee beans. "Chocolate-flavored?"

"You know it's my favorite," Quaid said.

She struggled with the jar lid.

"Need some help?"

"No, I'll get it."

Quaid walked into the sitting area and picked up the book, *The Changeling*, that he'd dropped on the floor. He tucked it into his inside jacket pocket, then glanced up to see Zaira studying him. "Thought I'd finish reading the story."

Her eyes sparkled as a smile touched her lips.

He walked over to the bookshelf, then ran his finger over the spines of several books.

"Your grandmother's journal is in the farthest most shelf, second row, sixteenth book."

She walked across the floor and handed him his cup of coffee. She sipped hers, and he kissed her cheek. "Thanks." He retrieved his grandmother's journal.

He opened the book, flipped through the pages, then tucked it into his pocket with the other. "What about Caryndian Bach?"

Zaira moved to the farthest most shelf. She pulled a ladder over, then handed her coffee cup to Quaid. She climbed up the ladder, and he smiled up at her. "Need my help?"

She looked down at him and smiled to see his gaze focused on her shorts. "I think I can manage." She looked back at the books, then pulled one out.

When she climbed down the ladder, he said, "What is it that you think you might—"

His words were never finished as the door jingled open. Both Zaira and he turned as Caryndian Bach walked into the shop.

CHAPTER 21

Caryndian smiled as Quaid held a cup of coffee in both hands. "I understood you were quite fond of Zaira's coffee, but I never imagined how much so."

"Would you like a cup?" Zaira walked over to the jars of coffee beans.

"Never quite acquired the taste, thank you, Zaira." He turned to see Quaid's blaster resting on the table.

Quaid's gaze followed his as he worked his way back to Zaira. He handed her cup of coffee to her. She took it and he drank more of his own.

"I understand you had quite a success of it today," Caryndian said.

"Rather," Quaid replied.

"So what book is it that you have there, Zaira?" Caryndian asked.

"Nothing that would interest you much," she

answered.

Caryndian walked over to the counter and reached his hand out for the book. "Let me see."

Zaira handed it to him as Quaid considered the distance to his blaster.

Caryndian thumbed through the pages, then frowned. "This is some kind of journal written by an Orion female copilot."

"Yes, interesting, isn't it?"

The magistrate put the book on the counter. Quaid glanced down at the book as he tried to read the name of the author. *Pelly Schoran.*

"What brings you here?" Caryndian asked.

"Coffee?" Quaid raised his cup to the magistrate. He slugged down the rest and set the empty cup on the counter.

"Quaid wanted to read *The Changeling.*"

Quaid pulled the book out of his pocket as Caryndian's eyes narrowed.

"And he was curious about his grandmother's journal."

"What would interest him about a copilot's journal?"

"This one interests *me.*" Zaira ran her fingers over the leather-bound book.

"What brings you here?" Quaid asked. "Kind of a ways from Riverine and the Rondovins are still on the run in the vicinity."

Caryndian stiffened.

"Zaira tells me you're not originally a Xenonian," Quaid continued.

"No, from Orion."

"Oh? Then answer me this. What is greater than God, more evil than the devil, the poor have an abundance of it, and the rich need it?"

Caryndian glanced at Zaira who shrugged. "It must be an Orion thing. I haven't a clue."

"I never was interested in riddles," Caryndian said.

"Nothing. Nothing is greater than God, nothing is more evil than the devil, though I can think of a few who come close, nothing is what the poor have and nothing is what the rich need."

Quaid kissed Zaira on the cheek, then edged his way toward the table where his blaster beckoned to him. "All school children on Orion know such a thing," Quaid said. "Did you know the one thing we have in common with Rondovins is our burial procedure?"

Caryndian glared at Quaid.

"I mean, everybody on Orion knows a carypsian coin is placed in the coffin with the deceased, but did you know the Rondovins have the same tradition?"

Caryndian smiled.

"You didn't know the Orion's have this tradition, or you didn't know what the Rondovins did with their dead?"

"Of course I knew the Orion's have this tradition. How would I know what the Rondovins do with their dead?"

Quaid smiled. "Do you know what the Rondovin war cry is?"

"Why should I know what it is?"

"I thought you might have learned what it was just in your line of business."

Caryndian glanced at the blaster.

"Ah, but you'd know what the Orion war cry was of course. You know—death to traitors!"

Caryndian smiled. "That's not the Orion war cry."

"You're right," Quaid said smiling. "I always rather liked that better, when the situation warrants it, of course. So you didn't say what brings you here. You're not interested in coffee…or reading."

"I'd heard Zaira had returned here. I thought she was alone, and I was concerned about her safety."

"So you had planned on rescuing her, just like you rescued those three Xenonian women in the midst of Rondovin-controlled territory? That was really touching, you know. I wondered how you ever managed to make it through all of those Rondovins camped out in the region without the women or you being sighted. Not only that, but it doesn't seem like the kind of job you'd normally perform."

"Are you implying—"

"Not implying anything. Thought it was quite clever how you managed such a feat. Why Drake and I had quite a time, got ourselves captured on more than one occasion, and in a pickle of a mess on several others. But now, we have the training to deal with such a crisis. However your job—"

"I was the only one who objected to you being made the Minister of Defense." Caryndian watched Quaid take another step toward the table. "Didn't think an outsider would be good for the job."

"Guess you were wrong."

"No," Caryndian said, shaking his head. "You've rather messed up my plans all along."

Quaid smiled. "If you must know, the riddle I told you, a Feronian related to me. An Orion wouldn't know the answer to it, in most likelihood. And as for the carypsian coin? Only the Rondovins are known to bury it with their dead. Those from Orion don't believe on paying their way into heaven." He took another step toward the table. *Distract him, Zaira.* "I wondered how you got the scar across your face." Quaid pointed to Caryndian's face.

Caryndian ran his hand along the scar. "My brother hit me with a saber when we were playing—"

"Ahh, yes. Rondovin children play with the ancients' weapons even when they're small. It's not long before they have graduated to more advance weaponry."

Caryndian smiled as he pulled a blaster from underneath his long gowns. "And Rondovins are known to hate coffee."

"So what now, Caryndian? I mean, are you going to kill Zaira and me and then remain as magistrate on Xenon?"

Turning his attention to Zaira, Caryndian said, "I waited long past my prime for you. Your father promised you to me. On the Rondovin home world, we have no problem with having a mate who's already been compromised." Zaira's eyes grew large. He smiled. "I'm afraid too many know about me here for me to continue to live here safely." He turned his weapon on Quaid.

Quaid dove under the table. The explosion shattered the glass table and knocked Quaid's blaster to the floor.

Quaid reached his hand out to grab the blaster, but Caryndian fired at his hand. He pulled it back as the blast ripped into the floor. Grabbing up a chair, Quaid used it as a shield while he jumped to his feet.

Caryndian aimed at him, but a jar of coffee beans sailed across the floor and struck him in the temple. He dropped his blaster and fell to the floor unconscious. Zaira ran to Quaid and hugged him tight.

He lifted her chin to see her eyes filled with tears. "Everything's all right, Zaira." He kissed her lips.

"That was our chocolate coffee." She pointed at the floor.

He smiled, then embraced her warmly. "Do we have anything we can tie him up with?"

The doorbell jingled. Carver and Martius rushed into the shop. "Drake said you were on your way over here, and we learned Caryndian was too." Carver stared at the prone figure of Caryndian on the floor. "Is he dead?"

Martius checked for a pulse. "Knocked out cold."

"He confessed," Zaira said.

"We have all of the evidence we need," Martius said. "Two of the Rondovins we captured told us all we needed to know."

"What will happen to him?" Quaid ran his hand over Zaira's arm. She nuzzled her cheek against his chest.

"He's killed Xenonians. The punishment is death."

Drake and Catarina hurried into the shop.

"Geez," Drake said when he saw Carynidan sprawled on the floor and plasma blasts to the table and floor. "You didn't tell me you were going to have this much fun. I would have come too."

Catarina hit him in the arm. "You had more important business to take care."

"True."

Martius opened the door to the shop, then signaled to a couple of Xenonians. Tagaron and another man walked into the shop.

Carver said, "Take him to the holding cell. He'll stand trial at once."

Tagaron glowered at Quaid holding Zaira in his arms.

"Tagaron," Martius said.

"Yes, sir." He helped the other man to carry Caryndian out of the shop.

Carver slapped Quaid on the back. "I'd say you've done a pretty good job for the early phase of your appointment as Minister of Defense." He looked at Zaira. "We'll see all of you for a celebration supper in three hours from now."

"Good job." Martius shook Quaid's hand.

Martius and Carver left the shop, and Drake said, "We're going back with them so they can drop us off at our place. We'll see you at the supper."

The room grew quiet again. Zaira said, "Well, Quaid, what do we do now?"

Quaid walked over to the glass door and locked it. "What I wanted to do with you the first time I laid eyes on you."

Zaira moved backwards toward the coffee counter. "What's up?"

"Have to clean up the mess." She waved behind her toward the glass without taking her eyes off him.

He took a few steps. She dashed for the counter. When she grabbed for Pelly's journal, he bolted the remaining distance across the floor. Grabbing her wrist, he began to tickle her. "How did you ever manage to get the lieutenant's journal?" he asked, as she squealed in giggles.

She dropped the journal on the floor. "I paid a year's allowance for it." She gripped Quaid's wrists while his fingers poised to strike again. "I must admit, the part about you was well worth the money."

Quaid glanced down at the journal.

"Of course, I found out why she liked you so much. Great maneuvers with the female persuasion in intimate situations. She was truly disappointed you weren't the marrying type."

"You said you thought I hadn't been with a woman before because I was so shy."

She smiled. "Well, I knew of the one woman. I wanted to know how many there really were. Martius asked Drake, but he only mentioned the one too."

Quaid broke free of Zaira's hands and pulled off his jacket. "Kind of getting warm in here."

Zaira backed away from the counter. "I have to clean up the glass, Quaid. What if we have company?"

"Door's locked." He unbuttoned his shirt buttons as

he walked toward her. "I thought you were getting a book off the shelf that would help convict Caryndian Bach of treason. Imagine my surprise to find it was Pelly's journal."

"I heard Caryndian at the door and I smelled his scent."

"His scent?" Quaid said, as Zaira backed into the sitting area.

"Yes. I'm very sensitive to scents."

Quaid raised his brows. "And mine?"

Her legs bumped against the soft cushions of the sofa, and she smiled. "The most agreeable musky, male scent with a hint of spice. I could always tell when you were nearby."

He closed the distance between them, his chest touching her breasts as he lifted her chin and gazed into her eyes. "I've never met a more tantalizing woman before in my life. I was so tongue-tied that first day, I was embarrassed."

She grinned. "I know. I was surprised I could have that much of an effect on you. I practiced for days before you arrived."

"Could have fooled me." He leaned her back on the sofa, then knelt before her. "I desired you more than I had ever wanted anyone in my life." He unbuttoned her blouse. He slipped her shirt over her shoulders and sighed deeply. "In all my travels, I've never seen such heavenly bodies." He kissed one breast, then the other with affection as she sank into the feather-filled cushions. "And your long legs just never quit." He ran his hands over her smooth thighs. He ran his fingers up her waist and leaned over to nuzzle her neck.

He sat beside her and yanked his boots off. "I wonder how Martius will view our lovemaking."

She pulled off his shirt and watched him stand and drop his pants. "He doesn't know the details. Just that your pleasuring me fulfills my fantasies. But he doesn't know how."

Pushing her legs apart, Quaid rested his knees between her legs on the sofa, then pulled at her shorts. "You could help, you know."

"I should be cleaning the glass off the floor, Quaid. What will my patrons think?" She smiled as he slipped her shorts down her hips.

"I dreamt of how it would have been had I been able to fulfill my own fantasies when I was here last." He nestled his face against her abdomen, and she ran her hands through his hair. "I can't believe I waited so long to pleasure you, Zaira."

"My brother warned me not to entice you too much. He feared you might not allow me to dissuade you when I did."

"The choice had to be yours." Quaid slipped her shorts to the floor.

"I knew you were the only one for me." She kissed the top of his head while he nuzzled his mouth against her breast. He ran his hand over her inner thigh. She lifted her hips slightly to welcome his advances.

He caressed her already swollen feminine nub, stroking, kissing her mouth with such passion, she felt she was lifting off in the Exiter again. She would always remember that fondly, that she had mated with him in his beloved spacecraft. And now, she would make love to him in her beloved book store and coffee shop. It just seemed the right thing to do.

There were no more words as the fragrance of coffee beans filled the air, mingled with the sensuous scents of their lovemaking. She writhed under his skillful fingers, reaching out for completion, gripping his muscular torso, loving him with all her heart.

He rubbed his stiff cock against her thigh, keeping it hot and ready for her, and she knew as soon as he made her come, he would enter her and make her come again.

She was so close to the outer edge of space, felt the jumping off point, felt herself free-falling right before the climax hit her, and she cried out with joy. "Omigod, Quaid. Do it again."

He smiled and kissed her deeply, at the same time plunging his cock between her folds. He pumped into her, loving his sweet and growly mate.

He didn't know which he loved more, making love to her here like he'd fantasized in the beginning, or making love to her on his ship that said he claimed her in his own element in deep space. He decided making love to her anywhere made him love her all the more.

He loved the way she caressed his back and gripped him tightly when she was coming again. He loved how she thrust her hips and moved her legs to give him deeper penetration. He loved the way she kissed him back as if she couldn't get enough of him. And he loved that she loved him just as much back.

She held her breath, closed her eyes, and held on. He thrust harder, rubbing her sweet spot, triggering another cry from her sweet mouth that said she'd come again. He kissed her and released, no need for protection after that first time. And he really loved that she was having his babies.

"Ahh," she said as he dove deep and he felt her climax tugging at him.

He massaged a breast, pumping into her until he was completely spent. He relaxed deep inside of her, and she kissed his cheek. "To think if I just had said yes that first day..."

He smiled. "I wouldn't have wanted you any other way."

She raised a brow, smiling at him.

He laughed. "Okay, I can't deny if you had said yes

the way you were teasing me with your hair, and smile, and clothes that first day I met you here, I would have wanted you then too."

She sighed. "We need to clean up the shop, and then I'll have to get a repairman to take care of the blast damage. But afterward, do you want to go for a swim?"

"Only if we do a lot of kissing before and after."

She laughed. "It's a deal."

EPILOGUE

Eleven months later, Quaid touched Zaira's silky hair as it draped over her milk-swollen breasts. He didn't think she could be any more beautiful than as a new mother. He still wasn't quite used to her turning into a jaguar, but she'd done so when taking him for swimming lessons several times. Which had led to her biting him accidentally, worried he was drowning, and dragging him to shore.

Now, *she* still wasn't quite used to *him* turning into a jaguar, *either*.

Suddenly, the sound of a baby's small cry pierced the serenity. He sighed and rose from the bed. "I'll get her."

He thought about Drake and didn't think his friend ever was so nervous as he was about getting ready for his and Caterina's own babies.

He hastened down the hall. By the time he reached the babies' room, both were crying and Quaid lifted one up into the crook of his arm, then gently retrieved the other in the same manner with his right arm. When he returned to the bedchamber, he smiled to see Zaira propped up slightly with pillows. She reached for one of the girls and rested her on her right breast, then took the other and did the same with her left breast. Their small lips encircled the protruding nipples and sucked at the milk for a couple of seconds, then drifted off to sleep.

She smiled to see Quaid frowning at the twins. "You'd think they'd drink more, and let you get more of a break in between."

"They can't drink very much before their tummies are full, Quaid."

She kissed each on the crown of their fuzzy heads, then waited for Quaid to return them to their beds. After he hurried to tuck the babies into their crib, he hastened back to the bedchamber. Finding the bed empty, he strode to the kitchen where pots and pans banged away. "You mustn't work yet, Zaira," Quaid scolded. He wrapped his arms around her flat waist as he kissed her cheek. "Tell me what I need to do to fix lunch."

"I'm not like Orion women. I'm perfectly fine. Having a baby is one of the easiest things for Xenonian women to do. And it's been six weeks."

"But you've had two babies."

"Makes no difference." She pulled freeze-dried bread out of a package. "I'll certainly be glad when the harvesters bring in our first whole grain wheat for making our own bread. I can't wait to try out several ancient cookbook recipes I've managed to find."

He wrapped his arm around her shoulder as he studied the gown that lightly veiled her over-sized breasts.

"I wondered when you would pleasure me again."

"But I thought that this would be too soon—"

"I was afraid you were shy about trying it again."

Quaid chuckled as he reached into her gown and ran his hands over her breasts. "I'm *not* shy."

"The babies are sound asleep right now. No telling when they will wake up again."

"Are you sure?" Quaid ran his tongue over her neck.

"*Our* lunch can wait."

He studied her eyes as their rich amber color had returned once she'd given birth and he could see the longing in them again. "If you insist."

"I do."

He swept her up in his arms and carried her back to their room.

In their bedchamber, Zaira dropped her gown to the floor, then watched as Quaid struggled with his buttons. She smiled. "I didn't think those from Orion would have so much difficulty with buttons."

"Only when I'm in a hurry."

She laughed. After climbing into bed, she ran her slender fingers in a small circular motion over the tips of her breasts. He fumbled with the last of his buttons while his gaze remained focused on her polished nails and the progress they made as they touched the dark epicenters. Finally, he tugged the shirt still buttoned, down around his hips. She laughed again.

"Come over here." Her voice had the same kind of sweet softness with a hint of power just yearning to be freed, like when she'd first met him.

"You captivate me like no other woman." He walked over to the bed and she pulled his pants zipper down with her long fingernails.

She moved with the same kind of long, drawn-out motion as she'd used with the buttons on her blouse, and he looked up to see the smile on her face. "Disappointed?"

"Very ready and long overdue, is more like it."

Her gloss-enhanced lips turned up slightly as her light touch made him groan. "Get much?"

"Not enough." His trousers fell to the floor.

She considered the sight of his full-blown erection wavering before her, and she looked up at him. "Want to do something about it?"

He slid into bed beside her. "What did you have in mind?"

"It's mating season on Xenon. Want to pleasure me?"

Quaid ran his fingers over Zaira's sensitive breasts, then kissed her cheek. "Never more than now." His gaze drifted to the sight of her curly hair covering her protected chambers. "Are you sure—"

She moved her legs apart for him. "Pleasure me, my husband. I cannot wait any longer."

With fingers deftly rubbing her most erogenous zone, he kissed her mouth fully. "How could I have ever doubted...," he said with a heavy breath. She bit his tongue playfully in response, then groaned as his fingers rubbed her rapidly between her legs in just the right spot. She arched her back slightly, and he slipped his steel-hard cock inside her.

"Ahh," she murmured as he thrust as deep as he could reach. Gripping at his muscular back, she groaned again. And then a deep-throated growl escaped her lips, and she opened her eyes to see his dimples as his smiled back at her. He relaxed and pulled her to lie on top of him. "I've wanted to do that in forever." She kissed his naked chest.

He lifted her chin and kissed her mouth with tenderness. "No more than me. You are heaven and earth to me."

One of the babies cried again and he groaned. "We should make them wait. Then they'll drink more the next time."

She sighed and kissed his nipple. "Go get our daughters."

He kissed her lips again. When she opened her eyes, his mouth gaped. "Zaira, your eyes...they're green again. They can't be."

"Yes, well it is all your fault, prince of Orion. Your sperm are oversexed, extra potent, great swimmers, and very mission-focused. Xenonian twins only have one set of twins, but I've mixed with an otherworlder and apparently you have determined that we will have more children."

"Another set of twins." He rose from the bed, spurred on by the urgent cries of the baby girls in the background.

"Little Quaid Lassiters." Her eyes sparkled with delight.

He laughed. "Tons of children, I knew it." He kissed her cheek, then hastened to dress before gathering up the twins for feeding time again.

Zaira knew Quaid was the right mate for her.

Already the people were rejoicing over Quaid and Zaira's daughters. Now he was going to have twin sons? He carried his girls back to Momma. He couldn't have been more pleased.

Shocked.
But pleased.

ABOUT THE AUTHOR

Bestselling and award-winning author **Terry Spear** has written over sixty paranormal romance novels and four medieval Highland historical romances. Her first werewolf romance, *Heart of the Wolf,* was named a 2008 *Publishers Weekly*'s Best Book of the Year, and her subsequent titles have garnered high praise and hit the *USA Today* bestseller list. A retired officer of the U.S. Army Reserves, Terry lives in Spring, Texas, where she is working on her next werewolf romance, continuing her new series about shapeshifting jaguars, white bear and cougar shifters, Highlanders, and having fun with her young adult novels. For more information, please visit www.terryspear.com, or follow her on Twitter, @TerrySpear. She is also on Facebook at http://www.facebook.com/terry.spear. And on Wordpress at:

Terry Spear's Shifters
http://terryspear.wordpress.com/

ALSO BY TERRY SPEAR

Heart of the Cougar Series: Cougar's Mate, Book

Call of the Cougar, Book 2

Taming the Wild Cougar, Book 3

Covert Cougar Christmas (Novella)

Double Cougar Trouble, Book 4

* * *

Heart of the Bear Series

Loving the White Bear, Book 1

* * *

The Highlanders Series: Winning the Highlander's

Heart, The Accidental Highland Hero, Highland Rake, Taming the Wild Highlander, The Highlander, Her Highland Hero, The Viking's Highland Lass, His Wild Highland Lass (Novella), Vexing the Highlander (Novella)

Other historical romances: Lady Caroline & the Egotistical Earl, A Ghost of a Chance at Love

* * *

Heart of the Wolf Series: Heart of the Wolf, Destiny of the Wolf, To Tempt the Wolf, Legend of the White Wolf, Seduced by the Wolf, Wolf Fever, Heart of the Highland Wolf, Dreaming of the Wolf, A SEAL in Wolf's Clothing, A Howl for a Highlander, A Highland Werewolf Wedding, A SEAL Wolf Christmas, Silence of the Wolf, Hero of a Highland Wolf, A Highland Wolf Christmas, A SEAL Wolf Hunting; A Silver Wolf Christmas, A SEAL Wolf in Too Deep, Alpha Wolf Need Not Apply, Billionaire in Wolf's Clothing, Between a Rock and a Hard Place (2017), White Wolf Christmas (2017), SEAL Wolf Undercover (2017)

SEAL Wolves: To Tempt the Wolf, A SEAL in Wolf's Clothing, A SEAL Wolf Christmas, A SEAL Wolf Hunting, A SEAL Wolf in Too Deep, SEAL Wolf Undercover (2017)

Silver Bros Wolves: Destiny of the Wolf, Wolf Fever, Dreaming of the Wolf, Silence of the Wolf, A Silver Wolf Christmas, Alpha Wolf Need Not Apply, Between a Rock and a Hard Place (2017)

White Wolves: Legend of the White Wolf, Dreaming of a White Wolf Christmas (2017)

Billionaire Wolves: Billionaire in Wolf's Clothing, Billionaire Wolf Christmas (2018)

Highland Wolves: Heart of the Highland Wolf, A Howl for a Highlander, A Highland Werewolf Wedding, Hero of a Highland Wolf, A Highland Wolf Christmas

* * *

Heart of the Jaguar Series: Savage Hunger, Jaguar Fever, Jaguar Hunt, Jaguar Pride, A Very Jaguar Christmas

* * *

Romantic Suspense: Deadly Fortunes, In the Dead of the Night, Relative Danger, Bound by Danger

* * *

Vampire romances: Killing the Bloodlust, Deadly Liaisons, Huntress for Hire, Forbidden Love

Vampire Novellas: Vampiric Calling, Siren's Lure, Seducing the Huntress

* * *

Futuristic/Science Fiction Romance: Galaxy Warrior

Other Romance: Exchanging Grooms, Marriage, Las Vegas Style

* * *

Teen/Young Adult/Fantasy Books

The World of Fae:

The Dark Fae, Book 1

The Deadly Fae, Book 2

The Winged Fae, Book 3

The Ancient Fae, Book 4

Dragon Fae, Book 5

Hawk Fae, Book 6

Phantom Fae, Book 7

Golden Fae, Book 8

Phantom Fae, Book 9

Falcon Fae (TBA)

The World of Elf:

The Shadow Elf

The Darkland Elf (TBA)

Blood Moon Series:

Kiss of the Vampire

The Vampire...In My Dreams

Demon Guardian Series:

The Trouble with Demons

Demon Trouble, Too

Demon Hunter (TBA)

Non-Series for Now:

Ghostly Liaisons

The Beast Within

Courtly Masquerade

Deidre's Secret

The Magic of Inherian:

The Scepter of Salvation

The Mage of Monrovia

Emerald Isle of Mists (TBA)

Hope you enjoyed this otherworldly tale!

Terry Spear

Made in the USA
Middletown, DE
05 January 2018